# my
## stepmother's
# secret

## BOOKS BY EMMA ROBINSON

*The Undercover Mother*

*Happily Never After*

*One Way Ticket to Paris*

*My Silent Daughter*

*The Forgotten Wife*

*My Husband's Daughter*

*His First Wife's Secret*

*To Save My Child*

*Only for My Daughter*

*To Be a Mother*

# my stepmother's secret

## emma robinson

bookouture

Published by Bookouture in 2023

An imprint of Storyfire Ltd.
Carmelite House
50 Victoria Embankment
London EC4Y 0DZ

www.bookouture.com

ISBN: 978-1-83790-329-0
eBook ISBN: 978-1-83790-326-9

*For Natalie*
*For teaching me about boundaries*

# ONE

*All roads lead to home.*

Despite the rain slapping against the windscreen, Gabbie could almost hear her father's words. Every time he left to catch a plane, she – wrapped around his legs, her head barely reaching his waist – begged him not to go. He'd laugh, gently extricating her fingers, lifting her into her mother's arms. 'If I don't go now, I won't be able to come home again.' Those were the days of picnics and playdates and trips to the park. When they were still *les trois mousquetaires* and life was simple and good. The days before she was the one who'd had to leave.

Years of living in London – and of Liam's preference for being in the driving seat – had left her out of practice for motorway driving. In her late teens, she'd had no issues negotiating the A12 late at night, thinking nothing of its lengthy unlit sections and frequent changes in speed limit. Now she jumped every time a juggernaut roared past her, sending a tsunami in its wake. It wasn't as if she was even looking forward to arriving at the house. Because her father wouldn't be there to greet her this time. Nor her mother.

A glance in the rearview mirror at the back seat confirmed

that Alice had fallen asleep, her blonde head bobbing from side to side, bright pink earphones framing her face. Olivia was still obstinately fighting fatigue, her frown illuminated by the glow from the mobile phone in front of her. It was a relief that she was quiet, at least. For the first stretch of the journey from London to Suffolk, she'd been a torrent of questions. Questions that Gabbie wasn't ready to answer.

As soon as the wipers shushed the windscreen clear, another sheet of rain took its place. Gabbie lifted the lever to maximum but it made little difference. Gripping the steering wheel hard, she leaned forward in her seat, trying to see a way through the deluge. Was it getting too dangerous to drive? Should she pull over? The hard shoulder would be even more dangerous, though, and where else could they go? *Just focus on getting there. Keeping the girls safe.*

'How much longer? We've been driving for hours.'

Having been silent for the last half an hour, Olivia's voice made Gabbie jump. She looked in the rearview mirror at her daughter's scowl. 'Not much longer. We're nearly there.'

What she'd mistaken for Olivia's acceptance had merely been her recharging for a second onslaught. 'I can't believe you're making me come. I have the party on Tuesday and I'm going to miss all the planning. It's the last one we'll all have together before everyone goes off to different sixth forms. My friends are meeting up tomorrow and now I won't be there. Why do I have to come?'

As if dealing with the weather outside the car wasn't enough, now she had to manage another hurricane of emotion from her daughter. 'Why' had become Gabbie's least favourite word in the English language. How naive was her younger self who'd thought the nappies and night-feeds stage was the difficult one? For a fleeting moment, she considered telling Olivia the truth as to why they were travelling in a torrential rainstorm to the last place on earth she wanted to go. But she dismissed the idea as soon as it came. Instead, trying to sound calm, she repeated what she'd already said twice in the last hour. 'We're going because I need to see Jill.'

'But you don't even like her. We haven't been here in years. Since before lockdown. Why do we have to come now?'

The vice of tension in Gabbie's stomach ratcheted up another notch. She hadn't been to the house since her father's funeral over three years ago and for the girls it was even longer than that. How was it going to feel, being in that empty house without him there? Worse, with Jill as their host?

Jaw tight, she tried to form the words she didn't have, but her lack of response was barely noted by Olivia, who was more interested in getting her own argument heard. 'And why do we have to come with you to Jill's house? And why does Dad not have to come?'

*It's not Jill's house, it's my parents' house. My house.* And what excuse could she give for Liam? She hated having to lie. 'Dad has to sort some things out at home. Anyway, it will be nice for you and Alice. Like a little holiday. It's a very pretty village. Don't you remember?'

'Pretty?' The word seemed to taste bad as it came out of Olivia's mouth. 'It's going to be so boring. Do they even have Wi-Fi?'

Much as Gabbie wasn't relishing her stay, there was nothing wrong with the village itself. It was pretty and quiet, just a few shops and one friendly pub which was tucked deep enough into the village to rarely attract anyone from outside. 'Well, maybe it will be a good opportunity to have some time away from your phone. A digital detox.'

Oh, the irony that Olivia didn't even reply because she'd returned to the eternal scrolling of the screen. She did have a point about the phone reception in the village, though. Hopefully the Wi-Fi was better than the last time they were here. Now, more than ever, Gabbie needed to be available for work.

A loud slap of rain on the windscreen brought her back to the road ahead. What was she going to say to Jill when they arrived? Their conversation earlier had been stilted, not least because it was the first time Gabbie had called in over two years. Even during lockdown, she'd only sent the most occasional of messages to check that she was well and didn't need anything. Jill's shock at her request was hardly surprising.

'You want to come here? Tonight?'

Her tone had been as unwelcoming as if Gabbie had suggested turning up at the house with a thirty-piece orchestra rather than just the three of them. 'Yes. I know it's short notice. I'll explain when I come.'

That was the part that was worrying her. How much was she going to explain? How much did she want to tell her? And how the hell was she going to find it in herself to ask that woman for help?

Jill had coughed; her usual tactic for stalling for time. 'Well, of course. This is your home. You're welcome here whenever you wish.'

It hadn't felt like home in over two decades, but she was desperate. They had nowhere else to go. And no one else to turn to.

# TWO

From the motorway, Gabbie turned left three times onto progressively quieter roads. The familiar Fernley Village sign – with its Constable-esque painting of a farmhand driving a horse and carriage – welcomed her to the place where she grew up. Now, driving at the requested twenty miles per hour, it was impossible to miss the bus stop where she and her friends had caught the *eleven minutes past the hour* into the next town, the bench where Sally Whittlestone had allegedly kissed Peter Colton for fifteen minutes, the park where her mother had pushed her on the swings until she'd complained that her arms were about to drop off. Long-forgotten moments unwrapping themselves like fine china that rarely saw the light of day.

Past the handful of shops that made up the high street; her father's house was on the other side of the village, halfway down a wide track. As they got nearer, her shoulders rose closer and closer to her ears. How was she going to explain to Jill why they were there?

The rain still wasn't letting up. As Gabbie turned the final bend, the gates of the house stood open in front of them, the house beyond. Behind her, Alice stirred and yawned, then gasped as she looked out of the window. 'I'd forgotten how big it was.'

To this day, Gabbie wasn't really sure exactly what her father had done for a living. He was a solicitor of some sort and his work involved a lot of international travel and meetings and dinners with important people. And it paid enough to buy a six-bedroom house on an acre of land in rural Suffolk. Though the leaded windows and dark wood frames weren't to her taste, she had to admit it was impressive. When she used to invite her primary school friends from the village home to play, they would look at her as if she was a princess and this was her castle. The first time she'd taken Liam home, his eyes had practically popped out of his head. In future visits, he'd never been comfortable here; although that was more to do with her father and Jill than the house itself.

The wet gravel crunched under the tyres as she pulled her car alongside Jill's beige Vauxhall. Even the woman's car was boring, nothing like the robust Land Rover her father had driven. Or her mother's shiny red sports car. It took every ounce of the strength Gabbie had left to keep her voice upbeat as she turned to the back seat. 'I'm going to knock. You wait here until the door's open, otherwise you'll get soaked. Can you bring a bag each when you come?'

The front door was solid oak which made a deep thud when Gabbie rapped the knocker. Underneath the small canopy over the door, her face was out of the rain, but it found its way down the back of her neck. She rapped again. Surely Jill was looking out for them? She tapped her foot on the flagstone. *Come on. Just answer the door.* She had her hand up to try again when the door began to open. She waved at the girls to join her: she wasn't going in alone.

Liam thought she hated coming to this house because of Jill, but it was the memories of happier times that were more difficult and painful. A lifetime ago, her mother would run down this corridor after her father had collected her from school. '*Ma cherie*, you're back, you're back.' How she would have loved her own girls to be wrapped up into her mother's Chanel-scented arms, swept into the sitting room for cakes and treats and a pile of tiny gifts just as she had been at the beginning of every school holiday.

Instead, they got Jill's cold smile. 'How was your journey?'

Gabbie nudged Alice into the hall. 'Fine, thanks. It's good to see you. You look well.'

In fact, she looked exactly the same as she had the last time Gabbie was here. Short layered hair, blunt bare fingernails and a sturdiness you might expect from someone who had spent their lives outdoors, on a farm or at the stables, perhaps. Gabbie – with her mother's slim French frame and long dark wayward hair – always felt like an incompetent child around Jill's solid practicality.

While Jill fussed at the girls to remove their wet shoes, Gabbie took the opportunity to run back out to the car for more cases and bags, hoping the cold rain would wash away the ghosts of being in that house again. Standing in that hallway, it was impossible not to feel the loss of her mother all over again. What would she have looked like if she was here? Would she still be wearing the vivid patterns, high heels and red fingernails of Gabbie's memory? She'd never understood what her father had seen in Jill; she was the polar opposite of her vibrant, exuberant mother. With the perspective of age, she could concede that he may have found comfort in Jill's steady familiarity in the early months after her mother's death. They had, after all, been friends for a long time. But, after that? How had he not tired of her in the years afterwards?

When she got back inside – having to knock again on the door that had been closed behind her – Jill was appraising Olivia and Alice, scanning them from head to foot. 'My goodness. Haven't you girls grown?'

Only Jill could make that sound like a criticism. Of course, to Alice, Jill was a near stranger, but Olivia had been twelve when her grandfather died and, up until then, they'd seen them both every few months. On the way here in the car, she'd been telling Alice what to expect. 'She's nice. She doesn't say very much, but I remember that she always gave me a present when we went to visit.'

Gabbie had had to bite her tongue to prevent herself from saying that those presents would have all been paid for from her father's money. To her knowledge, Jill had given up her job – some kind of boring admin work for a nearby dairy farm – when they got married and had spent the years since playing Lady of the Manor in their cavernous house.

'What does she do all day?' In her more spiteful moments, that had been the question she'd asked her father. Jill had no children of her own. She hadn't even been married before.

'She looks after me,' he used to say. 'And you know that's a full-time job.'

His wink didn't help to soften the resentment that was building piece by piece until she couldn't stand it any longer and returned to university early. In her last year, she'd barely come home at all. 'It's not my home anymore.' She'd ignored the hurt in his eyes.

Hovering in the hallway like visitors to a stately home was painful. 'Where shall we put our bags?'

Jill fiddled with the pearls at her throat, probably contemplating the mess that three unwanted house guests would bring with them. 'You can leave them there for now. I've made the beds up in your rooms and we can take them up later. Would you like tea?'

Gabbie was gasping for a drink, but wasn't ready to spend time clutching at conversation just yet. Being in this house took a little acclimatisation. 'Actually, can I show the girls up to their rooms first? Get them sorted.'

It was always like this when she came home. She and Jill circling each other like territorial birds. It had been worse when her father was here; she knew that he'd felt pulled in two ways and been angry because he shouldn't have had to choose.

'Of course. I've put you in your old bedroom and the girls are either side of you. Unless they'd rather share?'

'We'll sort it out. Come on, girls.'

She lifted the biggest bag – a large solid black case they'd been bought for a wedding gift – and started to drag it up the stairs, its weight bumping onto every step. Tactful enough to wait until Jill had retreated to the kitchen, Olivia stayed quiet until they were almost at the top before she started to grumble again. 'Why have we got so much stuff with us? There's more here than we took on our holiday and that was two weeks. You said it was only going to be a short visit.'

Gabbie had no memory of saying that, mainly because she had no idea how long they were going to be here. How long it would be before she'd be able to sort through the carnage of their life and find something worth saving.

Behind Olivia, Alice was moving up the stairs on her bottom, dragging a smaller bag as she went, with not a word of complaint. Gabbie could have kissed her. She should follow her younger daughter's lead, and force herself not to disappear down a black hole of self-pity. Yes, she didn't want to be here 'playing nicely' with her stepmother, but there were women in the world leading their children out of war zones; she and the girls were staying in a comfortable house in Suffolk.

Jill was a big fan of scented candles, oils and sticks in pots, so the higher up the stairs they went, the stronger the cloying scent of artificial flora became. When they reached the upstairs landing, Gabbie had to take a minute to catch her breath. Then she took a few more steps and pushed open the door to her teenage bedroom.

Last time she'd stayed here, the only change had been a

double bed instead of a single, but Jill had obviously had it redecorated again. Pale grey walls and a dark grey carpet were accented by bright yellow cushions on the bed and a painting of yellow roses. It looked like an anonymous hotel room, but she didn't hate it. She pulled the suitcase over to the large white wardrobe. 'I'll unpack later. Let's work out which rooms you want, girls.'

The room to the right of hers was very similar to her own, except the cushions and the roses were dark blue. And the one to the left was the same again, except the cushions were pink. It was such a stark contrast to the individually themed rooms her mother had created, full of pictures and objects from her travels. Of course, all of that had been swept away in a Jill-shaped tide as soon as she'd moved in. Where had those beautiful things gone?

Alice was bouncing on the bed with the pink cushions. 'Can I have this room? Can I?'

Olivia shrugged to show that she didn't care, so Gabbie nodded. 'Of course. I tell you what, why don't you both unpack your pyjamas and toothbrushes while I pop down and speak to Jill?'

She found Jill in the kitchen. This, too, had had the Jill whitewash: farmhouse-style cream cabinets, grey granite worktop and an oak table and chairs. The only remnant from her mother's day was the large Aga which also heated the house. Jill was lifting a kettle from the hob and filling a small enamel teapot. She turned as Gabbie entered. 'Everything okay?'

'Yes, the bedrooms look great.'

'I had them redecorated three years ago. I forgot that you still hadn't been here to see them.'

Guilt pinched at Gabbie, but she shook it away. It wasn't as if Jill was her mother. She shouldn't be expected to call her every week and visit every couple of months as she had when her father was alive. In any case, she sent her photographs of the children at Christmas, made them write a thank you card for the gifts she sent on their birthdays. 'Thanks for having us here at such short notice. We do appreciate it.'

Jill's voice was suspiciously bright. 'Of course. What about Liam? How is he? Did he not want to come with you?'

Clearly she was digging for information, and Gabbie was going to have to tell her at some point soon, but being around Jill turned her into a stubborn teenager. Old habits die hard. 'No, he's, uh, got some things to sort out at home.'

Jill nodded, her expression making it clear that she knew there was more to this than a social call. 'Are you sure you don't want something to drink? I've just made a pot of tea, or there's a jug of iced water and some glasses on the table there. What's he sorting out?'

Exhausted from the journey here and still reeling from the shock of that morning, Gabbie wasn't ready to explain everything yet. In a daze, she watched Jill carry the teapot over to the kitchen table and motion towards the opposite chair for Gabbie to sit down.

'He's really busy, actually. So we thought it might be best to get out of his way and leave him to it.' Gabbie picked up the jug of iced water and poured herself a drink; three of the cubes were stuck together and they fell as one into her glass, splashing water over the edge. She took a sip of the water, the sharpness of the cold soothing her tight dry throat. Jill was watching her, waiting for a better explanation. She needed to hurry; the girls could be back down at any minute. 'It's complicated. The thing is... I just need somewhere to stay for a few days.'

She hoped it would only be a few days. Jill sipped at her tea and frowned. 'Why can't you stay at home with Liam?'

Despite her own feelings, Gabbie didn't want to make Liam look bad in front of Jill. Until she knew the full extent of the situation, she would wait before spilling it all before her inevitable judgement. *Least said, soonest mended.* 'We just can't. We won't be able to go home for a while.'

Jill's eyes were as round as the coaster she'd slipped under Gabbie's glass. 'How long is *a while?*'

So much for *this is your home, you are welcome here anytime.* 'I don't know, yet. I'm sorry. And the girls don't know anything is up, so please don't talk about it when they're around.'

Jill looked offended at the very thought that she would be indiscreet. 'Of course, I won't mention it to them. But this doesn't make sense, Gabrielle. What's going on?'

For the second time in fifteen minutes, Gabbie could have kissed her youngest daughter when she snuck into the kitchen and leaned into the side of her. 'Can I go to the toilet here?'

'Of course, baby.' Gabbie took her hand to lead her back upstairs, but turned to Jill as she got to the door. 'I think we'll all get an early night. We can talk about this tomorrow.'

Jill nodded. 'As you wish.'

If Gabbie had a wish, it would be to be anywhere but here.

# THREE

*Don't look at the time.* Who was it that had given Gabbie that advice? That registering the time on her alarm clock would programme her brain to wake at the same time each night. Whoever it was, it was impossible to resist, so she knew that a 4 a.m. wake up was her new normal; lying awake, the noise of the day buzzing in her head. Except now, it wasn't concerns about Olivia having a boyfriend she hadn't met, or fear that she'd said the wrong thing to one of the mums at the school gate, or worry about meeting a deadline she should never have agreed to. Now the worries chewing at her in the darkness were much, *much* bigger.

In the half-light, her childhood bedroom was more familiar than it had been when she'd arrived yesterday. The fresh decoration just blurred enough that the walls were shadowed with the ghosts of her childhood posters, the collage of family photographs that she and her mother had spent a happy Saturday creating, the dressing table with fairy lights around the mirror that had been her tenth birthday present; so many happy memories that had been painted over in Jill's featureless grey. In the silence of the night, Gabbie lay still as tears crept from the corners of her eyes and past her earlobes onto the firm pillow.

She'd had so little time to gather her own girls' belongings together before leaving their house yesterday. Stood in the middle of Alice's room, she'd tried to work out the things she absolutely couldn't do without. Picking up teddies and dolls. Had Alice outgrown them? Hadn't it only been a matter of months since she would bring them down to the breakfast table every morning, feed them imaginary porridge from tiny plastic bowls? Every night, they would be kissed and read to before she tucked them into the end of her bed, their moveable eyelids closed until the next morning. Before Gabbie left the room, she'd even pulled the duvet from Alice's bed. Alice loved that cover with the puppies, had taken what felt like hours to choose it when they'd decorated her bedroom. However strange the bedroom she would sleep in that night, Gabbie had been determined that Alice would be wrapped in something familiar from home.

Then she'd done the same in Olivia's room. Around her mirror, pictures of her and her friends, dressed up to go out, at their prom, in PJs and pulling funny faces at a sleepover. Gabbie loved that Olivia was surrounded by good friends – it was all she'd ever wanted for both of them. A safe home, good friends and to know they were loved. Leaving that house had been so much harder for her than Liam could ever understand. The girls' bedrooms were supposed to be their refuge, their safe place. That's what she'd wanted for them, always. And now she'd stripped them of their possessions with no idea when – or even *if* – they would be back.

Closing her eyes, she tried the breathing exercises that would sometimes help to chase the noise from her mind so that she could sleep. At 5.30 a.m., the bedroom door opened and Alice was followed in by a glow of light from the hall. 'Mummy, I woke up.'

Gabbie held the duvet open for her. 'Come and get in bed with me, baby.'

Within minutes, Alice was tucked into the curve Gabbie made with her body, her fingers entwined in Gabbie's hair, soft breath warming Gabbie's neck. At a toddler group she'd taken Alice to when she was small – when she'd listened to three mothers expound their theories about making their children sleep in their own bed – Gabbie had stayed quiet: she cherished these moments with both the girls, this closeness, the knowledge that any pain or nightmare could be soothed away in her arms. If only the situation with Liam could be solved so easily.

Eventually, she must have dozed off again, but even the sleep she'd managed had been fitful and full of dreams. Just before waking, she'd been back at school, walking a long corridor, looking for someone or something. Whatever, or whoever, it was, she was unsuccessful every time. When she woke, it took her a moment to realise that she wasn't at school, she was in her childhood bedroom. Her mobile screen read 8.57. She hadn't slept that late in years. The bed was empty beside her. Where had Alice gone?

As soon as she was out on the landing, she could hear Alice's voice chattering away downstairs. Knowing how Jill felt about people 'parading' downstairs in their nightclothes, she ducked back into her bedroom, pulled on her jeans from last night and brushed her wayward hair into a loose ponytail before joining them.

Through the open kitchen door, she could see Alice standing on a step stool at the stove with a spatula in her hand, watching pancakes sizzle in a pan. The combination of hot fat and her daughter's loose curls sent a flutter of anxiety through Gabbie. Especially when Alice turned at the sound of her mother's footsteps and waved the spatula in greeting. 'Mummy, look at me! I'm making pancakes.'

Gabbie's fingers yearned to pluck her away from the stove. 'Watch what you're doing, baby girl. That's very hot.'

Jill looked over the top of her reading glasses. 'You're awake at last, then?'

Gabbie had forgotten how much Jill also judged people who lay in bed in the morning rather than 'getting the day started'. When she'd been home from university, she would purposely lie in bed until noon because she knew how much it made her stepmother's blood boil. Those were the days when she could sleep long like the innocent. 'I was awake in the night. I must have fallen into a deeper sleep than I realised. I'm not sure about Alice standing over a hot pan like that.'

Jill glanced in the direction of the stove, where Alice was using the spatula to prod at the batter in the pan. 'She's fine. There's nothing wrong with learning to cook early.'

Another of Jill's mantras. Gabbie was prevented from returning that serve by Olivia stumbling into the kitchen. 'That smells good. Pancakes for breakfast?'

Jill raised an eyebrow. 'Another late riser. I'm surprised you get anything done in your family.'

Olivia blushed, but she did stand her ground. 'Well, it is Sunday. The day of rest.'

Jill's glance at Gabbie expected a reprimand for Olivia's rudeness, but Gabbie wished she'd thought of it herself. When nothing was forthcoming, Jill changed her line of fire. 'Speaking of Sunday, it's Monday tomorrow. I didn't think to ask last night, but what are you going to do about the girls' school? State schools haven't broken up for the summer yet, have they?'

Maybe a stranger wouldn't have picked up on the disparaging tone Jill used for 'state school' but Gabbie heard it. 'Alice is only missing a week and Olivia is off anyway. She's had her induction days at her new sixth form college, so she's free until September now.'

Gabbie did feel guilty that Alice would miss the fun of the

last week of term, but she'd already had her end of year assembly at least. She'd been the cutest dormouse in any production of *Alice in Wonderland* that had ever been seen.

Jill wrinkled her nose as if the eggs in the pancake mixture had gone bad. 'Sixth form *college*? Does her school not have a sixth form?'

Gabbie wished she hadn't started this; she knew where it was going. 'It does, but she wanted a change. They don't offer the courses she wanted to do. She has her heart set on Film Studies.'

Jill turned towards Olivia who was trying to slink out of the room. 'Film Studies? Is that an A level? Shouldn't you be doing something more academic?'

She wasn't about to let Jill make Olivia feel bad. 'She can do whatever she wants to do.'

Jill kept up her interrogation of Olivia as if Gabbie hadn't even spoken. 'Did you not think about doing languages like your mother? She was always so talented at them. Your grandfather and I always thought she'd end up travelling the world.'

Clearly working from home as a translator had been a disappointment to them both. *Give with one hand, take with the other.* It was the same old story. 'Olivia, why don't you go and have a shower and then we can finish the unpacking we didn't do last night.'

Olivia smiled gratefully and disappeared. Gabbie helped Alice to lift a slightly charred pancake onto a plate and poured herself a coffee, her stomach too tightly knotted to want anything to eat. She needed to get some work done today, but it was more important to make sure the girls were settled first. 'What would you like to do today, Alice?'

Alice tilted her head to one side as if giving the matter serious consideration. 'Is there a park?'

There had been a park when Gabbie was Alice's age; she remembered it well. Her dad would often take her there on a

Sunday afternoon when her mother would take a nap – she hadn't had Jill's hatred for sleep – and he would play every game she wanted: she would be Rapunzel at the top of the climbing frame and he would rescue her, she would be the singing bird on a swing and he would push her into flight, he would be a scary monster chasing her around the green and let her stay just out of his reach.

'Yes. There's a park. After breakfast, you can get changed and I'll take you. Maybe we'll even persuade your sister to come with us.'

Alice shook her head. 'She'll just want to call her boyfriend again.'

Probably, Gabbie shouldn't be using her younger daughter as a spy on her elder one, but needs must. 'Really? How do you know about her boyfriend?'

'Because she talks really loud on her phone.' The way Alice rolled her eyes made Gabbie smile. And there was nothing wrong with Olivia calling her boyfriend. She just wished that she'd talk to her more about it, rather than keeping everything to herself. She would have loved a mother to help her navigate the teenage years and she was yearning to provide that for her own daughter. Responses to her gentle questions had taught her not to push.

Jill, on the other hand, was onto it like a bird on a worm. 'You let Olivia have a boyfriend? At sixteen?'

Though she knew they were guests in Jill's house, Gabbie couldn't take any more criticism this early in the morning. 'I can hear Olivia getting out of the shower. I'm going to jump in myself and then we'll head to the park and give you some space, Jill.'

Alice had been correct in guessing that Olivia didn't want to come. She looked at Gabbie as if she had two heads just for suggesting it. Gabbie wasn't surprised to see the eye roll – that's where Alice had got it from. 'I'm going to stay here and Face-

Time my friends. Seeing as I'm not allowed to actually see them.'

More guilt piled onto Gabbie's head. 'Okay, well we won't be long.'

They were actually hardly any time at all. The park was only a ten-minute walk from the house but, after five minutes on the swings, Alice announced that she needed to go to the toilet.

Concern crept over Gabbie. This had been happening more and more. 'Did you not go before we left, sweetheart?'

Alice hopped from one foot to another. 'I did! I did go. But I need to go again.'

'Okay, let's go back.'

Almost a month ago, the doctor's receptionist had made Gabbie feel like she was overreacting by worrying about how often Alice seemed to need the toilet, but she'd begrudgingly acquiesced to a phone appointment with the doctor. After asking about her general health, which was good, he'd just asked how much she drank. Alice did, admittedly, drink milk and water like a fish, so he hadn't been overly concerned. He'd offered her a 'non-urgent in-person appointment' which had been three weeks from then. It was also, Gabbie now realised, for tomorrow morning at 9 a.m. There was no way they were going to make that. *Dammit, Liam. You've messed up everything.*

Holding Alice's little hand in hers, they hurried back to the house and made it to the downstairs toilet just in time. When she came out again, Alice was ready to head back to the park, but Gabbie wanted to keep her safely wrapped up at home. Plus, the need to complete the translation projects that Mandie had sent was starting to scratch at her brain. 'How about I set you up with my iPad watching something while I get some work done and then we'll go to the park later?

Jill's sensible loafers appeared at the top of the stairs and then the rest of her came into view. 'An iPad? Wouldn't you rather do some painting? I've got my watercolours downstairs and you can sit at the table in the morning room with me and we can paint together.'

Gratitude and resentment fought for precedence as Gabbie saw how keen Alice was to paint with Jill. It would help her out to have the time to get this work done, though.

Jill also had a surprise for Gabbie. 'And while you were gone, I remembered that there's an old box of your things. When the decorator was here, I paid him to clear the loft for me and it was up there. I'll go and get the painting set up and then I'll get it for you.'

When she disappeared, Alice looked at Gabbie. 'What do you think will be in the box, Mummy?'

Gabbie had no idea that Jill had kept anything belonging to her. 'I have absolutely no idea.'

# FOUR

'Eurgh. This box is filthy.' Olivia screwed up her nose and looked at her carefully painted fingernails as if they were covered in something far worse than dust.

'Well, it hasn't been opened in a really long time.' Gabbie didn't like to think about how long it had been. Decades, probably.

After working for a couple of hours, Gabbie had needed a break. She'd made encouraging noises about Alice's artwork and then Jill had brought out the box she'd mentioned. The mystery of its contents had been enough to separate even Olivia from her mobile for the first time since breakfast.

Heavy yet fragile, they'd decided not to try and carry the box down the stairs, so all three of them sat around it in the middle of Gabbie's bedroom. Alice traced her finger across the lettering on one side of the dusty cardboard box. 'Whiskas.'

'It's cat food, sweetheart. It's just the box Jill used to keep the things in.' She didn't have fond memories of the cat Jill had brought with her when she'd moved into the house. An ancient, spiteful creature who'd viewed Gabbie with the same amount of disdain as her owner did.

Alice kept her hands safely by her sides as she peered inside the box, her cough sending dust motes into the air. 'And these are all your mummy's things?'

'Yes, I think so. I have a few pieces of her jewellery at home, but I'd forgotten that all of this was here.' All that was left of a life. Some scarves, photographs and postcards. The few items Gabbie had managed to rescue before Jill had cleared every last trace of her mother from this house more than twenty years ago. She'd been away at university but it'd ensured that she would never come back here to live. Never again would it feel like her home.

Olivia clapped her hands to get rid of the dust and then reached inside, bringing out a glittery shoe with a very high heel. 'Wow. Who was your mum, Cinderella?'

Alice pulled out its matching pair. 'She can't be, because there's another one.'

Memories of clonking down the hallway with those shoes slipping from her heels made Gabbie smile. 'She loved shoes. And boots. She had boxes and boxes of them.'

'Did she love jewellery, too? Haven't you got an earring like this?' Olivia held out a large square emerald surrounded by tiny diamonds.

'Yes, I have! Hold on a minute.' Gabbie leaned backwards to the bedside cabinet and pulled out the second drawer where she'd stowed her suede jewellery box. Since her father had passed her mother's jewellery onto her, there had only been one of these; she'd assumed the other had been lost forever.

But when she opened it, the first emerald earring wasn't there. Her heart plummeted. She must have left it at home, more concerned with gathering the girls' things than her own. Would she ever set foot in that house again to find it?

Thankfully, the girls were too busy rummaging in the box to notice. 'Look, there are photographs.' Alice pulled out a big pile and passed them to Gabbie, who skimmed through them. All were of her mother standing alone; different poses, different cities, but all very glamorous. Her father had always considered himself a proficient photographer, so she could imagine him taking his time to get the composition and angle just right.

Over her shoulder, the pictures elicited another 'wow' from Olivia. It was almost amusing; she'd never been this interested in the things that Gabbie wore. Olivia took the top photograph from the pile. 'She really knew how to dress, didn't she? Those clothes are amazing. She looks like a model or something.'

Gabbie leaned forwards to better see the one she was looking at. Her mother was standing on a bridge – Prague, maybe? – wearing cropped trousers and sunglasses that wouldn't have looked out of place on a poster for a Hollywood movie. 'Yes. She was beautiful, wasn't she, my mother? Your grandmother.' It felt strange to think that that's what she'd be to them. What would they have called her? Liam's mother had always been Grandma, but she couldn't imagine her own mother going for that. She would've shuddered and told them she wasn't old enough. She'd always looked younger than she was. And glamorous. All of Gabbie's friends had thought she was wonderful. 'Let's pretend we're sisters,' she'd say sometimes when she took Gabbie out for lunch. 'Just call me Margot. It'll be fun.'

Alice shuffled closer to Gabbie. 'What was she like, Mummy? Would she have loved us?'

Even thinking about it squeezed Gabbie's heart and made her eyes burn, but she didn't want the girls to see her sad. 'Well, you,' she nodded at Olivia, 'would probably have been whisked away for weekends in Paris or Milan where she would've paraded you around all the boutiques that she loved and you would've sat out the front of cafes drinking coffee and talking about the people who passed by. While, you,' she tickled Alice, 'she'd probably have taken for afternoon tea in big hotels and filled you full of cake and cream.'

Alice squealed as she tickled her. 'I do love cake very much.'

She'd thought about this before, of course. What her mother would've made of her two girls. It had been one of her first thoughts after the difficult birth she'd had with Olivia. *My mother should be here.* Spending a week in hospital afterwards, she'd had plenty of time to watch the mothers of the other women – newly grandmothers – visit and fuss and proclaim the child they held in their arms to be 'the spit of you when you were born'.

She'd ached then, feeling her mother's loss all over again. Because that's what happened, wasn't it? When you lose a parent, you also lose their presence at every significant event in your life from that moment until the day you die.

'Is this you?' Olivia held out a photo of a young Gabbie on her mother's lap, her arms wrapped around her like a shawl, their cheeks pressed close together. There was so much light and love that it almost took her breath away.

Alice took it from her sister. 'Mum, you look just like me.'

It was true. In the picture, the likeness was clear. She rarely looked at photos like these from her childhood; it was too painful. 'You're right, baby girl. Though I think that you're more beautiful than I ever was.'

Alice tilted her head as if she was giving it proper consideration. 'Maybe, yes.'

She had to laugh at her daughter's self-confidence. How she hoped she would keep that forever.

'I'm more like Dad.'

Gabbie couldn't tell from Olivia's tone whether this was something that pleased her or not. 'You do have his height and his lovely thick hair.'

It was enough to tip them out of the happy moment back into the reality of the situation. Olivia frowned. 'Why isn't he here? Why is he staying at home on his own when it's the weekend and he's not at his office?'

'I told you; he's got work that he needs to catch up on.' She hated lying to the children, but what else could she do? Olivia was as sharp as a tack. Even a little bit of the truth would be enough for her to find out everything. Whether it was for his sake or theirs, she wasn't about to tell the children the real reason that they weren't in their own house right now.

Alice had pulled out some more photographs and she held one up to the side of her face, pulling the same dour expression as her doppelganger in the photograph. 'You don't look very happy in this one, Mummy.'

Gabbie's stomach lurched when she saw it. She was twelve, her legs and arms didn't quite know how to compose themselves, her face so stern and eyes so full of fear. 'It was my first day at school. We were just about to say goodbye.'

She could still feel her utter devastation at the realisation that they really were going to leave her there. Her mother had cried. She'd tried to 'be brave' as her father had requested. *Don't make your mother worse.*

Olivia took the picture from her sister and scrutinised it like a historical artefact. 'It's so weird that you went to boarding school. Were you really rich?'

They weren't. Well, they'd been comfortably off, but nowhere near the league of most of the other girls who'd had live-in nannies and spent every school holiday abroad. 'It was just easier for my parents because my dad worked away a lot.'

That's how they'd pitched it to her. Her father's work took him all over Europe and he often needed her mother to go with him. Or wanted her to. Gabbie had never been sure which it was. Either way, it had clearly been his decision.

Alice hugged her knees. 'Was it fun? Like lots of sleepovers?'

Fun? That was not the first word that sprung to mind. 'To be honest, it was a little bit lonely.'

Maybe it was sitting there among the photographs of her

mother that caused the catch in her voice, but Alice moved closer and curled up against her like a kitten. 'You're not lonely anymore, Mummy. You've got us.'

Gabbie closed her eyes and rested her nose on the top of Alice's hair, breathing her in. 'That's right. I've got my lovely girls to keep me company.'

'And Dad.' She saw the flicker of fear in Olivia's eyes. 'You've got Dad, too.'

Deceiving them made her stomach twist, but it wasn't fair to make them worry when she didn't know for sure how things were going to turn out. 'And your Dad, too. Of course.'

Alice resumed her rummaging and brought out a pile of letters, loosely tied together with a ribbon. 'What are these?'

Gabbie recognised the handwriting immediately and it took her breath for a second. 'Oh, my. Those are the letters my mum wrote to me when I was at school.' She hadn't known that they still existed, assumed that they'd been lost. She took them from Alice's hands and ran her finger over the address in her mother's slanted script. There was something so personal about hand-writing; it was as if her mother's voice was here in the room with her.

'Will you read them to me?' Alice tilted her head to the side.

Normally, that cute expression would guarantee her daughter whatever she wanted, but Gabbie wasn't ready to read them even to herself. 'Maybe later, bunny.'

There was a soft knock on the door and it creaked as Jill pushed it open, intruding on the moment. 'I was going to start the chicken for lunch. Does it suit you all to eat around one o'clock?'

Gabbie unravelled herself from Alice. She didn't want Jill running around after them. It wasn't as if they were her actual family. 'I'll make dinner. You don't need to wait on us.'

Jill's look of offence threw her straight back to her late teens and the expectations of her whenever she came home from university. 'But I have it all planned.'

Before she could argue, Olivia surprised her by offering: 'I'll come and help you.'

That seemed to go down much better with Jill. 'Well, that would be lovely, Olivia. Thank you.'

Gabbie felt awkward at the idea of sitting around while they cooked, but she was relieved not to be in the kitchen with Jill, getting under each other's feet. This was difficult enough without that. Still, she couldn't just do nothing. 'Yes, thanks, Olivia. Alice and I can finish unpacking our bags while you're helping Jill.'

Olivia frowned. 'Don't do my suitcase. I'll unpack it myself later.'

If there was something secret in her case that she didn't want Gabbie to see, she didn't have the energy to worry about it right now. Especially when her phone started to buzz on the bedside table, moving towards the edge each time it rang. She picked it up to see Liam's number, then held it out to Olivia. 'It's your dad. Do you want to talk to him?'

Olivia pierced her with a look, as if watching her reaction. 'You speak to him first. And you need to answer quickly. It's already rung five times.'

'Okay.' She accepted the call. 'Hi, Liam.'

He sounded relieved that she'd answered at all. 'Gabbie. Hi. How's it going? Any movement on speaking to Jill?'

'We're all great, thank you. Good journey here, not much traffic.'

His voice hardened. 'Okay. Okay. I'm sorry, but I have my mind fixed on getting this mess sorted out.'

*Your mess*, she wanted to say, but not in front of the girls. Instead, she ignored his apology. 'Yes, the girls are right here. Did you want to talk to them?'

Before he answered, she held the phone out to Alice. 'Do you want to talk to Daddy?'

Alice loved nothing more than a chat on the phone, so she was able to back away and leave her to it. Because what was the point in talking to him if she had nothing that she wanted to say? She lowered her voice and spoke to Jill. 'I'll go to the supermarket and get us a bottle of wine to go with dinner.'

'Don't you want to stay and speak to Dad?' Olivia's tone was more challenge than question.

'Tell him I'll catch up with him later. I don't want to miss the shop. They close earlier around here on a Sunday.'

She snatched up her bag and slipped out before Olivia could ask again.

She wanted to shake off the feeling she'd had looking at that photograph. Shake off the memories of school.

# FIVE

*My Darling Girl,*

*I was so sad to leave you this afternoon that I had to write and tell you straight away how much I am missing you. When we got to the end of the driveway, I wanted to come straight back and get you, but your father told me how good this will be for you and what a good school it is. Maybe he's right. If we can both be brave, maybe we will laugh at our tears someday?*

*How is your room? And the other girls you are sharing with? Are they fun? The one with the long blonde hair looked as if she would be lots of fun. You should make friends with her. Do any of the other girls get packages from home? I will send you something every week to make you smile.*

*When I got home, I was very sad without you, so Jill came over and made lunch for us. Daddy and I are going away next week. He has business in Antwerp and he wants me to go, too. I think it will be really boring. Lots of dinners with the wives of his clients, but hopefully I will get some time to shop. What shall I buy you? Name anything you want and I will send it to you.*

*It will only be a few weeks until we see each other again. I will make the best plans for something to do. We will have one of our adventures. Do you remember the day we got in the car and just drove and drove until we found that beautiful river and we went swimming and had a picnic and we had to run around afterwards until our clothes were dry? Wasn't it fun? Let's do that again. Or anything else you want to do.*

*Be brave, my darling girl. Make lots of friends and have fun and remember that your mummy loves you very, very much.*

*Love Mama x*

Gabbie hadn't really thought that this day would ever come. When her parents – her father – had explained about the school and the fact that she would be boarding, it had come from nowhere.

'But why won't I stay at my school with Katie and Tricia? I've only been there a year.'

Her father had looked to her mother for help, but her arms were crossed, her tight mouth resolute. He tried again. 'St Catherine's is a really great school. There are tennis courts and a swimming pool and—'

'But I don't play tennis and I hate swimming. Ask Mummy; I hate my swimming lessons and I never want to go.'

Her mother had stepped towards her then, kissed the top of her head, tears in her eyes.

Despite her arguments, her father would not change his mind. She'd tried everything: tears, tantrums, begging. But his answer was always the same. 'You'll love it when you get there. Wait and see.'

Now it was September and the trees lining the entrance to

St Catherine's were turning orange and yellow. From the car window, Gabbie could see the grand old building sitting squat in the middle of playing fields; sounds of wooden hockey sticks clashing and the shouts of older girls rang through the air.

Her father's voice was resolutely positive. 'We're here.'

As arranged, Gabbie was met at the door by the housemistress, Miss Foster, a short solid woman with hair like a helmet, dressed mostly in brown. Beside her, Gabbie's mother looked like a bird of paradise in her scarlet coat and bright floral dress.

'Welcome to St Catherine's, Gabrielle. You can say goodbye to your parents now.'

Her father's voice was gruff as he pulled her towards him; his coarse tweed jacket scratched at her face. 'You're going to love it here, I promise.'

*No I won't*, she wanted to say. *I want to stay with you. I want to go home.* But she stayed silent, knowing it would do her no good. Her mother dropped to her knees in front of her and held her close, covering her with kisses. It was impossible not to cry then, as hard as she tried.


Miss Foster showed her to her dorm room and left her to unpack her things. The bedroom was quiet. Gabbie sat on the bed that was to be hers, feeling as wrung out as a damp bath towel.

What would her friends back home be doing now? Would they be passing notes at the back of Mrs Wallace's geography class? Making plans to meet at the park after school? She missed them so much that it actually hurt in her chest.

And her mum. When her dad had had to physically pull her away from their final goodbye. Telling her she was 'making it worse' for all of them. How could it possibly be worse?

Miss Foster had been kind, if not warm. As had the girl who had been selected to befriend her and show her around for the first week. Was there anything worse than having someone be kind to you because that's what they'd been told to do? It was so embarrassing. At least they'd left her alone now to 'get yourself unpacked and settled' before dinner.

The room was twice the size of her room at home, but there were four beds in it. Beside each one, a small table big enough for a lamp and maybe a book or two. She'd brought several favourites from home: their characters old friends whose company she would need now more than ever. The beds were neatly made, three of them covered in brightly coloured quilts with a teddy bear or cushions at the headboard. The fourth – the one she was sitting on – was hers.

Unshed tears burned at the back of her eyes as she thought of her own bed at home. The floral quilt cover that she and her mother had picked out on their last trip up to London, the rest of the books on her shelves that she'd read and reread, her dressing table with the lotions and potions that she and her mother would use when they were getting dressed up for a special occasion.

There would be no more celebrations for a while. Her nights would be spent here, with strangers, in a strange bed, in a strange house.

'How are you getting on?' The 'friend' from earlier poked her head around the corner of the door. Gabbie quickly wiped the tears from her eyes with the back of her hand. Afraid to speak in case the words became sobs.

The girl – she thought her name was Caitlin – came inside the room. Her long wavy hair was pulled back into a ponytail and it swished behind her. 'I know it's difficult on the first night. But you'll be okay. It's not as bad as you think. Honestly.'

Gabbie nodded, still not ready to trust her voice, but she attempted a weak smile.

'Come on,' Caitlin waved her to get up, 'you can unpack

later. Let's go and get some dinner. I can't promise it will be nice, but there will be lots of it.'

Gabbie followed the ponytail, glancing back once at the large suitcase by the side of her bed. Her mother had cried over it while they packed it yesterday, stroking her clothes as she placed them neatly inside. She knew – because she'd seen her do it – that she'd sneaked in packets of treats to make her smile when she eventually did get around to unpacking it here.

Gabbie hadn't cried then. Her father had been clear that she needed to be brave so as not to make her mother even worse. 'She's finding it hard that you're going, but she'll be fine once you're gone. And it will be the same for you, Gabbie. This is really great school; you're going to love it there, once you settle in. I know you will.'

This is all anyone had said to her about it. Even Jill, her parents' friend who was the one who'd found the school in the first place. A friend's daughter had been a teacher here and had convinced them all that it was the school equivalent of heaven on Earth. Jill was the one who'd brought the brochures to show them, the one she'd overheard speaking to her mother about it when she thought Gabbie was out of earshot. 'It's for the best, Margot. You know it is.'

But why was it for the best? How could it be better for her to be here, away from everyone she knew, rather than at the high school she'd been attending for the last year? No one had been able to give her a reason that she understood as to why they'd decided to send her away to school. Why her *father* had sent her away to school, when her mother – loyal to him though she was – clearly didn't want her to go.

Why did he want her out of the way? What had she done wrong? And why was Jill suddenly the person that he was turning to for advice?

# SIX

Being here was like stepping back in history. Not the local supermarket itself – which had kept up with the times and even had a shiny self-service till – but the way she felt about it. A cloud of grey had settled over Gabbie which seemed separate from the anxiety about Liam and the house.

It hadn't always been like this. In her earliest memories, the village had been the place she'd felt most happy. Whether it was ice cream after school with her mother in the cafe on the corner, or 'adventures in the forest' with her father in the woods behind the churchyard. Looking back, she'd lived a charmed existence wrapped in security and love. So why had it all gone wrong?

She could kick herself for offering to buy wine. It had been a reflex and she couldn't go back on it without raising suspicion. It didn't help that the supermarket was small and didn't have the choice – or special offers – she was used to in the large superstore at home. At least she didn't run the risk of bumping into someone who might ask why she wasn't staying at home. Or anyone who was going to ask her to do something, like the woman she'd stored in her phone as 'Mia's mum' who'd caught her at the school gate last Wednesday.

She'd jogged alongside Gabbie as she was dashing back home to her laptop. 'Hello! I'm so glad that I bumped into you. I've been meaning to ask you a favour.'

She pulled that face that people made to make it seem as if their 'cheeky' request was actually quite cute. Gabbie's heart sank. What was she going to have to do? 'Oh, yes?'

'It's my older daughter, Mia. She's struggling in French. I was wondering if you could help her out. We'd pay you of course.'

Tutoring someone's daughter was the last thing she wanted to do. Liam could never understand why these requests made her so anxious. It had been the same the week before when she'd agreed to join a book group with some of the mums from Olivia's old school so that they could stay in touch. 'Why do you always say yes to these things? When you know you're going to wish you hadn't?'

'They're Olivia's friends' mothers, what can I say?'

He shrugged. 'How about no, thank you?'

He made it sound so easy.

'What excuse can I use? What can I say I'm doing on Wednesday evening?'

He would look at her as if she was crazy. 'Why do you need an excuse? Just say no.'

Here, where she hadn't lived permanently for over three decades, she wasn't likely to run into anyone she knew. Which was why she was surprised to get a tap on the shoulder while she was staring at a bottle of passata.

'Gabbie?'

She turned towards the smiling face of a woman about her age with her hair scraped up into a plastic comb. There was something familiar about her, but she couldn't quite place her. 'Hello?'

'It *is* you!' She might not be sure who the woman was, but she seemed pretty clear that she knew Gabbie. 'My mum told me you were back. Jill called her this morning to say that she wouldn't need picking up for their art class tomorrow because you'd come to stay.' She laughed. 'Mum fancies herself the next Bob Ross, but my dad reckons that art class is just an excuse to meet up for lunch and have a few glasses of wine.'

The sound of her voice – and her ability to get through all of those words without taking a breath – must have turned a key on a door in Gabbie's memory. 'Tricia?'

Tricia beamed. 'Yes, it's me. Tricia Baxter, Bennett as was. It's got to be, what, twenty years since I've seen you?'

It was closer to twenty-five. Though Gabbie had played with the girls from her primary school when she came home the first few holidays, they'd drifted apart as the years had gone by. By their late-teens, they'd made it pretty clear that the 'snob' from the big house on the lane wasn't welcome to hang out with their group. It had seemed to coincide with the same time that they all got boyfriends.

'Yes. It must be that long. How are you? Are you still local?'

'Yeah, can't escape from the place. I married Craig in the end, big mistake, we're not together anymore. But we had two kids who most definitely weren't. A son and a daughter.'

Had Craig been one of the acne-ridden teenagers in the group she'd been excluded from? 'I've got two girls. Olivia is sixteen and Alice is eight.'

'Crikey. That's a big age gap. Same dad?'

*Wow.* She really wasn't afraid of a direct question. 'Yes. My husband, Liam.'

Tricia was obviously waiting for an explanation for the age gap but Gabbie wasn't about to give her one. Eventually, she moved on. 'My daughter is the same age as your Olivia. Maybe we should introduce them. Are you staying for a while?'

Something about her tone made Gabbie think that she

knew more than she was letting on. Surely Jill wouldn't have told Tricia's mother how suspicious their last-minute visit was? 'Yes, we're going to stay with Jill for a while. Summer holidays.'

Tricia arched an eyebrow. 'Really? Ours haven't broken up yet. I suppose yours go to posh schools with long holidays?'

Of course she'd assume that Gabbie's children had also gone to a private school. There was no way of explaining without telling her that she'd taken Alice out of school early and then that would open up another whole avenue of enquiry. She wanted to bring this to a close and get back to the house. 'I'm sure Olivia would love to meet up with someone her own age. Maybe we can arrange something.'

'Great. Shall we swap numbers? We can have a catch up and the girls can meet.'

Gabbie had meant it as a pleasantry. She wasn't expecting Tricia to be such a woman of action. She also wasn't sure they'd have anything in common or that she'd have the energy for social interaction right now. 'Actually, I don't have my phone on me and I've just changed my number.'

It was such an obvious lie that she was amazed when Tricia didn't call her out on it, but merely shrugged. 'I'll ask my mum to get your number from Jill. Then I'll text you and we can get something sorted for one evening.'

Gabbie pasted on her school-gate smile. 'Great. Sounds good.'

'I'll let you get back to your...' Tricia peered into Gabbie's shopping basket. 'Wine shopping. See you soon.'

'Yes. See you soon.'

Tricia turned to go then swivelled back. 'I'm sorry about your dad, by the way. I know it was a while ago, but, still, I'm sorry. My mum said he was a really nice man. Him and Jill used to go out with my mum and dad sometimes.'

Gabbie hated that Jill and her dad were the couple that

everyone remembered here. Almost as if her mother had never existed. That was probably the way Jill liked it. 'Thanks.'

Once Tricia had gone, the shelves looked even more depressing. It was like being back here at twenty, on a short visit from university, having to listen to her dad and Jill talk about their friends in the village as if they'd always been a fixture there. Only a handful of years after her mother's death and they were already married. It had been disgusting.

Her dad had taken her out to lunch to break the news. The Highwayman, on the main road out of the village. It had been the end of her first year at university and she was home for a week, before interrailing with two of the girls from her course. They planned to spend at least a week in Paris, flexing their language skills, before finding their way around as many other European cities as they could get to in a month.

They'd sat in the pub garden, her dad choosing a seat in the far corner. She'd been surprised that he'd ordered a whisky at lunchtime; now he was frowning at the ice cubes that the barmaid had dropped into it. 'I need to tell you something.'

She'd suspected it was coming. Even though Jill wasn't staying in the house this week, there was enough evidence around the rooms to suggest that she often did. The feminine hand soaps in the bathroom, her herbal tea bags in the cupboard – of course she was a chamomile drinker – and even spare clothes in the wardrobe of one of the bedrooms, which Gabbie had found when she'd gone snooping.

'You and Jill?'

She enjoyed the look of surprise on his face. 'Yes. I didn't know how to tell you. I was worried it might upset you. But she's been such a comfort to me since your mother died. A good friend. And, I suppose, it just gradually became more than that.'

She didn't want the grisly details. He thought that this was news to her, but she'd known for years that something was going on between them. Sipping at her pint of Adnams ale, she tried to think of a way to change the subject. What they did when she wasn't here didn't matter. Hadn't she spent her entire childhood not knowing what went on at home? There was no need to start now.

'We're getting married.'

She froze. *That* she'd not been expecting. Married? 'Why?'

He shrugged. 'Because we love each other.'

This had to be her idea. Jill. Any last vestige of feeling that she had for her mother's friend fizzed out like an extinguished candle. 'How nice.'

The dripping sarcasm wasn't lost on her father. 'Don't be like that. She thinks an awful lot of you. I want you to be happy for us.'

*I want you to be happy. I want you to be brave.* How many more times was he going to tell her how she should feel? 'Are you moving into her small semi in town or is she coming to live in your six-bedroom house, Dad?'

She knew she was being cruel, poking at him until he lost his temper, but he seemed determined to stay calm. 'That's not kind, Gabbie. To either of us. We have fallen in love and she will be coming to live with me in our house.'

Who was the 'our' here? His and her mum's? His and hers? 'It's hardly my house any longer then, is it? It'll be yours. Yours and hers.'

She spat the last word and he flinched. As always, he missed the source of her anger. 'The house will always be yours, Gabbie. When I go, it all goes to you. Jill is not after my money and, when you get over the shock, hopefully you'll admit that you know that.'

She'd laughed then, a bitter laugh older than her nineteen years. 'Do what you want, Dad. You always have. I'll be gone soon, anyway.'

They'd sat in silence then until he'd started to ask her awkwardly about her planned travels. Whether she needed more money or a lift to the airport. She'd shaken her head: she didn't want anything from him ever again.

She'd pretty much stuck to that over the years. When she left university and moved to a flat in Hackney she'd refused his offer to foot the deposit. But now, because of Liam and this horrendous situation, she was back begging the one person she'd never wanted to ask for help.

After throwing the bag of shopping in her car, she sat behind the wheel and called him. He must have been staring at his phone screen because he picked up on the first ring. 'Gabbie? Any news?'

'It might be nice to start with hello.'

He sighed. 'Sorry, love. I'm just on edge. I've just seen an email that says they've delayed the next court date by two weeks, to give us time to get the house on the market. I am hoping you've spoken to Jill and it won't come to that. We just need enough to show we can resume paying the mortgage.'

'I don't want to have to ask Jill for money, Liam. It's bad enough that we're having to stay here.'

She could hear the hardening in his voice, the shout that he was trying to hold back. 'I know you don't want to, but it's the only option we have. You do realise how serious this is, Gabbie?'

His heat turned her to ice. 'I think I understand that, Liam.'

He sighed. 'I know. Sorry. Shall I come up and speak to her?'

'No.' Jill's opinion of Liam was as low as her father's; he was the last person she'd be persuaded by. But it wasn't just that. Gabbie didn't want him here. She didn't want to even look at him right now. 'I will speak to her. You deal with the bank.'

His voice softened. 'I'm sorry. I'm really sorry about all of this. I will make it up to you, I promise. Once we've sorted all of this out, I will do everything in my power to make this up to you.'

Did she want him to make it up to her? Did she even want

him in her life any longer? He was presuming an awful lot to think that she would even want him to try. 'I have to go. Jill and the girls are waiting for me.'

Tonight, she would try to talk to her stepmother about money. As soon as the girls were in bed. And maybe she'd read some of those letters from her mother, too.

# SEVEN

*9th November 1992*

*My Darling Gabbie,*

*I know that you wanted to come home last weekend and I am so very sorry that you couldn't. There's been so much going on that I didn't have a chance to tell you that we wouldn't be coming to pick you up. I know that makes me a terrible mother and I am so sorry. I promise I will make it up to you next weekend. What would you like to do? Where would you like to go? Just name your wish and I promise that I will make it my command.*

*Jill has been at the house a lot this week and she has been telling me all the things that you're probably getting up to at school. It sounds like such fun. Like having sleepovers with your friends every night. Do you remember the sleepover we had here with all your primary school friends? When I woke you all up for a midnight feast like those books you loved so much?*

*I can't wait to have you home for the holidays – we have so much fun to catch up on.*

*Love Mama xx*

Coming back to school in November after the half term break was even more difficult than Gabbie's first day: this time she knew what she was coming back to. Even so, she had no idea that it was all going to get worse.

The time at home had been wonderful; her mother had packed six weeks' worth of fun into two. She'd seen her primary school friends, too. Tricia and the others had been really interested to hear all about school. She'd explained about the day – how they were woken for breakfast and then how the lessons were organised – and about all the fantastic facilities there – the pool, the tennis courts, the theatre with banked seats and proper lighting. She'd even made them laugh about how awful the food was – the jam roly poly they called Dead Man's Finger and the Brussels sprouts that could kill a man if thrown at force. But she hadn't told them how desolate she felt once she was back in her room, how lonely it was to sit in prep and not mind that the notes that were passed around never landed on her desk. She hadn't told them that she had no friends there at all.

Instead, she'd put all thoughts of school out of her mind and just enjoyed the freedom and happiness of being home. There, she woke up late to the smell of warm croissants and her mother's face lit up like a lamp when Gabbie padded into the kitchen to be wrapped in her Chanel-scented arms and turquoise silk dressing gown. She'd more than made it up to her for the times she'd promised to visit her at school and then had to cancel because of something – Gabbie assumed to do with her father – that had prevented it.

Her father had been pleased to see her, too, but he'd only had three days before being called to Munich for a meeting which ended up lasting a week. He apologised profusely, but Gabbie hadn't minded; since going away to school, she couldn't get over her disappointment in him. His betrayal in sending her away still stung. Plus, it meant she got to have her mother to herself.

Except, every day that he was gone, Jill would visit. She would just appear mid-morning on the pretence of having something to return, or with a gift from her garden or a cake she'd baked. Her mother welcomed Jill in for a coffee or to have a slice of the cake with them. Gabbie couldn't help but be resentful at having to share her precious hours with her mother giving Jill the positive version of her life at school.

It was Jill's fault that her mother didn't take her seriously when she'd told her that she didn't want to go to the school any longer. 'I hate it, Mum. No one talks to me. The girls are snobby and the teachers are so strict.'

Her mother's face had clouded over, the sadness on it so profound that she hadn't wanted to make it worse by telling her about the nights she'd cried into her pillow and screwed her eyes tight to imagine herself back at home.

When her mother had brought it up in Jill's company, though, Jill had shaken her head and smiled. 'It's just the settling-in period. You'll get used to it and then you'll love it. Join some teams, maybe?'

Her mother had looked from Jill to Gabbie and smiled. Gabbie had bitten her tongue and done the same.

And now she was back at school, sitting on her bed, refilling her tuck box with the treats that her mother had urged her to choose from the sweet shop in the village, before she and her father – returned from his trip – drove her back to school.

Five minutes before they got to the school, his voice had been stern. 'Now, you two, let's not make this worse for you both with another long drawn-out goodbye.'

As she'd watched them drive away, her mother had looked

back at her from the passenger window. Looking as much of a prisoner as Gabbie felt.

On the way to her room, she was obviously taking up too much space in the corridor, because a sixth former in hockey kit smacked into her shoulder with a bony elbow. It didn't bother her too much; there was a clear ranking order at school and she knew that she was near the bottom. It wasn't personal; to this girl – to all the older girls – she was someone to ignore. In fact, she hadn't realised how easy she was to ignore until she'd come here. How easy to overlook. How invisible. Was it the way she held herself, head down, scurrying to Maths, English or lunch like a harvest mouse? Or was it her ordinary looks, her lack of excellence in lessons or on the hockey pitch? Either way, other than an occasional smile or pleasantry, she'd had no real interaction with any of the other girls since she'd got here. Maybe Jill was right. Maybe she needed to try harder to be liked.

If her parents weren't going to take her out of the school, she'd need to try and make at least one friend. Maybe she could force herself to train harder at hockey or netball, get selected for one of the teams. Drama group would be another option, although that would involve her standing on stage in front of an audience and even imagining that made her shudder.

Jill had given her a lecture the afternoon before about the amount of money it was costing her father to send her here and how important it was that she make the most of the opportunities he was giving her. It was almost as if Jill was appointing herself a third parent and it was most definitely not wanted. If she did make an effort, show her parents – and Jill – that she'd tried her best but she still didn't want to be here, maybe then they would listen to her and let her come back home and go to the high school with her old friends. She would do it. Push herself out there and try to make friends, get herself noticed.

If only she'd realised how preferable it could be to be invisible. How much worse it could be to be seen.

# EIGHT

Sunday lunch had been strained – Jill's disapproving face when Alice pushed every piece of vegetable except the carrots to the side of her plate set Gabbie's teeth on edge – and she'd been glad to keep her promise to take Alice back to the small park, ensuring that she visited the toilet before they went this time.

When they got back, Jill was speaking to Olivia in the kitchen. From the hallway, she could hear Olivia asking questions about Jill's art class and the people she'd mentioned from the village. Though Gabbie was proud of her politeness and friendliness, she couldn't help feeling irritated that Jill was getting the best of her daughter.

The rest of the afternoon crawled by. Jill got a text from Tricia via her mother, asking for Gabbie's number. Gabbie only discovered that she'd sent it when she got a message.

> Hi! Lovely to bump into you. Jill gave me your number and she said you've no plans for tomorrow. I've got a half day tomorrow. Why don't you and your daughters come over? About four?

Gabbie read it three times. There was no way out of it and, to be honest, she would quite enjoy some adult company with someone who knew nothing about her current situation. Unless Jill had messaged Tricia with what she suspected along with her telephone number.

> Great. Text me your address and we'll pop in.

At teatime, Gabbie made sandwiches for them all. Jill raised an eyebrow when she cut the crusts from Alice's, but she didn't actually say anything. It had been a late night for an eight-year-old the day before and, by seven o'clock, Alice was yawning.

Jill looked over the top of her reading glasses. 'Hand over your mouth, Alice. It's clearly about time you were in bed, little lady.'

It was bedtime, but that wasn't Jill's decision to make. 'Are you sleepy, Alice?'

Usually, there would be a resolute *no* to that question, but she must be going through a growth spurt because she'd almost welcomed bedtime in the last couple of weeks. 'Will you come with me, Mummy? Can I sleep in your bed with you?'

Gabbie would have loved to curl up with Alice and black out the rest of the day in sleep, but she needed to finish the translation work from earlier. If she lay down in a warm bed right now, she wouldn't be getting up again. 'I'll read you a story but I can't stay all night.'

She was surprised when Olivia stood up. 'I'll take her.'

Alice was thrilled; she loved her older sister. 'Will you read my story, too?'

'Okay. But only once.'

Gabbie smiled as she watched them go. Sometimes their big age gap was a lovely thing.

Without them here, the air between her and Jill was colder and she was grateful that she had the perfect excuse to escape.

'I'm going to go back to my laptop in the morning room and get this work finished.'

Jill nodded. 'Don't stare at the screen too long; you'll never get to sleep tonight.'

Gabbie dug her fingernails into her palms as she left to prevent herself from replying.

With the door to the morning room shut behind her, and her laptop set up on the table, Gabbie could finally breathe again. There was something about reading French which always soothed her. She'd been halfway through her degree before she realised that, in her mind, she always read French in her mother's voice: it had been both a comfort and a source of pain. Most people assumed that she'd been brought up bilingual. 'It's easy for you with a French mother,' her local friends used to moan. But that hadn't been the case. Her mother had always spoken English at home aside from the odd phrase or endearment. 'I don't want your father to feel excluded,' she would say. But that didn't explain why she hadn't spoken French to Gabbie more often when they were alone.

And then, of course, she'd gone away to school. There, she'd kept silent about her mother's nationality, not wanting the weight of expectation on her in Madame Fournier's classroom. But maybe it was imprinted on her DNA somehow, because languages came easily to her. When the time came to choose her A levels, and then her degree, choosing French had felt right. Not only because she was good at it, but because it was a way to stay connected to the mother she'd lost.

Becoming a translator had been an obvious career path and Gabbie had always loved it. Though she wasn't the creative type exactly – she'd never believed the lie that everyone had a book in them – translating one language into another required an ability to use language accurately, but also effectively. Choosing the right adjective to convey the strength of expression sometimes felt like composing poetry.

The texts Mandie from the translation agency had sent had nothing of poetry about them, though. Press releases from an international logistics company and web pages from a PR company in Quebec. Her eyes were tired and she tried to rub some life into them before she started. She'd been at it for about forty minutes when the door to the morning room opened and she looked up to see Olivia standing on the threshold, as stiff as a board. 'Hi, love. Everything okay? Did Alice make you read that story ten times again?'

Olivia's face was white. She looked as exhausted as Gabbie felt. 'Alice is asleep. She hasn't got a clue what's going on, thank goodness.'

She was so hard to read lately. Was she angry? Upset? Both? 'What is it, Olivia? Are you still cross about missing the party on Tuesday?'

She was expecting more remonstrances about how she didn't understand what it was like to be the only one who wasn't going. How Gabbie was ruining her life. She wasn't expecting what she actually got.

'Are you splitting up with Dad?'

*Ouch.* She wasn't pulling any punches. But Gabbie wasn't ready to answer that question. Even to herself. 'What makes you ask that?'

Olivia stepped into the room, her arms straight at her sides, fists clenched. 'You bringing us here, Dad staying at home, you barely speaking to him before we left. I'm not stupid. I'm not a child.'

No, she wasn't a child, but she wasn't an adult either. Gabbie could remember vividly how that felt, the tug of childish ways, the pull of adult promise. Both at once and neither at the same time. If only she could make Olivia realise that it would all be okay.

It was difficult to convey that right now, though, when she'd no idea whether they were going to be fine. How would it be for the girls if this was the end for her and Liam? And even if they managed to – somehow – find a way out of this mess, how could she trust that he would not put them back in this position again?

This wasn't the time for that conversation, though. 'Love, you just need to—'

'I'd go with him.' Olivia cut her off with the jut of her chin. 'If you leave Dad, I'm staying with him. I'm not moving out of our house.'

Her words cut into Gabbie, sharper than a knife. How had they got to this? So far away from one another. The little girl who had gone to sleep every night with her tiny fingers twisting Gabbie's hair. Her breath soft and sweet on Gabbie's cheek.

Until Olivia turned three, they'd been inseparable. Although she'd gone back to work six months after Olivia was born, Gabbie had had the luxury of only taking on a limited number of translation projects that she could work around looking after the baby. It had been exhausting – at times she'd been typing with her eyes half-closed and a sleeping baby Olivia strapped to her chest – but it meant that she hadn't had to sacrifice a single moment.

Maybe that's why it had been so difficult to leave Olivia with strangers when she started preschool. Her first morning had been torturous. Gabbie had packed her a little bag with a snack and her favourite teddy – a much-loved fluffy panda who wasn't so much black and white as black and grey – and had made sure that her clothes were easy for her to pull down and up if she had to go to the toilet. She'd tried to think of every eventuality that her tiny little girl might encounter and prepare her for it.

Liam thought she was being over the top. 'It's only three hours, Gabbie. And the preschool staff know what they're doing.'

Of course they knew what they were doing, but they couldn't watch all the children at once, could they? And Olivia was so precious; she couldn't bear the idea that she would need her mother and Gabbie wouldn't be there. It brought tears to her eyes even thinking about her wandering alone in that room full of strangers.

But Olivia had amazed her. Clutching her Peppa Pig lunch bag, she'd taken the hand of the nursery teacher and waved goodbye to Gabbie as if she'd done this every day of her life.

'But that's good, isn't it?' Liam had been completely confused when she'd called him, gulping down huge sobs, from the preschool car park.

'Yes. Of course it is.' She'd pulled down the glove compartment to search for more tissues. 'She doesn't need me at all.'

He had been gentle then. 'You've done a good job, Gabbie. She was ready to go because you gave her everything she needed.'

That had started her sobbing all over again.

She wanted to cry now, too, seeing the anger in her daughter's face. Anger directed at her. 'You're not going to have to choose who to live with because no one is moving anywhere.'

She'd always sworn that she wouldn't lie to her children, but she was getting dangerously close now. If Liam wasn't able to persuade the bank to give them more time – and she wasn't able to persuade Jill to lend them some money – then they might all be moving somewhere. Who knew where? Her stomach lurched at the very thought.

Olivia clearly hadn't finished wounding her. 'And why are you being so horrible to Dad? He wanted to speak to you earlier and you were just shutting him out.'

The irony nearly made her laugh out loud. *Her* shutting *him* out? He was the one who'd kept a massive, earth-shattering secret, not her. But she couldn't say anything about that to Olivia. How would she even begin to understand what Liam had done and why? If Gabbie couldn't get her head around it, how was a sixteen-year-old going to?

'The thing is, Olivia, there are lots of parts to being an adult which are complicated. Situations come up that you've never encountered before and you have to deal with them in the best way you can. No one tells you what to do. There're no right answers.'

Olivia's gasp made her jump. She raised a trembling hand to her mouth. 'Oh, no. You really are getting divorced, aren't you? I didn't think it was really real. Please don't. Is it my fault? Because I've been difficult lately and—'

'Hey, hey. No. Absolutely not. None of this has anything to do with you. There's no talk of divorce. We just have stuff to sort out. Come here.' She pulled Olivia towards her and was surprised that she didn't resist. It felt so different hugging her these days. Like holding another woman rather than a child. Though she still had an inch on her, it wouldn't be long before Olivia was taller than she was.

Awful though the situation was, she was enjoying this moment of Olivia needing her reassurance. Resting her face against her hair, she closed her eyes and breathed in. Now Olivia's voice was softer, younger and her words pulled Gabbie back down a tunnel to over thirty years ago. 'When are we going home, Mum? I just want to go home.'

She wished so much that she could click her heels together and take the three of them back there. To a week ago when their lives were average and everyday and safe. Olivia couldn't possibly know how much her words were like knives. How could she? Gabbie had spoken so little of her time at boarding school – keeping any anecdotes positive and cheery – that her daughter would have no idea how her words had echoed Gabbie's own, over three decades before.

# NINE

*22nd November 1992*

*My Darling Gabbie,*

*Are you getting excited for Christmas yet? While we were away, Daddy had to go to lots of meetings, so I had time to go shopping for presents and I might have bought some lovely things for a girl you know. One of them might already be on its way to you as I write!*

*I think I have persuaded your papa to have a Christmas party at the house. Would you like to invite your new friends to come? Your letter told me lots of nice things about school, but you haven't mentioned any of the people you've met. Haven't you any gossip for your poor mother?*

*Jill looked after the house while we were away and she has moved so many things around that I don't know where to find anything. Your father keeps telling me how much better everything is now that it's organised properly, but I liked it better the old way.*

*Hope you enjoy the little gift!*

*Love Mama xx*

It started with the Belgian truffles.

Her mother had accompanied her father on one of his trips to Brussels and had sent Gabbie a selection box of the most beautiful chocolates she'd ever seen. Each individual square chocolate had been handcrafted to a different design: stripes and swirls and dots and criss-crosses. Others were shaped like flowers – roses and tulips – or engraved with swirly French writing.

They were too perfect to eat and there was still no one with whom Gabbie might share them. Instead, she'd stowed them into the tuck box under her bed, intending to have one each day whilst she read a book.

If Gabbie was invisible, Jessica Swanley-Thomson was a beacon. Thick blonde hair, big blue eyes and a voice that could cut through ice. Never alone, it would always be clear whatever thoughts were in her entitled head because she would be loudly proclaiming them to whichever acolyte was currently hanging on her every word.

Gabbie didn't know which of her roommates had told Jessica about the chocolates, but she almost jumped when Jessica sidled up to her after prep and asked about them. 'It's not surprising that you don't have any friends if you keep all your treats to yourself rather than share.'

For a moment, she had no idea what she was talking about. Her heart thumped with the pressure of trying to understand. 'Sorry?'

'Your posh chocs. Don't you think it might be nice to let your friends have some?'

Now she was really confused. What friends? 'Would *you* like one?'

She tried – and failed – to keep the stammering desperation from her voice. Jessica shrugged. 'If you're offering, we wouldn't say no.'

Gabbie knew that this was her chance. If Jessica liked her, that opened up the possibility of friends everywhere. 'Do you want to come now?'

'Okay.' Jessica turned to the girls slowly packing away their books, clearly waiting to follow wherever she might lead. 'Come on, Gabbie has chocolate.'

She hadn't expected quite so many of them to follow her back to her room. She leaned underneath her bed and brought out the white cardboard box; pulled out the drawer of sweets, sitting in brightly lined dimples like jewels. The collective sigh of the girls gave her – for just a moment – a fleeting pleasure. These were her chocolates and she was sharing them with her new friends.

Jessica, of course, took the first one. It was the centrepiece; the perfectly crafted pink rose which was double the size of all the others. Though Gabbie had planned to save this one for last, it didn't matter. It was a small price to pay. She offered the box to the next nearest girl – Serena – who took it from her hands and spent forever choosing between a white chocolate square and a milk chocolate heart.

'Come on!' One of the girls behind nudged Serena so hard that the chocolates jumped in the box. 'You're taking too long.'

Serena snatched up both chocolates in one swoop and passed the box on. From that point on, it took seconds for the box to be passed around from one eager hand to another. Gabbie's heart fluttered; she couldn't stop them. *Not all of them*, she wanted to say, *please not all of them.*

The girls were such a noisy hubbub of laughter and groans of sugar-infused pleasure that, once they left, the silence in the bedroom was all the more deafening. Gabbie could only stare at the crumpled empty box on her bed and avoid the pitying looks from her dorm mates.

It was then that she realised that this was not the start of her inclusion into their group. They'd taken what they wanted and now they were gone. She'd been picked up and dropped like a disposable napkin. As far as they were concerned, she no longer existed.

Once a week, all the girls were required to write a letter to their parents. As everyone had been at school, following their usual routine, these must have been the most mundane of epistles. Not wanting to upset her mother, Gabbie's had always been a list of the lessons she'd done that week with all the things she'd learned. She tried to find something of interest to comment on – the flowers in the garden or an interesting anecdote from one of the teachers – but it wasn't easy.

This time, though, she'd reached the limit for being brave. She was going to tell her parents the truth. About the theft of the chocolates, the loneliness, the dull misery that was her constant companion. And she did.

Once the letters were written, they had to be checked by the housemistress, Miss Foster. After her early kindness, Gabbie now knew her as a formidable woman, with a huge chest and eyes that looked in slightly different directions. Gabbie was terrified of her; she had a booming voice that pinned you to the wall whether she was reprimanding you for running in the corridor or merely telling you to hurry up and finish your breakfast.

Gabbie was good at English, her spelling and punctuation possibly the best in the class, so it couldn't have been that which caused Miss Foster to frown at her letter. She realised that this might possibly be the first time that she'd told anyone about her unhappiness. Maybe she should have come to see her before now and asked for help. Is that what she was going to say?

But Miss Foster merely flicked out her arm from the elbow

so that the paper audibly sliced the air. 'No. You can't send this home. Your parents are too busy to read about silliness among girls. And you don't want to upset them, do you? Go and write them a nice letter now, please.'

She bent her head to continue marking the set of exercise books in front of her, her fountain pen scratching red ink across the page. She didn't even look up when Gabbie hesitated. 'Off you go, then.'

With legs like lead, Gabbie returned to her chair and took up a fresh sheet of paper. If she wasn't allowed to write the truth, she would have to wait until she next saw her mother in person.

# TEN

Tricia's house was the middle in a set of three terraced houses. Her front garden was small but neat and the door knocker so shiny that Gabbie could see the reflection of her sunglasses in it.

Alice had opted to stay home with Jill, so it was just the two of them. Gabbie wished that Olivia hadn't put on so much make-up, but she understood the need to keep herself a little hidden. Weren't her sunglasses doing the self-same job?

The tall dark-haired girl who answered the front door looked as if she'd had the same idea. 'Hi. Are you Gabbie and Olivia? I'm Elsa. Mum's in the kitchen. Come through.'

She led them through a small lounge to the kitchen where Tricia was taking a tray of black smoking discs from the cooker. 'Dammit.'

Elsa started to laugh. 'Impressive, Mother.'

As Tricia dropped the baking tray and its contents into the sink, the smoke alarm behind their heads started to emit its piercing beep. Without missing a beat, Elsa pulled a chair underneath it and climbed up to turn it off, while Tricia flapped her arms about to move the smoke.

'And that's how we welcome guests in our house.' Tricia

laughed. 'I was planning to impress you with some homemade cookies, but I was listening to this really good podcast called "Best Friend Therapy" and I lost track of time. Do you like podcasts?'

Elsa groaned. 'Mum! Enough with the podcasts. Please can you just be normal for five minutes?'

'Normal is overrated, Elsa. I tell you and your brother that every day.'

Elsa's brother chose that moment to walk into the kitchen. 'Is something on fire?'

'This is my son, Matt. And Elsa you've already met. You must be Olivia?'

'Yes,' Olivia nodded. 'Pleased to meet you.'

Matt must have been almost six feet tall and he had the same dark hair and olive skin as his sister. By the way she blushed when she spoke, his good looks hadn't been lost on Olivia.

Matt yawned and stretched his arms above his head. 'I was just about to make something to eat, but I can come back in a bit?'

'No, you kids stay in here and sort yourselves out with some food. I've made a pot of coffee for Gabbie and me to take into the garden.' She looked at Gabbie, 'Unless you'd prefer tea?'

'Coffee in the garden sounds great.' She touched Olivia's elbow to check that she was okay with being abandoned, but Elsa was already showing her a picture of her recent prom dress on her phone. Olivia smiled at Gabbie and nodded that she was fine to go.

The garden was a neat handkerchief of green bordered by bright pink pots of flowers. Tricia had set a table and two chairs with mugs and an insulated coffee pot. 'Sorry about the lack of biscuits.'

'Please don't apologise. This is lovely. A real sun trap.'

Tricia looked pleased. 'Well, it's small, but it's mine. All mine.'

'So it's just you and the children here?'

Tricia picked up the coffee pot and started to pour. 'Yep. We had a four-bedroom place near the park, but that was sold during the divorce. We moved in here about eighteen months ago.'

'It's lovely. You've done a great job on the place.'

'Most of the credit goes to Elsa. She's an art student so she knows about these things. Matt wields a paintbrush and does what she tells him and I just pay for the materials. Milk?'

'Yes, please. No sugar.'

She took the cup that Tricia passed her. 'Is it harder? Being a single parent?'

'Mine are older now, and my ex was a waste of space, so not really. Maybe if they'd been younger, I might tell a different story.' She screwed up her eyes. 'Why do you ask?'

Gabbie wasn't ready to start unburdening her problems just yet. 'No particular reason.'

Laughter travelled out of the kitchen, Olivia's among it; Gabbie was pleased she was enjoying herself.

Tricia sipped her coffee. 'So, how long will you be staying with Jill?'

'I don't know yet. It depends on a few things. My husband's job and holidays and stuff like that.' She was trying to be vague but she could see that she was merely stoking Tricia's curiosity. She wished she knew what Jill had told Tricia's mother.

'Well. It'll be nice to spend some time with you while you're here.'

Gabbie shifted in her seat. 'I'm sorry that I was so rubbish at keeping in touch after I went to university. I didn't even know you'd got married, much less that you'd split up with your husband.'

Tricia waved away her apology. 'Don't be silly, we all get

busy. I could just as easily have called you. And me and Craig splitting up was a long time coming.' She sighed. 'I found out that he'd slept with someone else. Someone he met through work. I threw him out, obviously. But the kids were distraught and he begged to come back. Promised me he'd never do it again and I, like an idiot, believed him.'

'So he did do it again?'

'Of course he did. Once he'd been let off the hook once, he thought he could get away with it again. Like the podcast says, "what you permit, you promote."'

Elsa hadn't been wrong about her mother's podcast obsession. 'And that's when you split up?'

'Yep. Fool me twice and all that. I was worried what the kids would say. I mean, he's a good dad, always has been. But I was honest with them second time around and they understood. Matt was really angry with his dad for a while, but they're getting there. Craig is living with a new girlfriend – poor cow – and they've met her and everything.'

Gabbie admired her honesty, but this was different to her situation. She was really angry with Liam right now, but it wasn't as if he'd had an affair. That would have been something she could definitely never forgive. The jury was still out on whether they could make their way back from their particular problem.

'So, how's work? Are you still translating?'

'Yes. I work from home and can work it around the kids, which is great. How about you?'

'I'm a legal secretary. I went back to school a few years ago and did the qualifications. I'm still studying, but I love it.'

'Good for you, that's fantastic. So you work for a solicitor?'

'Yes. I've always been fascinated by anything about the legal system on TV. Once the kids got older and I had more time, I decided to go for it. You only get one chance at this life. You have to take it.'

It had been a long time since she'd met anyone as positive as Tricia; being with her was like being given a long cool glass of water on a hot day. 'You're amazing.'

'Yeah, well. It took me a lot of therapy to get to this stage but, yes, I'm pretty happy.'

Something else occurred to Gabbie. 'Your legal firm, what kind of work do they do?'

'All sorts. A lot of it is family law but that includes quite a lot. Divorce, custody, financial.' She counted them off on her fingers.

Though she didn't want to lay out her problems before Tricia, it would really help to speak to someone who knew the law. 'Do you think I could make an appointment to see someone at your place?'

Legal advice wasn't cheap, she knew that. But she still had that money in the account that she'd been saving for a new kitchen.

If Tricia was shocked, she was professional enough not to show it. 'Of course. I'll ask Jane to speak to you. She's great. And if I tell her that you're a friend of mine she'll probably have a chat with you beforehand so that she can tell you if it's worth your while engaging them for whatever it is you need.'

'Thank you. That would be really great.'

Before she did that, she was going to need to call Liam and get the full details of what he'd already done. She didn't want to spend a precious phone call with a solicitor admitting she didn't know what had happened and looking like even more of a fool than she already felt.

Two hours later, Gabbie and Olivia were being waved goodbye by Tricia and Elsa from their front door, promising to get together again soon.

Jill's house was only a ten-minute walk away. Once they were out of earshot, Gabbie nudged Olivia. 'How was that?'

She was delighted to see a smile on Olivia's face. 'Great. I really like Elsa. We've swapped numbers and she said that if I'm stuck for something to do, I should just text her.'

'I'm pleased. Maybe we can spend some time with them while we're here?' She'd overheard Elsa telling Olivia about her plans for the week when they left and it had sounded like she was suggesting that Olivia was welcome to join her.

Olivia nodded. 'Yeah, that'd be good. Can we go home for the night tomorrow, though? It's just, I have that party, the one that everyone from my old school is going to. Remember?'

She hadn't forgotten. But with no house to go back to and no access to all the clothes except the ones they'd packed to bring here, there was no way that Olivia was going to be able to get to that party. 'I'm sorry, love, but I'm not sure that we can.'

Olivia stopped dead in the street. 'But I have to go. Everyone is going to wear their prom outfits again and it'll be the last party we'll have before everyone goes off for the summer and then loads of people are going to different schools and colleges. It'll be the last time we're all together. I have to be there.'

Olivia looked distraught. Just like that, the pleasant atmosphere of the last couple of hours was torn apart.

'I'm sorry, but I just can't see—'

'You don't understand. Mum, please.'

She hated saying no, hated not being able to give Olivia what she wanted. 'I would if I could, honestly I would. Come on, we need to get back to Alice.'

Olivia started to walk, but she looked straight ahead and said nothing all the way home. Gabbie understood her desire to be with her friends more than anyone; it wasn't fair that she was the one having to bear the brunt of her anger when all of this was Liam's fault. What could she do to make this better?

# ELEVEN

*Darling Gabbie,*

*It was so wonderful to see you on Saturday! I am so pleased that I put my foot down with your father and refused to go on his boring trip to Munich.*

*And how delightful that we should bump into that friend of yours and her parents. Why haven't you mentioned her before? Did you say her name was Jessica? We must try and meet up with them in the Christmas holidays!*

*Did I tell you that Jill had wanted to come with me when I visited you? I said she could, but then I realised that I wanted it to be just us, so I left without her. She was so cross when I got home. But it was lovely to have just mother and daughter time, wasn't it? I can't tell you what a weight it was from my shoulders that you are making friends. I knew that you would, my clever, beautiful daughter. Because who could fail to love you?*

*You'll notice from the postmark that I am not at home yet.*

*The house is so big and lonely without your father home and I just know that Jill would come over expecting us to meet for tea, so I have taken myself away for a few days. Wish you were here with me!*

*Love Mama xx*

Every half term, there was one exeat weekend when there were no Saturday lessons and students were allowed to leave the school until supper on Sunday. Sometimes students would go home for the night; for others, their parents would come and take them out for the day and bring them back early. When Gabbie's mother came to take her out for lunch on an exeat Saturday without her father, Gabbie resolved to tell her how unhappy she was – despite trying very hard to fit in – and beg to be allowed to leave.

It was drilled into the girls how lucky they were to be at St Catherine's. When Gabbie had first enrolled, she hadn't given much thought to the financial cost to her parents. They'd always been comfortably off and, when she'd been at primary school, she'd known that the other children regarded her as the rich kid from the big house. At St Catherine's, though, she was in a much lower financial league. The girls there would talk about the nannies who had raised them, the housekeepers who let them sneak warm cakes from the kitchen at home; some of them even had chauffeurs to drop them to school at the beginning of each term. Quite soon, Gabbie learned how the rich can sniff out who is their equal and who is not. And she was deemed most definitely not. Maybe that's why no one wanted to be her friend.

Due to a last-minute business trip for her father, it was to be just her and her mother that weekend. Speaking to her alone, Gabbie knew that she would be able to make her mother understand just how much she missed home. Her mother had big plans for them and had booked a room in a five-star hotel seven miles from the school for them to stay for the night. Gabbie didn't want to spoil the whole of their time together so, for the Saturday afternoon and evening, she kept her sadness locked away and allowed herself to be sucked into her mother's orbit.

Their final few hours together included Sunday lunch in the hotel restaurant. A vast space filled with white tablecloths and crystal glasses. Whispered conversations and the chink of silver cutlery surrounded them on all sides. Once they'd placed their order, Gabbie took a deep breath. Now was the time. But, when she opened her mouth, someone else's words replaced hers.

'Hello, Gabrielle. I didn't expect to see you here.'

To her horror, she turned to see Jessica Swanley-Thomson standing beside their table. But this was a different Jessica. One that was all smiles and appraised Gabbie's mother like a work of art. Beside her, a set of parents who looked exactly like her: blonde, attractive, wealthy.

Her father was also looking at Gabbie's mother, and he clearly liked what he saw. 'How nice to encounter one of Jessica's friends out in the wild. How are you finding the school, Gabrielle?'

Gabbie's tongue felt too big in her mouth; she could barely push the words past it. 'It's fine, thank you.'

Her mother was much more effusive. 'Well, this is wonderful. I've been asking Gabbie about her friends. So nice to meet you, Jessica. I'm sure you girls have lots of fun together.'

Jessica looked at her mother like she was a model, her voice saccharine sweet. 'Oh yes, we do. Gabbie is always kind enough to share the lovely treats you send her.'

Her mother beamed. 'Then I shall have to send more for you all.'

Then passed a few pleasantries between the parents, but Gabbie barely registered their conversation. Her mother looked so pleased that she'd finally found a friend that, even once the three of them had left for their own table, she could no longer summon the energy to tell her what was going on.

Of course, it hadn't helped matters back at school, where Jessica regaled her group with a description of their surprise meeting before calling out to Gabbie. 'How did your mother have a daughter that looks like you? She must have been so disappointed. Is your dad really ugly?'

Every comment was met with rapturous delight from the other girls. An adult observer would have known that this was in no small part due to relief that it wasn't directed at them, but to Gabbie, these were poison darts of truth that made her sink even further down inside herself.

At every turn, her attempts to tell her parents how unhappy she was had been thwarted. First the censorship of the letters home, then the interruption of her lunch with her mother. She'd even tried – and failed – to speak to her parents about her loneliness on her weekly allotted phone call. But how could she possibly pour out her heart with a queue of irritated girls behind her who would find her tears and whispered pain a delicious treat to share at teatime?

Her only option was to stick it out and wait until the Christmas holidays. Once she was at home, she would be honest and tell them how she felt. Even if she was ashamed to have no friends and guilty that her mother would be upset. During her time at home, she would be able to explain everything, tell them the truth of how she felt, whatever the consequences.

# TWELVE

When they got back from Tricia's, Olivia disappeared upstairs and Gabbie slipped off her shoes in the hall and called out for Alice and Jill. 'We're home. Where are you?'

Jill's voice echoed from the back of the house. 'We're in the morning room.'

The morning room was adjacent to the kitchen at the back of the house. When she'd been around Alice's age, it had been her favourite place in the house. The large window let in the early morning sunshine and she had blurred but beautiful memories of sitting at this same oval table eating crêpes that her mother had made for breakfast. Then the walls were a bright egg yolk yellow. Now, like most of the house, they were a cold vanilla.

Once she'd moved in, Jill preferred to use this room when she invited the local women over for coffee or afternoon tea. Privately, Gabbie had called it the moaning room – all they did was sit around and discuss their husbands and any of their friends who were absent that week – and she'd avoided ever having to go in when they were there.

When Gabbie pushed open the door today, though, she found that the china tea set and starched tablecloth had been packed away and Alice was sitting at the oval table with Jill, surrounded by paper and paint and glue. 'Crikey. Where did all this come from?'

Jill glanced up at her, but kept snipping. 'My friend from the choir has grandchildren Alice's age. When I told her you were here, she kindly dropped off all of these craft materials.'

More people who knew that Gabbie and the children were here. Had she taken out an advert in the local paper?

Alice waved something brightly coloured. 'Look, Mummy, Jill showed me how to make a paper chain of people. I'm going to stick some eyes on them and give them all different colour hair.'

That must be why Jill was cutting up short lengths of wool in various shades of brown and yellow. They seemed so comfortable with each other that it had the opposite effect on Gabbie and she hovered by Alice's side, not sure where to insert herself so as not to disrupt their project.

'Why don't you take a seat?' Jill nodded at the chair opposite, relinquishing her scissors and pushing the wool strips towards Alice. 'The hair is done, Alice. Shall I start sticking the sequins on for buttons?'

It would be churlish to refuse to join them. As she sat down, Gabbie took in the pile of fragmented people shapes who must have been Alice's first attempts. She loved the way Alice stuck the tip of her tongue out of the side of her mouth as she concentrated hard on transferring the plastic eye from her finger to the face of one of her creations. 'Did you used to sit here and make things with your mummy?'

It was obvious that Jill was purposely not looking at her; no one needed that much concentration to stick a sequin onto a dress-shaped piece of card. 'Not that I remember. My mum, your grandmother' – still the word felt strange associated with Margot – 'wasn't really into this kind of thing.'

She hadn't meant to sound so dismissive. Some of her happiest memories were drawing or painting or colouring with the girls. Then she would pin up their work in the kitchen, or frame it for the wall. Some of them still hung in the hallway at home and it was painful to imagine them looking out on their abandoned rooms.

Jill smiled at Alice. 'Your grandmother didn't like mess much.'

Alice looked surprised. 'Did you know Mummy's mummy?'

Why was Jill so surprised that Alice didn't know that? Did she expect Gabbie to have told her? 'Oh yes. We were friends. Well, actually I was friends with your grandpa first.'

*And last*, Gabbie thought. Once her mother was out of the way.

Alice loved a life story. Finished with the eye sticking, she dipped a thick paintbrush into the pale pink paint and dabbed at the hands and feet of the paper people. 'How did you know Grandpa, Auntie Jill?'

They'd decided on the moniker 'Auntie' because Gabbie wasn't comfortable with anything more than that. 'We went to school together; we grew up in the same street.'

Alice scrutinised Jill as if imagining her at school. 'So why didn't you marry Grandpa first?'

If Jill was uncomfortable with this line of questioning, she didn't show it. 'Because when he met your grandma, he fell head over heels in love.'

As Jill spoke, Gabbie folded a strip of purple paper into a concertina. She could feel her chest tightening. She didn't want to hear any of this. She knew it all, of course: how her father had introduced Jill and her mother, how they'd become close friends. When she was young, she could remember many afternoons spent at Jill's house with her mother, or meeting her for tea in a fancy cafe. Before she was old enough to know what tact was, she would ask Jill why she didn't have a husband or a child of her own.

But Alice had other questions. 'What does *head over heels in love* mean?'

Before it toppled, Gabbie reached out for the jar of water that Alice was using rather enthusiastically to clean her paintbrush. 'It's an expression, sweetheart. It means you fall so much in love with someone that you can't help yourself.'

Alice screwed up her face as if they were both crazy. 'And it makes you fall over?'

Jill laughed. 'Something like that.'

Paintbrush poised mid-air, a slow nod suggested that Alice was trying her best to understand. 'And then Grandpa fell over in love with you?'

Every time she said the word 'love' the tension in the room went up a notch. But Olivia saved them by sloping into the morning room, her phone welded to her hand. 'Everyone is on the WhatsApp group talking about the party tomorrow and what they're going to wear. I can't believe you're stopping me from being there.'

Gabbie understood that feeling, but what could she do? It wasn't only that they were two hours away; if she took Olivia back home for the party, she would have to explain why she couldn't get into her own house to get ready for it. 'There'll be other parties.'

She hadn't thought Olivia's face could get any darker. 'Not like this one. Everyone is going to be there.'

Alice looked up at her sister. 'Is your boyfriend going to be there?'

Quick as a flash, Olivia picked up another paintbrush and dabbed a blob of yellow paint onto Alice's nose. Alice screamed and then collapsed into giggles.

Olivia had a smile for her little sister, at least. 'What are you making here, squirt?'

'Paper people.' Alice painted glue on to the head of her next victim and then started to lay the wool hair across it. 'Did you know that Auntie Jill was friends with Mummy's mummy? But she was friends with Grandpa first.'

Gabbie couldn't sit through this again. 'I'm going to make a drink. Would anyone like tea?'

It took her three attempts to remember where Jill kept the cups and then the teabags. It didn't matter how organised someone's kitchen was, it was never the way you would have done it yourself. She wondered whether her own mother would have laid it all out differently. Not that she had many memories of her mother in the kitchen beyond breakfast pancakes, to be honest.

Though she'd had to walk out into the hall to get into the kitchen, there was actually a hatch that connected it to the morning room so she could hear their conversation perfectly. As she'd left to make the tea, Olivia had picked up a piece of paper and was cutting out more people. She sounded much brighter than she had when she first came downstairs. 'What was Mum's mum like?'

There was a pause before Jill answered. 'She was very beautiful. That's where your mum gets it from. And you two girls.'

Gabbie felt herself blush at the unexpected compliment.

'Mummy says that her mum was lots of fun.' That was Alice.

'Does she?' Jill's tone was hard to read; what would she say? 'Well, I think she was a lot of fun. Exciting, I suppose. You never knew what she might do next. One minute you thought you were coming to dinner, the next she would have you in the car being driven to the theatre. You just never knew.'

'I wish we'd met her.' Hearing Olivia's sigh squeezed at Gabbie's heart. The pain of missing her mother had never been so sharp as the moment the nurse had lain Olivia on her chest for the very first time and she'd become a mother herself.

She could hear the metallic snip of Jill's scissors. 'Well, I think your mum is a lot like her.'

Olivia laughed. 'Mum never does crazy things. She's always at home.'

'Daddy does crazy things though.' Alice lowered her voice to a whisper. 'Sometimes he lets me have ice cream for breakfast if I don't tell Mummy.'

How had it happened that she was the boring parent who stayed at home and he was the one they idolised? It wasn't fair. If only they knew what that exciting daddy had got them into.

'Dad would let me go to this party.' Olivia's sullen tone was back. 'I don't see why I can't go back home and stay at our house with him.'

'Maybe your mum wants you with her. Why is the party so important?'

'Because everyone is going to be there. And things will happen and they will be talked about for days and days and I won't be a part of any of it.'

'And was Alice right about your boyfriend being there?'

There was only a momentary pause. 'Yes. He'll be there.'

'And you're worried about that?'

Gabbie waited with her hand on the tap, about to fill the kettle. She was interested in what Olivia had to say.

'There's going to be loads of girls there. And he's really popular.'

'I see. And you're worried that these other girls might be a temptation for him?'

She was surprised to hear Jill talk to Olivia like this; even more surprised that Olivia didn't sound as if she minded. 'Sort of. Some people drink at these parties. Something might happen.'

'I understand.' Jill hadn't missed a beat at hearing that

sixteen-year-olds were attending drunken parties. 'But the thing is, if he's got you, why would he be interested in other girls?'

'That's nice, Auntie Jill, but I'm not sure if it's true.'

'I disagree. You're clever and kind and beautiful. He needs to know how lucky he is to have you.'

Jealousy ate at Gabbie. These were the conversations that she should be having with her daughter. Jill hadn't even had a child of her own. What did she know about this?

She needed to get back in there. The kettle would take forever on this Aga and she'd hear it whistle from the other room, anyway.

She filled a glass with water for Alice and made her way back to the breakfast room. Anyone surveying the scene would assume that Jill was a grandmother crafting with her two grand-daughters. But that wasn't what it was, and Gabbie didn't want any of them getting too close.

'Here's your water, Alice. What can I do?'

Olivia pushed her chair back. 'You can take over from me, Mum. I'm going to call Dad and see if he'll come and get me for the party.'

She didn't want to have another argument; let 'fun dad' be the bad guy for once. 'Okay.'

Olivia stopped in her tracks. 'Really? You're not going to stop me?'

She knew she was safe. There was no way Liam – who didn't even have a car right now – was going to be able to pick Olivia up and take her to stay at his friend's house with him, without having to tell her a whole lot of things he didn't want to explain. He would have to – for once – be the one who said no.

She felt almost guilty when Olivia practically ran from the room in excitement, but she'd tried to tell her, hadn't she? Jill looked up at her. 'Is that a good idea?'

Gabbie was the parent here, not her. 'Well, we'll see in a minute, won't we?'

But she was regretting it already. Talking to Liam about the party was only going to make Olivia more upset. Again, she wished that she could wave a magic wand and make everything okay again. Doesn't every mother try to make things better for her children? Even if she doesn't go about it the right way. Even if she ends up making it worse.

# THIRTEEN

*Darling Gabbie,*

*I know that you didn't want me to say anything to the school, but I have been so upset, thinking of you being unhappy. Even your father thinks that it's unacceptable they allow the other girls to exclude you and that we have to do something.*

*You'll probably know this by the time this letter reaches you, but he called to speak to your housemistress this evening. He said that she was very kind about it all and she thinks it's because you haven't involved yourself in any of the extra-curricular activities. She thinks that you might find some like-minded people if you do that. What do you think?*

*She also said that she will speak to you about the girls that are being unkind. She has dealt with situations like this before and believes it's the best thing to get you all together so that it can be sorted out once and for all.*

*Please try, my darling, and write back and tell me how it goes.*

*Love Mama xx*

*PS Jill insisted on sending you those awful thermal pyjamas. I will find you some beautiful ones in Milan next week and send them to you instead.*

Gabbie's meeting with Miss Foster was as brief as it was devastating.

Miss Foster's rooms were on the bottom floor of the house which also included the girls' dorms. It doubled up as her office and sleeping quarters, so this was where she would summon any of the girls that she needed to speak to. This was only the second time that Gabbie had been here; the first was the afternoon that she'd arrived at the school.

Her stomach was somersaulting as she knocked on the heavy wooden door.

'Come in.'

Inside, a room perhaps twice the size of Gabbie's dorm included a single bed with a navy blue blanket, a red and yellow Persian rug, an oval wooden table with two chairs and what looked like a basic kitchen area with a toaster and a kettle in the corner. To Gabbie's left, Miss Foster sat at an old-fashioned desk with a green leather inlay.

'Don't stand there dithering. Come in and sit down. Do you know what this is?' She tapped the navy ledger on her desk.

As she lowered herself onto the hard angular armchair nearest the desk, Gabbie shook her head. 'No, Ma'am.'

'This, Gabbie, is my bible. Not the holy kind. But equally important when I am keeping records about all of you girls. Everything that I need to know is in here. It's where I plan out who is going to share a dorm with whom, where I record any issues that arise, any problems and their resolution.'

She paused on the word 'problems', then again on the word 'resolution' to make her point very clear before she continued. 'I don't think you are giving this school a chance, Gabbie. I think, from speaking with your parents, that you have been used to having a lot of things your way. When you are in a school, you are part of a community. You need to get on with it.'

Acid rose in Gabbie's throat. She could do nothing but nod. What had her parents said to her housemistress? And why, when she'd begged them not to?

'Your mother seems to think there is a bullying issue. But I have explained to her that we don't have bullies at this school. This has all, I feel, been merely a matter of getting off to a bad start. So I am going to do something for you that I never normally do. Do you know what that is?'

The only thing Gabbie knew was that it wasn't going to be what she wanted, which was to leave this school behind. It had taken her so long to pluck up the courage to speak to her parents about it at Christmas. And they'd betrayed her.

'No, Ma'am. I don't know.'

'I am going to move you into another dorm. The only way for you and Jessica to sort out this issue is to spend time together. There is a spare bed in their dorm which makes it very easy. You will move in this evening.'

It was as if someone had their hands around Gabbie's neck and were pushing her windpipe with their thumbs. Move into the dorm with Jessica and her gang of horrible friends? There would be no escape from them. Ever. 'It's okay, Miss Foster. You don't need to move me. I will be fine where I am.'

'Nonsense.' She shut the hardback book with a hollow slam. 'It's done. You can move your things during prep this evening.'

Carrying her packed case from her current dorm to the new one, Gabbie felt like a prisoner on death row. She had thirty minutes to herself in the room before the others returned. Did they already know that she would be there? How were they going to react? She covered her face with her hands and cried and cried.

Her new dorm-mates obviously had been informed, because – when they burst into the room half an hour later – none of them looked surprised.

Jessica had a smirk on her face that Gabbie wished she had the confidence to wipe off. 'You're here, then.'

Gabbie continued to unpack her clothes into the small chest beside her single bed. 'Yes. I've been moved here.'

'We know.' Jessica sat on the end of Gabbie's bed; picked up the satin pillow which had been a gift from Gabbie's mother. Gabbie itched to snatch it from her; she didn't deserve to touch it. 'We are supposed to become friends.'

Behind her, the other girls laughed, clearly enjoying the show. Gabbie's eyes burned, but she wasn't about to give them the satisfaction of crying. 'You don't have to be my friend. It's fine.'

Jessica's eyes widened theatrically. 'You don't want to be our friend? Well, that's not an option. We're stuck with you now, and you'd better not go telling tales on us again.'

# FOURTEEN

Much as Gabbie wanted to stay with Alice at the table making paper people, this was too good an opportunity to get some more work done. She retrieved her laptop from the sideboard, and balanced it on her lap, sitting in the armchair in the corner of the room while Alice chattered away to Jill.

Lots of people assumed that, as a fluent French speaker, she translated documents into French. But almost all translators translated from their second language into their first. French might have been her mother's language, but it was not her mother tongue. The press release she was working on was almost done. All it needed was a final read-through but, try as she might to keep focused on it, she had one ear on Jill and Alice's conversation and the other straining for Olivia. What would Liam say to her about the party? Would he tell her the truth about the house?

It didn't take long to find out. Within five minutes, Olivia came thundering down the stairs, two at a time.

Gabbie wasn't particularly proud of her smug pleasure in Liam being the one who had incurred Olivia's wrath for possibly the first time ever. She was tired of always being the bad guy. To protect Alice from the fall out, she met Olivia in the hallway and pulled the morning room door closed behind her. 'What did your dad say?'

Olivia stomped to a halt in front of her with her arms crossed, looking to all intents and purposes like a petulant four-year-old. 'He said that I couldn't go to the party.'

Gabbie held out her hands. 'You see. I told you that—'

'He told me that I couldn't go to the party because *you* want me and Alice here with *you*. He said he wasn't about to go against what you wanted.'

*What?* Of course he had. How hadn't she seen that coming? Why had she thought that, with everything he'd done, he might just take the rap for one tiny thing? Any energy she'd had, drained from her. 'Well, it doesn't matter. You can't go and that's that.'

'You are so unfair.' Olivia burst into tears and flew back upstairs.

Gabbie wanted to follow her, to comfort her. But what was the point?

Jill hovered with a cup of tea. The kettle on the Aga had obviously finally boiled. 'That didn't work out well.'

She could really do without parenting advice right now; especially from Jill. 'Yes, well, the fun parent can do no wrong.'

'I know how that feels.'

What the hell was she talking about? 'You don't have any children.'

Jill flinched, then shook her head. 'I didn't mean me. Your father would often say those exact words about your mother.'

This was nothing like that. Nothing like that, at all. 'My mother was a fun parent. But she was always there for me. She was the one who visited me at school, who took me out for the day, who made sure I had everything I needed. She was nothing like Liam and I am nothing like my father.'

She hadn't meant to raise her voice, but she clearly had

because the handle to the morning room door squeaked and Alice stepped into the hallway, trailing her strand of paper people behind her. 'Mummy, why are you shouting?'

She took a deep breath and forced on a smile. 'Sorry, sweetheart. Mummy was just cross about something. It's not important. Look at your people. They're amazing!'

Alice beamed and pulled them out to show her. 'I made all of us. Daddy, you, Olivia, me and Auntie Jill.'

She held them aloft for further praise; Gabbie wanted to tear the paper Jill from the end of the chain. 'They're wonderful. Why don't you put them back on the table to dry and then you can pack away Jill's friend's craft things.'

'They're my craft things now, Auntie Jill said. And she said that I can leave them all out on that table so that I can use them whenever I want.'

Did she now? The same woman who had brushed toast crumbs from the table from in front of a teenage Gabbie while she'd still been eating breakfast was suddenly completely fine about an array of paper and paint being left scattered across a table indefinitely?

Jill shrugged. 'I don't really use that room any longer. I thought it would be nice for her to have everything set up so that she can use it anytime.'

It *would* be nice for her, so Gabbie wasn't about to get petty, but she didn't trust this new version of Jill one bit. Leopards don't change their spots.

When her phone rang and she saw it was Liam, she walked out into the garden so that Alice wouldn't overhear their conversation. 'Why did you tell Olivia it was my fault she couldn't go to her party?'

His sigh on the other end made it sound as if he considered himself the injured party. 'What else could I say, Gabbie? It's not as if we can tell her the truth.'

Gabbie was beginning to consider whether keeping the

truth from Olivia was the best idea. 'On the subject of the truth, I need to speak to you about where we are with everything that's going on and what you've already done. I want to talk to a solicitor and—'

'You don't need to speak with a solicitor. I'm sorting everything out.'

She was losing her patience with his interruptions and obfuscations. 'I need to know what's going on, Liam. In detail.'

His tone flipped from defence to attack. 'I've told you what's going on. We just need a chunk of money to get us through this, then I'll get a new job and everything will be okay.'

How could he be so sure? What made him assume that this was what she wanted, too? He needed to know that she was not just rolling over and accepting this. 'Liam, you seem to think I've already forgiven you. I don't know if I can trust you again. I'm so angry and—'

'Of course you're angry. I have been an absolute idiot. But I am going to make it up to you. I am going to make everything okay again, I promise.'

'But how can I know that—'

'I'm going to get help. I'm going to sort myself out. That's why I don't want Olivia to know. I never want them to know. I'm going to make it all okay, as if it never happened. Trust me, Gabbie. I won't let you down.'

Why was it that when she spoke to him her resolve to get to the bottom of everything just crumbled? He made it seem as if they could get through all this, that they could be a family again. 'I don't know, Liam. I—'

'Just speak to Jill. That's all you need to do. I will do everything else.'

Once she'd hung up, Gabbie paced around the garden. Whichever way she looked at it, she was going to have to swallow her pride and ask Jill for financial help. All these years of refusing to let her dad give her any money, and now she was going to have to beg his widow for the money he would have given her willingly.

Upstairs, she paused outside Olivia's bedroom. Had she given her enough time to cool off before attempting to talk to her? She'd learned to her cost the repercussions of trying to reason with her eldest daughter when she was this tightly wound. Far better to let her have time to uncoil before expecting a reasonable conversation.

But, when she knocked gently on her door, it was pulled open to a cloud of perfume and a freshly painted face. 'I'm going out.'

She stepped back in surprise as Olivia walked past her. 'Out where?'

Olivia paused at the top of the stairs and frowned at Gabbie's obvious stupidity. 'With Elsa, of course. She just sent me a text to say that she's going to the Village Inn garden with her brother and his friends.'

Much as she liked Tricia's children, Gabbie wasn't sure about this. 'A pub garden? You're only sixteen, Olivia.'

The eye roll made a reappearance. 'Really, Mum? Am I?'

She could definitely live without the sarcasm, but didn't want to start another fight. She took a deep breath and kept her voice calm. 'You have to be eighteen to go to a pub without an adult.'

'We'll be with adults. Matt is nineteen. And we're going to sit in the garden and I'm not going to drink or anything. Elsa's sixteen and she's allowed to go. Call her mum if you want?' The last was accompanied by a provoking jut of the hip.

Gabbie knew the Village Inn. It was very quiet, owned by a couple that Jill and her father had known for years and was always full of families and older people. If Tricia was letting Elsa go, maybe it was okay.

It would also ameliorate the party situation and her guilt at letting Olivia get her hopes up. 'All right, but only for a couple of hours. I want you to come home way before it starts getting dark.'

This time the eyes nearly disappeared into the back of her head. 'Don't worry. I'll be home before I turn into a pumpkin.'

As Olivia swept down the stairs, Gabbie stayed where she was and closed her eyes. Parenting was so hard. Not the actual doing of it, but the knowing what to do. How did you ever know that you were making the right choices, the right decisions, the right rules? She'd always said that she took her hat off to single parents who had to do all of those things on their own, with no one to buffer or be a sounding board. If she made up her mind to leave Liam, was this what she'd have in store?

She hadn't meant to be so sharp with Jill, either. That was hardly the way to win someone over to helping you out. It was a good thing that she and Alice were getting along so well. If she could see how devastating it would be for the girls to lose their home, maybe she would be generous. They'd been here for two days and Gabbie still hadn't had the courage to bring up the money situation. Was there any point in humiliating herself in asking? Either way, she'd no choice. With Olivia out, and once Alice was in bed, this evening was the best opportunity to speak to her.

Not for the first time, she wished her mother were here. There had been several times in her life when she'd thought the same thing. If her mother were still here, in this house, she would click her fingers and make everything better for the girls, just like she had for Gabbie when she was their age. Like she had on her thirteenth birthday. Because of all the memories Gabbie had of her mother, that was the strongest and most beautiful.

# FIFTEEN

*14th March 1993*

*Darling Gabbie,*

*I know that you kept saying that you didn't want a party but I am so glad that you changed your mind and I PROMISE that I'll make it SO much fun. Your father will be away again, so I can be there for the whole weekend. It'll be such a hoot to be just girls. Don't press me for any more information because I want it to be a surprise!*

*I can't believe that my little girl is turning thirteen! It seems like you were a baby a minute and forever ago. I keep dreaming of all the fun things we can start to do together now that you are older.*

*I have decided to redecorate the house this week, too. My first priority is to make your bedroom beautiful for when you are home. It's going to be another surprise but I am making it very grown up and suitable for a teenager! Maybe some of your friends from school might like to come and stay in the holidays?*

*Love Mama xxx*

When her thirteenth birthday loomed, Gabbie's mother had insisted that they do something special. She'd been up for the weekend – alone again – and had suggested that she arrange to take Gabbie and 'all her friends' out for a birthday lunch.

In the light of Jessica's 'warning', she'd led her mother to believe that everything was fine now at school, but she hadn't been able to keep the blush from her cheeks when she'd said she'd prefer it to be just the two of them.

Her mother narrowed her eyes. 'What do you mean? It's your birthday. We always have a party for your friends.'

It was true, they'd had some fantastic parties back in the village. Fancy dress and clowns and candy floss. But she'd had actual friends to invite then. 'I don't need that kind of thing anymore. I'm nearly thirteen now.'

Her mother had laughed, that infectious giggle that had heads turning appreciatively in their direction. 'You're never too old to celebrate your birthday. In fact, they get better as you get older. We can make it so much more fun. You can have a grown-up birthday. Those are the best kind.'

She could feel herself being pulled into her mother's enthusiasm, but there was no way around it. She'd have to admit the real reason for her reticence. 'I don't know who I'd invite from school.'

There was something in her mother's face that suggested she knew more than she was letting on. 'What about the girls in your dorm? Like the blonde girl that we met at the Grove Hotel. Jessica, was it? Let's invite them.'

She'd felt sick at the very thought, but somehow her mother had coaxed her into it with the promise that she would 'make it all wonderful'. Right there and then she'd called Jessica's parents – congratulating herself for having the foresight to take their number last time they'd met – to find out whether they'd allow their daughter to spend a precious part of the next exeat weekend at a birthday party for Gabbie. Apparently they'd been delighted.

For the week before, her stomach had been in pieces. Even if the girls came, how were they going to behave in front of her mother? Humiliation seemed inevitable. Would her mother – who was loved by everyone she met – be ashamed to have a daughter so unpopular? There was only one thing worse than being rejected: the rejection being witnessed by the person she loved and admired most in the entire world.

In the end, though, it had been perfect.

Gabbie's mother had reserved a whole room at the White-croft Hotel and had booked two cars to drive the girls there in style. A man in uniform escorted them from the entrance to a pair of double doors, which he opened to reveal a large round table laden with plates of sandwiches and tiny cakes. Eager for their share of the treats, the girls were a hubbub of polite thanks and smiles. Gabbie had only nibbled at the sandwiches, tensely watching all of the girls' reactions to her mother's questions and stories about places she'd been and things she'd done. Anxiety loosened its clutch on her little by little as she watched the rapture in the girls' faces as her mother told them about her brief career as a model in London and the famous actors she'd met in her work.

But that wasn't the best part of it.

As they got to the end of their afternoon tea, her mother clapped her hands. 'Girls. I have a surprise for you. Who likes to dress up?'

For one awful moment, Gabbie thought that her mother had got it uncharacteristically wrong, envisaging princess costumes and tiaras that would ensure she would be the laughing stock of the school. Even the other girls looked at each other uncertainly.

But she needn't have worried. When her mother swept

them into an adjoining room, they were met with three clothes rails of stylish modern clothes that looked as if they'd been stolen from a catwalk in Paris. Even better, there was a make-up artist and a hairstylist ready to turn six thirteen-year-old school-girls into glamorous young women.

Jessica actually gasped.

The next two hours were bliss. The girls were in and out of the two makeshift changing rooms – two floral sheets pinned across two corners of the room – trying on sheath dresses and sequinned tops and impossibly high shoes. Among them all, her mother flitted like a butterfly, buttoning and arranging and suggesting and laughing. She could see the adoration in the eyes of all her schoolfriends as they looked at her beautiful, glam-orous mother. Bonnie, a shy girl teased about her weight, looked at herself in admiration in one of the three full-length mirrors propped at one end of the room as Gabbie's mother clapped her hands and pronounced her 'beautiful'.

Having spent so little time together recently, it would have been easy to be jealous of the attention that her mother gave the other girls if it wasn't for the way she returned to Gabbie's side every few minutes. To kiss her cheek, or urge her to try a chiffon scarf around her neck or tell her how beautiful she was. Instead, the envy went the other way; Gabbie could feel it coming off the other girls in waves. *I wish my mother was like that.* She soaked it up like sunshine in the first days of spring.

At the end of the party, four of the girls returned to school, but Jessica's father came to collect her for dinner in the nearby hotel. When he suggested that the four of them eat together, Gabbie held her breath for the expected rejection. Instead, Jessica smiled and nodded. 'Yes, let's do that.'

During dinner, her mother continued to entertain her and Jessica with stories, some of which Gabbie had never heard before. She spoke to them both as if they were women, rather than little girls, and Gabbie could see by Jessica's expression that she was enjoying it as much as Gabbie was. By the time they returned to their hotel room, she was exhausted but happy. It had been the best birthday she'd ever had.

Even better, the school she returned to the next day was a different place altogether. She was seen. She was envied. She was *someone*. Jessica decided that her star had risen high enough that she would align herself to it. On the way back to their room after supper, she linked arms with her again. But this time she was offering rather than taking. 'My father bought me some of the magazines that your mother recommended. Do you want to come and sit on my bed and look through them?'

The next few weeks she floated in a bubble of acceptance. No, it was better than that. As if she were her mother's proxy, the girls would ask her opinion about the make-up and clothes they loved to read about. She still missed home, but loneliness no longer gnawed at her in the night. She had her mother to thank for that. Her kind, thoughtful, beautiful mother. Who always made everything better.

Until she couldn't.

# SIXTEEN

Though she was clearly exhausted, it took a while to get Alice into bed. First she was hungry, then she was thirsty, then she wanted a second story and for Gabbie to lie with her until she fell asleep. If she was honest, Gabbie had no desire to go downstairs and face Jill, anyway, but she couldn't put off telling her the truth any longer.

As she lay listening for Alice's breath to settle into the shallow rhythm of sleep, she had to fight to keep herself awake as exhaustion threatened to claim her. Initial shock over, all she wanted to do now was curl up in a ball and hope their problems would soon be over. But each time she closed her eyes, all she could see were those images from the doorbell app on her phone: two men so wide that they filled up the screen. Dressed in black, with faces like bulldogs, they wouldn't have looked out of place at the entrance to an exclusive nightclub. The larger one, his hair as dark as the clothes he wore, pushing something through their letter box. Then the roar of the truck as they towed Liam's silver Audi. She screwed up her eyes then blinked furiously as if the images were grit that she could wash away.

Lifting herself from the bed slowly, she leaned over Alice to check that she was asleep, before creeping out of the bedroom. It brought back memories of the night after night that she'd done this when Alice was a baby. Such innocent times. When everything was good.

At the bottom of the stairs, she could hear the soft voice of a TV crime detective coming from the sitting room. Her father and Jill had always loved those programmes, trying to beat each other to the identity of the killer. Well, she had another mystery for her to solve right now. She took a deep breath and opened the sitting room door.

One glance at her face and Jill reached for the remote to turn off the TV, lifting her legs from the footrest and shifting back into the deep-seated tapestry sofa to give Gabbie her full attention. 'Alice asleep?'

'Yes. It took a little while.'

Gabbie sat on the matching sofa on the opposite wall, then regretted it. It made her feel as if she was about to take a job interview. Or be interrogated by the police. 'So, I need to ask you something.'

Jill had obviously been expecting this since they'd arrived on Saturday night. 'You need something from me?'

She'd expected this to be difficult, but it was much worse. Fluent in two languages, yet she'd no idea how to phrase what she had to say. She could only approach this slowly and hope that the words she needed would come. 'There's no subtle way to say this. We've got financial problems. Big problems.'

After putting Alice to bed on Friday night, she'd found Liam slumped on the sofa like a dead man, his face white and drawn, as if he hadn't slept in weeks. He'd looked up at her as she'd come in, then let his head fall heavily into his hands. 'I can't do this. I've tried, but I can't do this. It's all gone wrong, Gabbie. It's all gone wrong.'

Anxiety had fluttered in her chest as she'd sat next to him on the sofa. 'What are you talking about? What's gone wrong?'

He'd reached out and clutched her hand. 'You have to understand. We needed more money. My job just isn't sustaining our lifestyle, the girls are getting more expensive, we'll need to support Olivia through university soon. It all adds up.'

Now her heart started to race. 'What is it? You're scaring me, Liam. Just tell me.'

His faced creased as if he was about to cry. 'I can't. It's too awful.'

Nothing could be as awful as the catastrophic possibilities streaking through her brain. 'Just tell me, Liam. Whatever it is, we can fix it. Just let me help.'

He covered his face with his hands. 'Don't say that. You're too good for me. I don't deserve it.'

Jill was staring at her, waiting for her to explain. 'We have run into difficulties with paying our mortgage. We've missed some payments and now the bank has taken the house and we need to get it back. We need to prove to them that we can pay and we don't have long to do that.'

She knew she wasn't making sense. Without the vital piece of the puzzle that she was withholding, Jill didn't have a chance of seeing the whole picture and they both knew that.

'You're keeping something from me, Gabbie. I've known you long enough to recognise the signs. You look just like your...' She paused. 'What has Liam done now?'

Gabbie couldn't bear the dismissive tone to Jill's voice. However angry she was with Liam, the instinct to support and defend him from her stepmother's judgement ran deep. 'Why do you assume straight away that it's Liam? It could be me. I could have overspent on credit cards or...'

Why couldn't she think of another example of how she could have burned through a huge amount of money? Jill merely raised an eyebrow. 'It's not you, though, is it? What has Liam done?'

Gabbie felt like a recalcitrant teenager, being scolded for getting home late. 'If you give me a chance, I'll tell you.'

When Liam had started to sob, Gabbie couldn't bear it any longer. She hadn't seen him cry since the girls were born. And those had been tears of joy; these were most definitely not. She wrapped her arms around his shoulders 'It's going to be okay. I'm here.'

He let her hold him for a while and then pulled himself out of her arms, looking into her eyes. 'It's my fault. I've been gambling. With our money. I thought I could handle it, but I can't.'

Gambling? This was such an unexpected answer that Gabbie thought she'd misheard him. When had he been gambling? 'I don't understand. When...? What...?' She couldn't phrase those questions in her head, much less articulate them. This was a bad dream. It couldn't be real. But the look on Liam's face was real enough.

Though they both sat on the same sofa – Liam with his elbows on his knees, leaning towards her in semi-supplication – she stayed perched on the edge, pinching her thumb as she listened to him speak.

'It started small. Online. A few bets on the football. Sometimes roulette or the slots. Just something to do, really.'

Something to do? He'd stayed at the office late so frequently in the last year that she'd assumed he had things to do coming out of his ears.

'When work got intense, it was a good way to unwind. I found myself doing it at lunchtime; I could even do it at my desk, blocking out all the noise around me and just focusing on that.'

He made it sound like some kind of mindful meditation. 'How much were you spending?'

'Not much at the beginning. Fifty pence. A pound. Then it was a fiver. A tenner. If you spend more, you win more.'

'And you lose more.'

He frowned. 'Well, yes.'

'Sounds terribly exciting.'

Her sarcasm wasn't lost on him and his expression became more defensive. 'Actually, it was. I know you are going to mock this, but I actually had a system. And it worked. Remember that weekend in Madrid? The hotel with the marble floors? Paid for with my winnings.'

How did he have the front to look so proud about that? That holiday had been incredible. But she'd thought he'd had a bonus at work. And that was last year. He had been lying to her even then?

'How long has this been going on?'

He looked down at his hands, where he was picking at his fingernails. 'I'm not sure. A while.'

'When did it start getting serious?'

He sighed, but didn't look up. 'I had a few losses. Nothing that I couldn't cover, but I'd reached my limit on some of the sites. So I took out a credit card to cover them. I was only going to need it for a month or two, so I wasn't worried about the interest rate.'

He paused. Was he contemplating his own naive stupidity, as she was? 'And I'm assuming you didn't pay it off?'

He looked up at her then and, if it wasn't for the anger boiling inside her, she might have felt sorry for him. 'I ended up having to get another one. And then others.'

Her fingers itched with the desire to shake him. He wasn't some stupid kid who didn't know how the world worked. 'At what point were you going to tell me?'

He held out his hands. 'Honestly? I wasn't. My plan was to get enough money together to clear everything and then I wouldn't do it ever again.'

Jill's face got whiter and whiter – and her mouth tighter and tighter – with every word of Gabbie's story. As soon as Gabbie paused for breath, her response practically burst from her. 'How did you not know? How could he have been frittering away all of your money and you had no idea?'

Hadn't she asked herself the same questions? Running over and over in her mind the times that he had stayed up later than she had, scrolling on his phone. Or the times that he had been irritable and snappy for reasons she couldn't fathom. Or, in contrast, gregarious and generous, suggesting impromptu weekends away. 'I don't know. He works – worked – in a bank. He just dealt with that side of things. When it came to any financial decisions, we talked it all through, but he did the paperwork, managed the accounts. There was no need for me to check up on him. I trusted him.'

Her voice faltered with those last three words. But her obvious distress earned her no sympathy from her stepmother. 'Oh, Gabbie. You've been so naive. So stupid.'

It was one thing to tell herself this. Quite another to hear it from the person she liked least in the world. 'You can call me whatever you want, Jill. But that doesn't change the situation. We need money to save our home.'

If Jill understood what Gabbie was asking – and how could she not? – then she wasn't answering yet. 'And what's happened to Liam's job? Wasn't he always talking about how well he did? How much commission he could earn?'

Shame reddened Gabbie's cheeks as if the transgression were her own. 'Not any longer.'

Liam had tried to explain it to her, tried to make her understand how it had happened. 'I know this sounds crazy to you, but I had it under control. All I needed was to clear the debts I had and then I could clear my head and sort everything out. But then Covid happened and lockdown and I was working from home and the commission wasn't what it was and I couldn't keep up the repayments on the credit cards. So that's when I did it.'

'Did what?'

He took another deep breath. 'I added the credit card debt to the mortgage.'

A chill seeped through Gabbie's body. 'How much?'

He didn't directly answer her question. 'Once the debt was cleared, I could cover the payments on the mortgage. It was tight, but I could just manage. The trouble was, I didn't have any money left over to actually do anything else.'

She knew what was coming next. 'So, you carried on gambling?'

He nodded. 'But then it got worse. I lost my job.'

Just when it looked like they were getting to the bottom of this, it got deeper. It was like trying to escape from quicksand. 'You've lost your job?'

Again, he nodded. 'I needed money, so I started moving money around between my accounts. Cross-firing, it's called. Switching money between accounts, writing cheques and moving funds before they'd cleared.' He twitched at the sound of her fingers drumming on the table. 'It doesn't matter on the details. It's illegal. Instant dismissal. They had all the evidence. I'm lucky they didn't call the police, but I had to clear my desk and leave immediately.'

Her mouth was almost too dry to get the words out. 'When? When did you get fired?'

'A month ago.'

*Deeper and deeper.* 'And where have you been going every day when I thought you were at work?'

She pretty much knew the answer to this question; his face merely confirmed it. 'Trying to get the money back. But it was like a snowball rolling down a hill. It just got faster and faster and bigger and bigger and it was out of control and I just couldn't catch a break. I just couldn't control it. Every day I was just chasing my losses.'

She couldn't believe what she was hearing. 'Why didn't you tell me? Why were you keeping this to yourself?'

'Because I know what a stupid, stupid fool I've been. And the money I've spent, the money I've added to the mortgage, it's like I've stolen from you.'

Like? *Like?* That was the final straw. 'You *have* stolen from me. From all of us. I don't even know what to say, Liam. This is all so unbelievable. And this is why those men were knocking on the door yesterday? They're debt collectors?'

He nodded. Then swallowed. 'And there's more. It's worse.'

How did this get any worse? 'What?'

He pulled a crumpled envelope from underneath his thigh, its rough edges torn violently apart. 'I've had a letter. From the bank.'

Gabbie's chest hurt; she wasn't breathing. 'Yes?'

'They're going to repossess the house.'

After that, he broke down into tears, his shoulders shaking as he finally gave into the sobs. Gabbie was frozen. Take the house? Her house? Their home?

There wasn't a trace of sympathy on Jill's face. 'So that's why you came in such a hurry on Saturday?'

'Yes. I didn't want the girls to be there when... when the men came. They still don't know anything about what's happened.'

'They don't know about Liam gambling away all of the money you had?'

Each time Jill attacked him, she had the urge to protect. 'I don't want them to think badly of him.'

Jill was shaking her head slowly from side to side. 'I can't believe what I'm hearing. I really can't.'

How could she, who'd never been a mother, possibly understand? 'He's their father and they love him. What else do you expect me to do?'

'Tell the truth? Why *do* they think you dashed here in the

pouring rain when you haven't been near me in the last three years?'

'I just told them I had things to sort out with you.'

'I see. And what would those things be?'

It was excruciating. Why was Jill making this so hard when she must know what Gabbie was going to ask? Was she punishing her for something? 'We need money to pay our arrears. And money in the bank to prove we can pay in the future. We need your help, Jill.'

When Liam had suggested it, she'd been adamant that this was the last place she wanted to come for help. He'd started by apologising again, his eyes rimmed red. 'I am so sorry.'

She still didn't know how to handle this. 'How have you let it get to this stage without realising you were out of control?'

He held out his hands. 'You can't possibly understand, Gabbie. You came from money. Your huge house and foreign holidays and posh education. Money is different for you.'

Was he making this her fault somehow? 'What difference does that make, Liam? That has nothing to do with this.'

'But it does. I want to be able to give you all the things you deserve. You and the girls. I can't keep up with everything, and the wins, well, they give me the opportunity to spoil you all.'

Her stomach squeezed at the thought of how many of Liam's impromptu gifts – his last-minute plans to eat out at a nice restaurant, the jewellery he'd bought her 'just because' – how much of that had come from the proceeds of an online slot machine or a fortuitous hat trick at a football match? 'I wouldn't have wanted to be spoiled if I'd known that's where the money had come from. We can't lose the house. This is our home. Our girls' home.'

Liam rubbed at his temples. 'I have tried everything with the bank. Rearranging the payments or asking for a mortgage holiday, but I've run out of options.'

Again, this wasn't making sense. 'But this is a joint mortgage. How am I only finding out about this now? Surely, they would have written to me about it?'

He frowned and looked down at his hands. 'I've been having the mail redirected. To a PO box. I bring the other letters back and leave them on the mat.'

It was almost like having someone's arms around her waist, squeezing tighter and tighter with every beat of this story. Redirecting the post was so... premeditated. 'There must be something we can do. They must have an option for us. A way we can do this? I can take on more translation work. There's plenty of it going at the moment.'

Her mind was racing for a solution. Running numbers through her head. Her wages would be enough to cover their household bills and their food, but there would be less than a hundred pounds or so over. Not nearly enough to cover the mortgage.

There was something about Liam's expression that made the squeezing start again. 'That won't be enough. We need a sizeable chunk of money *now* to clear it. I think it's time we talked to Jill.'

Jill? Her stepmother? Where had that come from? 'What are you talking about, Liam? How is she going to help?'

He frowned at her in annoyance as if she was being purposely obtuse. 'Oh come on, Gabbie. She's living in that big house that belonged to your dad. You've never had a penny of his money. She owes us. She owes you.'

He expected her to go begging to the person she hated more than anyone else in the world to bail out his bad behaviour? She couldn't believe that he was asking her to do this. There was no way she was going to Jill and asking for help. She could just imagine the look on her face when she refused. *Your father was right about him.* 'No, Liam. I am not asking Jill for help.'

'I know you don't get on. But you did once, didn't you? When your mum was still alive? You liked her then? And if you tell her that you need the money – we need the money – if you tell her we are about to lose the house, maybe she'll help?'

Was he losing his mind? 'Why would Jill want to help me? We barely speak. I haven't even seen her for three years.'

'But you have to try, Gabbie.'

'No. There is no way I'm going to that woman and begging her to help me.'

'Gabbie, we have no choice. If I can't call the bank and tell them we have money coming, they're coming to repossess the house this afternoon. You have to ask Jill.'

She'd been silent then, unable to think of another solution. 'If I do this, you have to get help, Liam. There are meetings for this. Gamblers Anonymous.'

Liam exhaled a long breath. 'I will.'

His obvious relief wasn't reassuring. 'You have to promise me.'

'I promise. As soon as you leave, I will find a meeting and go.'

Of course, she didn't tell Jill all of this, but it didn't matter anyway because her answer was immediate and firm. 'No.'

Gabbie wasn't sure that she'd heard correctly. 'Pardon?'

Jill raised her chin. 'I said no. I'm not going to bail out your feckless husband.'

Gabbie swallowed. 'But this is not about him. It's about me and the girls. Our home.'

Jill tilted her head on one side, appraising Gabbie like a racehorse with an injury. 'So, you've left him, then? Liam? You're ending the marriage?'

'I...' How did she answer that? She was angry with him, so angry. But he was completely broken and so sorry for what he'd done. 'I haven't decided what I'm going to do.'

Jill's laugh was dry and derisive. 'Of course you haven't.'

'I have to think of the girls!' She hadn't intended to raise her voice. Her hands were trembling and she lowered her voice again before she spoke. 'They're my first priority. I don't expect you to understand.'

Jill winced at the sharpness of her tone, then nodded. 'I understand, Gabbie. Believe me, I understand.'

The air between them crackled with unsaid words that stretched back years. As their present silence stretched to breaking point, Gabbie expected Jill to speak, to yield, to offer a hand of help. But she didn't. And if she could be cutting, then so could Gabbie. 'That's your answer? You're happy to sit in this huge house that my father paid for and leave us homeless?'

Jill shook her head. 'I'm not happy about any of this. You're welcome here as long as you want to stay. Or as long as it takes to sell your house and find somewhere new. You must have a lot of equity in that place.'

What did she know about their equity? 'What do you mean?'

Jill frowned. 'Equity is the difference between the amount of your mortgage and—'

'I know what equity is. I'm not an idiot.' Gabbie had been a fool not to be more involved in their family finances, but that wasn't because she didn't understand it.

'Well then, you'll know that you must have built up quite a lot of it. Especially as your father gave you a very generous sum of money to add to your deposit when you bought it.' Jill folded her arms as if she'd made herself very clear.

But she must be confused. 'No, he didn't. I've never taken a penny from my father since I left home.'

Her father had offered money towards the house, like he always had. *You might as well have it now while you need it. You'll get it all one day anyway.* But she'd refused.

Now Jill was looking at her with weight in her eyes. 'Maybe *you* haven't.'

She didn't want to even entertain what Jill was clearly

suggesting. 'We didn't want his help. We told him no thank you.'

'And yet, Liam accepted the money all the same. Quite a sizeable amount, if I remember correctly.'

Despite her loose, light T-shirt, Gabbie felt hot and clammy. Surely this wasn't true? Liam knew how she felt about accepting help from her father. 'I don't believe you.'

Jill shrugged. 'Believe whatever you want. Clearly, that's working out well for you.'

That was unbelievably cruel, even for her. 'It can't be true, because if we had lots of equity, the bank would lend us money and they won't. Liam has tried.'

This was supposed to prove her point, but the shock in Jill's face winded Gabbie, too. Jill recovered first and spoke through tight lips. 'Then it sounds as if you have a big problem on your hands. Your father gave you money that your husband has lost. I am not about to let him throw away even more. Please don't ask me this again.'

Gabbie stared at her own hands as Jill rose and left the room. As they'd been talking, she hadn't realised how she'd moved further and further forward in her seat, practically begging Jill to help her. Now she crumpled backwards. What had she expected from the woman who had taken her father from her, and her home?

Her head was spinning with the ramifications of their conversation. Was it true that Liam had already taken money from her father and never told her? Did Jill mean it, that she was not going to give them anything at all? And, more urgently, what the hell was she going to do now?

# SEVENTEEN

The clock on the bedside cabinet beamed 3.57 a.m. across the darkness.

Gabbie shifted herself to face the warm little body beside her. How long had Alice been beside her? Before they'd arrived, it had been years since she'd snuck into bed with her in the middle of the night. It was amazing how much space she could take up with those little arms and legs.

In sleep, she looked like a baby again: long lashes brushed the top of her flushed cheeks, her mouth pushed out into a soft pout. Her beauty always took Gabbie's breath away. How had she and Liam made such beautiful creatures as their two daughters?

After her conversation with Jill had ended so badly, Gabbie had spent the rest of the evening in her bedroom, tucked into bed, attempting to work with her laptop on top of the quilt, waiting for Olivia to come home. Still raw from Jill's reaction, it had been a huge relief that Olivia hadn't come home ready to spar again. In fact, she was in a much better mood altogether, and was unusually chatty about her evening when Gabbie asked how it had gone. Perched on the end of Gabbie's bed, she'd pulled her knees into her chest and smiled. 'Yeah, it was really good. Matt is so funny; he was making everyone laugh.'

Everyone? 'Who else was there?'

'Just me, Elsa, Matt, some of his mates. They were really cool, too.'

A bunch of nineteen-year-old boys? 'Were they all drinking?'

'Of course. It's a pub, mum. But they weren't drunk if that's what you're asking. And a couple of them were driving, too. Before you ask, Elsa and me just had J2os.'

Driving? That was the next thing for Gabbie to worry about; the fact that Olivia's friends would be starting to turn seventeen in September. She would have a few months before Olivia would be able to learn to drive, but in the meantime, she would have to accept that she was going to be getting in cars with people who had only recently passed their test. Something else for her brain to catastrophise in the middle of the night.

At least Olivia had gone to bed seemingly happy last night. And she hadn't mentioned the party again. With luck, the novelty of Matt and Elsa would keep her occupied long enough for Gabbie to sort out their housing situation. Which, after her conversation with Jill last night, felt even more urgent.

Gently, Gabbie pushed Alice's knee into less sharp an angle. Maybe that was what had woken her up. She tried to close her eyes and go back to sleep, but her mind was firing off random thoughts like tinder sparks, as if it was trying to see which one would catch alight and start a blaze of anxiety to keep her awake.

First thing tomorrow she would start to look into this business with the bank. She'd do some research, speak to Tricia's solicitor and then call Liam. The time for just leaving this up to him was over. Before turning over onto her right side, she stole one more look at Alice, listening to her soft breath, watching the twitch of her lips. On the bedside table was a gift that Alice had presented her with at bedtime last night. A heart-shaped drawing of the four of them that she'd made that afternoon. 'So you can put it on your bedside table and pretend you are back at home.' What a sweet, easy child she was.

She must have drifted back to sleep eventually, because she woke around 9.30 – was there some kind of enchantment on this house that made her sleep late? – to see Alice sliding a cup onto her bedside table. Milk sloshed over the top of it and onto the glass surface.

Gabbie dragged herself from the clutches of deep sleep. Where had that been in the middle of the night when she'd needed it? 'Please be careful, sweetheart. It might burn you.'

'It's not hot. It's just milk. I wanted to make you tea, but Auntie Jill said it was dangerous to carry hot things upstairs and she said you might not want a drink yet anyway. I was supposed to let you sleep. Auntie Jill said you needed a rest.'

Well-meant as it might be, Gabbie wasn't comfortable with Auntie Jill making all the decisions around here. 'How long have you been up?'

Time had no real concept when you were eight. 'A long time. Auntie Jill was up. We made pancakes for breakfast again and Auntie Jill made a face on mine with strawberries and cream.'

'Did she? And you're all dressed already?'

Alice nodded proudly. 'Auntie Jill and me went for a walk to the shop to get milk. Guess how many cats we saw on the way?' Not waiting for Gabbie's guess, she held up four fingers.

'Wow. That's a lot. I'm going to jump in the shower and get dressed and then we could go out and explore some more if you like?'

Alice looked less keen. 'Can we go out later? Auntie Jill is going to show me how to do knitting in a minute.'

This was getting ridiculous. 'Is Olivia up yet?'

'Yes. She's in the shower. She's going to see Elsa.'

That did it. 'Right. Let's get this day going.'

Once she'd had a super-quick shower in the other bathroom and pulled on some jeans, Gabbie walked into the morning room to see Alice – long knitting needles poking out from her fists – massacring a square of wool. Beside her, Jill was watching and encouraging. 'That's it. You're really getting it now. What a clever girl you are.'

After Jill's refusal to help them last night, Gabbie had the urge to snatch away the knitting, followed by her daughter. 'Morning.'

How did Jill have the front to turn and smile as if nothing had been said? 'Good morning. Would you like some coffee?'

'It's okay. I can make it.' Alice looked up at the sharpness of Gabbie's tone, so she softened her voice. 'You're much better than I am at knitting. I tried once or twice but couldn't make head nor tail of it.'

Though she was talking to Alice, Jill stuck her nose in as usual. 'Ah, well. All you need is patience and someone to teach you.'

Was that a dig at her or her mother? Either way, it rankled. 'My mum always said that knitting was for old people. She preferred cashmere with a designer label.'

Jill's smile stiffened. 'That sounds like your mother. Come on, Alice, let's go upstairs and find the wool.'

Almost as soon as she'd filled the kettle and put it on the Aga, Gabbie's mobile rang with a local number that she didn't recognise. She picked it up, expecting it to be Tricia, but there was a clipped professional voice on the other end. 'Hi. Is that Gabbie Johnson?'

'Yes. Speaking.'

'Hi, I'm Jane Grieg from Capel & Ash solicitors. Tricia asked me to give you a call?'

Good old Tricia. 'Yes, thank you so much for calling so quickly.'

Gabbie sank down on to one of the hard, uncomfortable chairs around the kitchen table. This was embarrassing even over the telephone. 'Our house is being repossessed by the bank. My husband has been dealing with it up until now. We missed a few payments on our mortgage' – was it worse to admit that she hadn't known about that or pretend that she had? – 'and the bank wasn't willing to give us time to find the shortfall.'

There was a pause at the other end. 'I see. And did you have legal representation with you when this went to court?'

Gabbie's heart fluttered. Liam hadn't even mentioned going to court. 'I... er... I don't really know to be honest. My husband has been doing everything.'

This was excruciating. Jane – a professional woman – must think she was absolutely pathetic. She thought herself pathetic. Why hadn't she pushed for more information yesterday? Why had she let Liam cut her off when she asked?

But Jane's tone was kind. 'I see. Well, this kind of thing can be a complete shock. What I can say is that banks are usually open to making arrangements wherever possible. They will want to know what kind of repayment schedule you are able to offer. Are you expecting to have any additional sources of income?'

Again, she couldn't avoid sounding weak and uncertain. 'I'm not sure. It's complicated. But obviously, I want to do whatever I can to avoid losing our home.'

'Of course. And when does the repossession order take effect? Usually you have at least a month.'

A month? Liam had known for a month that those people were coming to throw them out onto the street? 'It already has. We had to move out three days ago.'

There was another pause at the other end. 'Ah, then that's slightly more complicated. But it's not a lost cause by any means. Look, what I suggest is that you get all the paperwork together, get the full story from your husband about the procedures he's been through and then make an appointment so we can go through everything and make a case to the bank. How does that sound?'

It sounded like she needed to speak to Liam again as soon as possible and find out what he'd actually done to stop this. 'Thank you. I'll speak to him and be back in touch as soon as I can.'

'Great. The sooner the better in these cases. Once they put your house on the market, it all gets a bit trickier.'

Once Jane had gone, Gabbie was left feeling nauseous at the thought of a 'For Sale' sign on their lawn, strangers walking around their house, hoping to get a bargain price at the expense of the previous owners who hadn't been able to keep hold of their home. She needed to get on this straight away. The kettle started to scream on the Aga and she moved it onto another ring, all thoughts of coffee pushed to one side. She googled 'Repossession' on her mobile. The first three suggestions were YouTube videos about how to make money by buying repossessed homes. Money from misery. She just wanted to cry.

There was no time for feeling sorry for herself. With Olivia and Alice occupied, this was a perfect time to call Liam. He picked up on the second ring and sounded out of breath, as if he was running at the same time as talking. 'Gabbie? I've been trying to call you. How are you? Please tell me you have news?'

In the background, she could hear noises and chinking. Was that glasses? Or machinery? 'Where are you? You sound out of breath?'

'Me? No, I'm just walking, trying to find a bench so that I can talk to you, hold on.'

He muffled the other end of the phone – presumably with

his hand – and then he was back again. The background noise had gone. 'Okay, I can focus now. What's happening?'

She had questions that she wanted answered first. 'Did you go to court? With the bank? I've spoken to the lawyer and she said we would have been sent a court date.'

'You've spoken to a lawyer?'

How did he have the cheek to sound defensive? 'Yes. A friend of a friend. It doesn't matter. Did you go to court?'

What should have been a yes or no answer surely didn't require the pause he gave before speaking. 'It's complicated. There were a lot of letters. There was a lot going on.'

This was like speaking to Olivia when she was covering up the fact she hadn't done her homework. 'Did you go to court, Liam. Yes or no?'

'No. I missed the date somehow and then they wouldn't reschedule and...' He trailed off.

He must know as well as she did that there was no excuse. 'I don't even know what to say to you, Liam.'

'Gabbie, please. I know I've screwed up. You have every right to be really angry at me, but please, just give me a chance. If we can sort this out, I will never do this again. I will spend the rest of my life making it up to you. Please, honey.'

'Even if I did forgive you, how are we going to sort this out? There is no money. You have no job and there are only so many hours of translation work that I can physically do in a day.'

'Ask Jill for money.'

It was almost pleasurable to burst his bubble. 'I have asked Jill. She said no.'

'What? She can't say no. She has to—'

'Why do you keep saying that? She has no obligation to give us anything.' Gabbie could hear her voice getting louder but she couldn't stop it. Had she ever shouted at him before? Had she ever shouted at anyone?

'I'll come up there. I'll speak to her.'

'No.' The last thing she wanted was him here. And she knew that she had even less chance with Jill if Liam added his voice to the conversation. 'Do not come. I'll speak to her again. But I need you to send all the house paperwork to me. Everything.'

It was as if he wasn't listening to her. 'I want to see the girls, too. You can't stop me from coming to see them.'

She couldn't bear the thought of him here. She needed time away from him to get her head straight. Plus, one look at Liam and they could kiss goodbye to Jill ever helping them. There had to be a way to put him off for a while. 'And what are you going to tell the girls when they ask why they can't come home?'

His silence spoke volumes. Then, 'I miss you all so much.'

There was so much pain in his voice that, despite her anger, her heart went out to him. It was so much easier to stay angry when she was alone with the cold hard facts than it was when she spoke to him. This was Liam, her Liam. The man who brought her flowers for no reason and made her favourite breakfast and brought her back from the brink of losing her mind at Olivia by making her laugh.

Thinking about this Liam and the Liam who had gambled away all their money, lost their house and – she'd now discovered – hadn't even turned up for the court date was like thinking about two completely different men. Had he just lost his mind? Was he in some sort of crisis? And why, for the love of God, had he not been able to come to her?

Tears filled her eyes. 'I just can't cope with seeing you yet.'

'I understand. But soon?'

At some point she was going to have to decide what happened next for them. 'Yes, soon. But first, I need to get the paperwork to the lawyer, and see what she can make of this mess. Then we can talk.'

Once he'd gone, she closed her eyes and sat, wanting to calm herself again before returning to Alice. Whatever she decided, the girls would be her first priority. As long as they were okay, she would make anything work.

'Mum?' The door to the kitchen opened and Olivia's head came into view. 'Can I talk to you for a minute?'

# EIGHTEEN

The water in the kettle was still hot and Gabbie poured them both a tea. 'I thought you had plans to see Elsa this morning?'

Olivia had taken a seat at the kitchen table. In front of her, there was a place mat of the Eiffel Tower and she picked at the side of it with her fingernail. 'I do. I'm heading over there in a bit.'

Gabbie added plenty of milk and a teaspoon of honey into Olivia's tea. 'Are you going to her house or are you off out?'

Olivia took the cup from her hands and blew on it. 'I don't know yet.' She sipped at it. 'When I was upstairs, Tom called me.'

Though Gabbie knew that Tom was the name of Olivia's boyfriend, they hadn't had a proper conversation about him. She was ridiculously grateful that Olivia might be about to confide in her. It was what she'd hoped for. That, as she grew into a woman, they would be close like this. Not best friends – that would be odd – but that they would talk and share and support one another; like equals. She tried, though, to keep the eagerness from her voice. 'That's nice. Is he well?'

The twitch of Olivia's lips made her realise that this had

been a stupid question. 'He's fine. He really wants me to go to this party.'

Gabbie's heart sank. This again. 'Sweetheart, we already talked about this. We can't—'

'No, listen.' Olivia held up her hand to cut her off. 'We came up with a plan. Dad must be planning to come up, right? If he comes today, I can go home with him, I can go to the party and stay a few nights, see my friends. Then he can bring me back at the weekend before he has to go to work on Monday. Or maybe I'll just stay there until you come back?'

There was so much wrong with this plan, not least that Liam was neither living at the house or going to work. As Olivia was privy to neither of these facts, it was getting increasingly difficult to explain to her why she couldn't – at sixteen – just stay in the house while her dad was at work. 'Your dad is working really late this week. Even this weekend.'

She hated lying to her. At least, with all the late nights Liam had had recently, the lie was believable. Late nights, ironically, that he had been lying to Gabbie about.

'I'm not a child. I know why Alice needs to be here, but not me. I'm sixteen. I can stay at our house on my own. I could be going out to work. I could legally get married. I could be having a baby.'

The mere thought of that made Gabbie shudder. 'I know you're old enough to stay at the house alone; that's not the point. I want you here with me. To spend some time with Jill. That's not a lot to ask, is it?'

'Why? We're not doing anything here. It's boring. Usually you don't want to be here, either. I don't get it.'

Of course she didn't get it. How could she, when she didn't have the full facts? 'I do understand, Olivia. I know that you just want to be with your friends. I do remember what it was like to be sixteen.'

Olivia laughed unpleasantly. 'Do you? Because it doesn't

feel like it. You always go on about how much fun your mum was, all the times you did exciting crazy things, but all you seem to want to do is stop me having fun. It's one party. That's not a lot to ask, is it?'

The tone of that last sentence hit deep and Gabbie had had enough. 'I'm done, Olivia. I've said no about the party three times now and you keep coming back to me. You're not going and that's final.'

Olivia stood up so quickly that the chair clattered to the floor. 'You're so selfish. I hate you.' And she ran from the room.

The door rattled in its frame as she slammed it. Gabbie closed her eyes. She had no more energy to go round this again. Olivia's words hurt, but they weren't the first time they'd been uttered in this kitchen. She could still remember the look on her father's face when she'd said it to him. She'd known she was hurting him, too, but she hadn't been able to stop herself.

Almost immediately, the door was pushed open and Alice's face appeared around it. 'Are you okay, Mummy?'

She must have heard Olivia's shouting. 'I'm fine, sweetheart. Olivia is just cross about the party again.'

Jill followed her through the door. 'Sorry, I told her to give you some space.'

The only space Gabbie wanted was from Jill. She sat up straight and held her arms out to Alice. 'That's okay. Alice can come to me whenever she wants.'

She gave her a squeeze and kissed the top of her head. 'Have you finished your knitting? We could go out somewhere if you like?'

She wanted to get out of here herself. The walls were bearing down on her with the weight of their shared history. She needed some air.

'I just need to finish and then we'll go, okay?' Alice tilted her head to one side in the manner she'd copied directly from Gabbie. It made her smile.

'Okay. Hurry up then.'

As soon as she'd run from the room, Gabbie let her head fall back into her hands. Jill crossed the room and refilled the kettle. 'Are you really okay?'

Right then, she wanted to share the burden so much that even her stepmother would have to do. 'I hate saying no to the girls about anything. I can't bear it.'

Jill put the kettle back on the Aga and turned to look at her. 'But you have to say no, don't you? As a parent?'

She knew she shouldn't open herself up to Jill's black and white view of life. 'Of course you do sometimes. But having fun with her friends is not really a lot to ask, is it?'

Being in this house, the conversation she'd had on the phone to Liam, the risk of losing her home, there were so many emotions coursing through Gabbie right now that it needed the merest scratch for them to all come gushing out.

And Jill's condescending attitude was far more cutting than a scratch. 'Having fun is not the be all and end all though. There are more important things for a parent to supply.'

After last night, Gabbie didn't have the patience to take Jill's judgement on the chin. 'Really? I think having fun is pretty damn important. I had a mother who made everything fun. Every moment that I spent with her was wonderful; she was never the one who stopped me doing anything; right up until I lost her, I know that she did everything she could to make me happy.'

Now it was Jill's turn to lose her patience. 'This again? Oh for goodness sake, I assumed you'd grown out of this, Gabbie.'

The shock of her words made Gabbie sit up straight in her chair. 'Grown out of what? Loving my mother?'

Jill shook her head. 'You speak about Margot as if she was a saint. But you hardly knew her.'

That was unbelievably cruel. 'Well, pardon me for being only thirteen when my mother died and for spending most of the year before that away from her because my father thought it was the best thing for me.'

Jill was still shaking her head. 'You have absolutely no idea, do you? I knew you were spoiled, Gabbie, but I never knew you were stupid.'

Where had this come from? 'How dare you speak to me like that? If my father was here you'd never—'

'No, of course I wouldn't. I didn't, did I? The whole time we were married when you treated him as if he'd betrayed you. Because he wouldn't let me. He thought it was best for you to perpetuate this ridiculous myth about your mother being this wonderful creature who loved you.'

Now she could see where this was coming from. Jealousy was an ugly beast. 'My mother *did* love me. And she *was* wonderful. The days I spent with her were the best days of my childhood. Maybe even my whole life.'

As much as she disliked Jill, she'd never actually tipped into hating her. Right now, though, she was dangerously close.

'Listen to yourself. *Days* that you spent with her. Anyone can be a fantastic mother for a day, or even a week. But that's not enough. A mother needs to be there all the time, day in, day out. For the boring minutia of parenting. The school uniform shopping and the daily teeth cleaning and the homework help-ing. That's being a mother.'

Gabbie had heard enough. 'That was hardly her fault! Dad sent me away when I was twelve years old. She couldn't see me. Weekend visits and school holidays. That's all she had. All we had.'

She could feel her breath coming in shorter and shorter bursts. All of the disappointment and fear and anger of the last few days was tumbling over her. But she wasn't going to cry. She wasn't.

If Jill could see her distress, it wasn't making her pull her punches. 'And how many of those weekend visits did she actually make? How much of the summer did you spend together?'

Gabbie screwed her eyes shut to stop any tears. Pictures of tea in cafes, picnics in parks, shopping trips to impossibly glamorous department stores, last-minute flights to Paris or Barcelona. She'd planned to do all the same things with her own daughters; why did she not do it more?

When she opened her eyes, Jill was watching her, waiting for an answer. 'We spent all of our holidays together.'

Jill tilted her head to the side, like a school teacher waiting for her student to work out the answer to a problem. 'Really? Because I was there, Gabbie. And that's not how I remember it.'

Of course she was there. Always in the background. Supposedly her mother's friend. But everyone knew how that had turned out. 'Why are you being so awful about her?'

Jill sank down onto the chair opposite, the fight seeping out of her. 'I'm not being awful. I'm trying to tell you the truth. Because this pedestal you've kept your mother on is about to topple and crush you.'

# NINETEEN

*28th March 1993*

*Darling Gabbie,*

*I was so happy to get your last letter and hear that school has been better. I am glad that your friends enjoyed your birthday party and that they like the clothes they chose. Of course you, my dearest girl, were the most beautiful of them all.*

*Your new bedroom is finally finished and I am so excited for you to see it! As well as your new bed, there is a beautiful cerise sofa bed for when your new friends come to stay. Jill tried to persuade me to buy something 'neutral' like grey or – can you believe it – beige! That woman has no idea about what looks good.*

*I know that I promised I would come and see you this weekend, but I have been called away to visit a friend in need. I know that this is the second time in a row that I've changed the plans, but I know that you will understand and I will make it up to you by taking us both away to Paris as soon as you finish school for the year.*

*Love Mama xx*

Towards the end of an English lesson, Mrs Spearman – the headmistress – had sent for her. Gabbie spent the long walk up the echoing corridor to her office worrying at the hem of her blouse, trying to think what she could possibly have done wrong.

Mrs Spearman was a stern woman, slow to smile and quick to reprimand. But that day her face was kind. 'Why don't you sit down, Gabrielle.'

She was so focused on Mrs Spearman's piercing blue gaze that it took her a moment to realise that there was someone else in the room. Her father.

At thirteen, she was more than tall enough for this hard wooden seat, but she clutched it with both hands to stop herself from slipping at Mrs Spearman's words. 'Your father has come to take you home. I'm going to give you both a moment.'

It was so strange to see her father there that her initial thoughts were confused. It was only a few moments before the fear returned. Was it the words themselves, the unfamiliar gentleness of Mrs Spearman's tone, or the hand she rested on Gabbie's shoulder for a moment before she left the room that sent alarm bells ringing?

Six months before, one of the girls in the year above had lost a younger sister, a baby, only a year old. She'd been called to Mrs Spearman's office, too. They hadn't seen her again until the beginning of the following term, when she'd returned, white faced and tainted with loss.

Gabbie turned to her father. Grief lined his face like a furrowed field. She knew and yet she didn't believe it. 'Dad? What is it? What's happened?'

'My darling, I'm so sorry. I'm so very sorry.' He reached for her but she couldn't move, holding onto the sides of that chair as if it was the only thing keeping her upright.

She shook her head at him. 'No. No. No.'

'There was a car accident.'

Her legs were numb, trembling beneath her. 'No. No.'

Her father wouldn't stop talking. 'She wouldn't have felt any pain. The doctor said it would have been instant. She didn't suffer, darling. You must understand that.'

'No. No.' She put her hands over her ears. If she didn't hear it, it wouldn't be true.

He reached again for her arm. 'Please, Gabbie. You have to be brave. You have to be my brave girl.'

*I don't want to be brave. I am sick of being brave.* The words screamed in her brain but they never left her mouth. She let him pull her close and hold her as she collapsed into deep, painful sobs. Her beautiful mother was gone.

The other girls had clearly been told to stay away from the dorm room while she collected her things. As she reached to the back of the drawer in her bedside cabinet, her hand found the torn truffle box. She held it in her lap and let the tears fall into the empty tissue-lined holes. She had to drag her suitcase down the corridor to the entrance where her father was waiting; the few girls in the corridor lowered their heads as she passed.

She'd wanted to go home for so long, but not like this. The two-hour drive began with her father trying to engage her in conversation, but even he gave up after her monosyllabic responses. She stared out the passenger window, seeing nothing but the droplets of rain chasing one another through the steam of her breath.

Pulling up outside the house, she still expected her mother to throw open the door and welcome her home. Instead, it was Jill – in a black dress – who met them on the front step. 'I'm so sorry, Gabbie.' She took her in her arms but it felt so stiff, so formal, that it merely served as a reminder that she would never again feel the soft warmth of her mother's embrace. Gabbie didn't even have the energy to lift up her arms. She just stood there, a bag in her hand, like a refugee from another life.

Jill released her and smoothed down her own dress. 'I've made sandwiches for you both. I'll brew some tea and bring it through to the sitting room.'

Gabbie didn't question why Jill was there. Hadn't she always been around? But she was in no mood for polite conversation. 'No, thank you. I'll just go to my room.'

Jill started to say that she should eat something, but her father held out a hand to stop her. 'You go on up and have a lie down if you want.' Gently, he took the bag that she was still clutching. 'Some sleep might do you good.'

Her bedroom at home had been one of her favourite places in the world. But now it was so full of memories that made her claustrophobic with grief. The bed where her mother had lain beside her after a nightmare, singing her fears to sleep; the clothes in her wardrobe that they'd shopped for together, her mother urging her to try brighter colours, sharper styles; the very paint on the walls that her mother had chosen when she'd decorated her room to surprise her. She was everywhere; she was nowhere. Gabbie fell face down onto her bed and gave herself up to the tears that she couldn't escape.

She stayed in her room until the following morning, pretending to be asleep whenever her father and Jill came to check on her. Jill had slipped a sandwich and a cup of tea onto the table beside her bed. She let them go dry and cold, unable to even consider eating. Eventually, she dragged herself from her bed and forced herself into the shower.

For ten days before the funeral, she haunted the rooms of the house, unable to settle for long on the sofa, the kitchen stool or her bed. Even her books – always a refuge from loneliness – were no help: the words danced on the page in front of her eyes. Her father tried to reach out to her, suggesting walks or taking her out for lunch or to a film, but she didn't have the energy to walk to the car. It was even exhausting watching Jill flying around everywhere: making tea for visitors from the village, cooking huge meat pies and casseroles that choked Gabbie as she tried to follow Jill's insistence to 'keep your strength up.' How could she? Her only strength was dead.

Jill's clearance of her mother's ornaments and pictures was explained away too quickly and easily. 'There will be so many people here for the wake. They will just get broken.' But Gabbie felt their absence like a missing tooth; running her fingers across the places they should be. It was like losing her mother all over again.

The funeral itself was a blur. Aware of bodies dressed in black on all sides, she kept her face forward, her hand inside her father's. There was nothing of her mother in the dour hymns and the hushed eulogy. Her mother had been laughter and excitement, not murmurs and melancholy. Why did they not celebrate who she was? *She wouldn't want this.*

Her mother's things didn't reappear on the shelves at home in the following week. Worse, objects disappeared from elsewhere – heavily patterned Moroccan serving dishes hidden at the backs of cupboards, brightly embroidered cushions from Malta stowed inside the ottoman at the bottom of the stairs. Colour drained from the house like water from a leaking cup.

Gabbie couldn't stay here; it was too difficult to be in the house, even in the village, without her mother. Maybe she didn't like school, but, thanks to her mother, she did at least have some friends there now. Eight days after the funeral, she spoke to her father.

'I want to go back to school tomorrow.'

Her father looked startled. 'But they said you could take as long as you needed. Jill thinks that—'

'I don't care what Jill thinks.'

It would be easier to be back at school. Her mother had

never been there with her, so she wouldn't have to face these constant reminders of her absence. She could even squint her mental eyes and pretend that her mother hadn't gone. At school, nothing would have changed. She had her new friends and they'd loved her mother too. They would help her through this, wouldn't they?

# TWENTY

Jill looked as if the words she was uttering were causing her pain, but Gabbie could only think that she was enjoying it.

'Your father sent you away to boarding school because he didn't trust your mother to take care of you when he was away working.'

Surely she could see how ridiculous this lie was? 'Then how can you explain why she was the one who came to see me at school more often? She was the one who would take me out for the day? He clearly trusted her to be able to do that.'

Jill nodded. 'I don't mean that she couldn't take care of you. It was that sometimes she wouldn't. She would get an invitation to go somewhere or do something and she would just go.'

Gabbie had absolutely no memory of anything of the sort. 'I don't believe you. Why wouldn't he tell me this?'

'Because he didn't want you to think badly of your mother. He knew how you felt about her, Gabbie, how much fun you had together. He didn't want to sully the image you had of her.'

Those words rang in Gabbie's head. Wasn't that what she was doing with the children? Making them believe only good things about their father? 'But that wasn't fair on him.'

Jill shrugged. 'He used to say to me: "She already thinks I'm the bad guy for sending her away, Jill. How can I shatter the one thing she thinks was good about her childhood?"'

Could Jill's version of events be true? He carried the blame for it all that time? 'And what about you? You didn't care about my mother. Why wouldn't you have told me at some point over the last three decades?'

Jill was shaking her head slowly. 'You're wrong. I did care about your mother very much. We were friends. But I didn't like the way she treated your father.'

'What do you mean?'

Jill placed both hands on the table in front of her as if she was about to push herself up. 'No. I've said too much.'

'You haven't said anything. But you have started and now you have to tell me.'

This time, Jill spoke slowly as if she was translating every word to soften its blow. 'She was a free spirit, your mother. It was what he loved about her; what we all loved about her. She was the first one to come up with a plan of what to do or where to go. She could make a trip to the supermarket an adventure.'

This was true. She would sometimes give Gabbie ten pounds and tell her she could buy whatever she wanted for their dinner and they would eat it. She seemed slightly disappointed when, by the third time she did it, Gabbie eschewed buying sweets and cakes for meat and vegetables. 'I remember how much she made him laugh.'

It wasn't just laughter; it was total delight. He'd worshipped her mother. And who could blame him? When the other mothers were so much less than her.

'She did. She made us all laugh. But she wanted everything to be like that. All the time. And that isn't real life, is it?'

That wasn't fair. 'She could be serious when she had to be.'

Jill took another deep breath. She was clearly ramping

herself up for a revelation. 'She cheated on him, Gabbie. Several times.'

Up until now, she'd been considering everything Jill was telling her, at least giving it the time of day. But this was a step too far. It was clearly a complete lie. 'No way. She wouldn't have done that. And he wouldn't have put up with it, either.'

The way Jill was telling this story, her father was being portrayed as victim, as if her mother had had the control. But that wasn't the man he was. He was strong, he was powerful. The man had been an international lawyer with clients all over the world.

'It's true. She would disappear for weeks altogether. She'd go to a party somewhere and then stay, and then meet a group of people who were travelling somewhere and just go with them.'

At the back of Gabbie's mind, a memory whispered. Stories her mother had told her. 'But that was when Dad was working away. She would be on her own, so she would go and visit friends. It was why she couldn't always...'

She stopped. That was more than she wanted to say.

But Jill was nodding. 'Go on. That was why she couldn't always, what?'

Gabbie pressed her lips together. 'Nothing.'

There was no way she was going to admit to Jill what she was thinking. That there were times when she'd watched the clock in the school hall move through the minutes as she sat there, coat on, waiting for her mother to arrive. The sympathy from her house mistress when, after calling to speak to Margot they'd been told that she'd been 'unavoidably detained'. That was the phrase they always used. She'd never known whether that was Margot's actual words or their translation of whatever excuse she'd given them.

But Gabbie had always blamed her father for that. It was his work that made things difficult for her mother. He always needed her with him and left Gabbie alone at school. It was his letters that asked her not to ask her mother why she hadn't come.

'How could she have done this? Dad was always demanding she went away with him. She said she hated it, that the people that they met were really stuffy and boring, but she went because that's what you have to do when you're married to someone.'

She remembered how strongly she'd felt the injustice of it. That these boring men and their wives got to spend time with her beautiful mother when they didn't deserve it. That she and her mother had had to sacrifice their precious time together because of them. Because of her father.

Jill moved her hand as if she was about to reach for Gabbie's but then changed her mind. 'She wasn't away with your father, Gabbie. He went on most of those trips alone.'

Gabbie pressed her hand to her chest. Was this true? Her mother had lied to her? Worse, had used her father as a reason why she couldn't visit her at school?

'But why send me away?'

'Because he thought he was keeping you safe. As you got older, he thought it was more likely that she might take it into her head to disappear for a weekend and he would be on the other side of the world.'

This wasn't true. Surely? What parent would do that? Have a whole other life? Put themselves before their child? 'She would never have done that.'

Jill continued as if she hadn't spoken. 'He even asked me if I would keep a check on things. Pop in unexpectedly, make sure that everything was okay.'

She felt sick. That's why Jill had been over so often? Her mother had said it was because Jill was lonely. Because she had no family of her own. 'If that's true, why didn't he ask you to look after me instead of sending me away?'

'He did. But your mother wouldn't have it. Ironically, the woman having the affairs was also incredibly jealous. She wouldn't have me "taking over", as she put it.'

None of this made any sense. 'Why did he send me back after she died, then? Why not ask you to look after me?'

Jill frowned. 'Because you wanted to stay at school. That's what you told your father. He asked you if you wanted to come home and you said no. Your father kept all your letters from school. He even printed out all of the emails you ever sent him. They're still in the cupboard in our bedroom. I can show you.'

Jill left the room, then reappeared with a square brown leather box which looked as if it came from a previous age. She opened the lid to reveal a neatly filed collection of letters and emails. Gabbie recognised her childish handwriting on the front of the envelopes. These were the letters they'd been forced to write home every weekend whether they had something to say or not.

When she didn't take them, Jill placed them on the table in front of her. 'They belong to you more than they do to me. It's up to you whether you read them or not.'

'I still don't understand where this has all come from. If you're telling the truth and my father wanted everything about my mother kept secret from me, then why are you telling me now?'

Jill was still standing as if she wanted to leave her alone with the letters from the past, but she looked her in the eye. 'Because I'm worried that history might repeat itself. And I'm telling you while you still have a chance to do the right thing.'

# TWENTY-ONE

2nd May 1993

*Dear Dad,*

*I have settled back into school and my lessons are going well. My friends are looking after me so you don't need to worry.*

*I got the top score in the last French test and Madame Fournier awarded me a certificate which will be sent home to you.*

*I hope that you are keeping well and that your trip to New York goes well.*

*Love Gabbie x*

For the first two weeks after her mother's death, everyone at school treated Gabbie like a fragile vase. Girls she didn't know would look at her with pity, then turn to whisper about her to their own friends. The girls in her dorm had mumbled their condolences – one had even left some chocolate on her bed – but she had no one special to comfort her or hold her close.

Even Jessica had kept her distance. Gabbie had been confused and hurt. Hadn't these girls become her friends? And now they were acting as if she had an infectious disease. Their silence was preferable, however, to what was to come.

Though they had money, Gabbie had been raised not to be wasteful or demanding. So when her new school shoes disappeared and she had to write to her father for a replacement pair, she'd been very apologetic. Then, when her hockey stick went missing, followed by her geometry set, her father had been understandably irritated. 'I know things are difficult, Gabrielle, but you need to be more responsible.' Her face burned with the certainty that the girls behind her in the phone queue knew more about the disappearance of her things than she did.

Bewildered by her dorm-mates' behaviour, she tried to catch Jessica on the way to prep one afternoon. Hurrying to catch her in the hallway, she reached out to touch her elbow. 'Jessica? What's going on? What have I done to upset you all? I thought we were friends?'

Jessica merely stared at the hand Gabbie had reached towards her until she dropped it. 'Friends?' She'd practically spat at her. 'Friends? What gave you that idea?'

From that point on, she became the butt of every joke. The letters that passed her by during prep were accompanied by sniggers in her direction. Her grief for her mother was still as raw as an open wound and Jessica's increasingly sharp comments and cruel taunting were like salt. How had Gabbie been so stupid as to believe they liked her? Clearly it had only been her mother who had managed to win these girls over with her glamorous clothes and cosmetics and, with her mother gone, those bonds had snapped like a thin thread of cotton.

But then Jessica had decided to take it up a notch. 'If you want to be friends with us, you need to earn it. Do the proper initiation. After lights out tonight, you have to knock on Miss Foster's door and run back here.'

Dares were common, but Gabbie had always been a good student and her heart thudded just thinking about it. 'What if she catches me?'

Jessica had laughed at her. 'By the time she hauls herself out of bed and gets to the door, you'll be back here. Don't be a baby.'

That afternoon, Gabbie's stomach had churned with the thought of what she was planning to do. She'd pushed her mashed potato around the plate at dinner, left her milk untouched at teatime. Why did they want her to do it? If she was daring, would it impress them? Desperately lonely, if this was all it took to win back their friendship, she would do it. She would take the dare and show them all.

But now, in the dead of night, she wasn't so sure. Then Jessica shook her by the shoulder. 'It's time.'

All the girls had torches for midnight trips to the bathroom; Gabbie's had a wrist strap which she posted her hand through to make sure that she didn't drop it. The parquet floor was cold and hard on her feet, but she didn't dare to put on her slippers for fear they would make a noise.

Everyone in the dorm was awake and watching her from underneath their bedcovers as she slipped out of the door. The corridor was dark and the light from her torch chased shadows across the walls. The cold air bit into her bare ankles at the bottom of her pyjamas.

At the end of the corridor, steps wound down to the ground floor. They creaked with indignation as she slowly made her way downwards, her stomach flipping over with each step. On the way back up, she would have to be a lot quicker.

She turned left, past the boot room, past the stationery cupboard, until she came to Miss Foster's door. In the dark, it looked more intimidating than ever before. Any thought she may have had of pretending that she'd knocked was taken from her before it even began: Jessica was hanging over the rail at the top of the stairs, watching, hissing at her, 'Get on with it!'

She looked back at the door and knocked.

Jessica's voice hissed again from the stairs.

She knocked again. Louder this time. A voice came from within. 'Who's that?' And she ran.

Back up the stairs, she followed the flash of Jessica's heels along the corridor and back into the dorm where she threw herself into bed, heart thumping louder than the sound of the footsteps that were coming up the stairs. Though she had her eyes screwed tight, she could sense the presence of Miss Foster as she looked into their room, muttering under her breath,

Once they were sure that she'd gone – this time the squeaky stairs were a helpful messenger – someone switched on a lamp and the girls collapsed into giggles. 'That was so much fun.' Jessica was beaming at her and Gabbie couldn't help enjoying the moment in the glow of her approval. It was, she had to admit, a little bit exciting to have done something she shouldn't. She'd been brave and now things would go back to the way they were. She wouldn't be alone any longer.

Except it didn't stop there. A couple of days later, Jessica dared her to steal tuck from another dorm. Then she made her call things out in science class when Dr Alma turned her back. Each time, the dares got riskier in terms of being caught. Gabbie was frightened to do them, but she was more frightened of going back to being invisible to her new friends. If she could earn her place by doing what they wanted, then that was what she'd have to do.

They were due a big maths test. Gabbie was a proficient mathematician and wasn't too troubled about it. Jessica, apparently, was.

'You need to steal one of the maths papers for me.'

She'd discovered – Gabbie didn't know how – that the papers were copied the week before and kept in the maths office before the test day. Jessica's plan was for Gabbie to sneak out of prep and go and get one. Prep – where they would complete any private study set by their subject teachers – was supervised by a sixth former. They would wait until Sonia Thompson was supervising them, because she had absolutely no control in there and it would be easy, Jessica insisted, for Gabbie to sneak out and back in again without being seen.

This felt like a step too far and maybe Jessica realised this because she also added, 'This will be the last thing. No more after this. Then you'll be one of us.'

It really would be the last thing, because when Gabbie crept out of the maths classroom with the paper in her hand, her maths tutor Mr Thread was waiting for her with folded arms.

In the end, she got off pretty lightly. Perhaps it was because she'd lost her mother so recently. Or perhaps it was because she was such a good student that they knew that she'd been put up to this by someone else. Not that she ever told them that. In fact, she hadn't told them anything: she'd just stood in the middle of Mrs Spearman's office and cried.

Her father had been called and she'd had to speak to him on the telephone. For one blissful moment, she'd thought she might get expelled. To her embarrassment, Miss Foster actually intervened on her behalf and spoke about how difficult she must be finding it after losing her mother, especially as she'd had 'friendship issues in the past'. When her punishment was handed out, it was six weeks of early inspection. Every morning, before room inspection, she would have to go to the PE changing rooms in the basement of the main building – ironically nicknamed 'Hades' despite its sub-zero temperature – and sweep them out before hurrying back up to her dorm for their room inspection.

Despite having to set an alarm to wake herself half an hour before the others, she actually didn't mind the time she spent in 'Hades'. It was quiet and she was alone. It was also the place where, two weeks in to her punishment, she found an unlocked door that led outside the building.

# TWENTY-TWO

Once Jill had gone, Gabbie continued to stare at the box of letters. Unlike the ones from her mother, she had no desire to read them, knowing that they would only contain a censored version of whatever she'd wanted to say at the time. Even so, she would imagine it would be easy to scratch the fragile veneer and see the pain underneath every carefully constructed sentence.

Her phone dinged with a message. A text from the mother she'd spoken to at the school gate back in London.

> Hi Gabbie, I've spoken to Mia about the French tutoring and she said Tuesday nights are best for her. She's so busy with her dancing and sports clubs on the other nights. You know what it's like! Does that suit you? Thanks sooo much for this!

Irritation prickled at Gabbie. Not only had she not offered a regular tutoring slot, but she was expected to fit in around a teenager's social schedule. She didn't trust herself to answer without sarcasm right now, so she closed it down. Then realised that the mum would see that Gabbie had read it. Opening it back up again, she typed:

> Hi. I'm away at the moment without my diary. Will let you know.

Even as she typed, she could almost hear Liam in her ear. *Just say no.*

She also had a slew of Facebook notifications, one of which was a request to join a group for the book club she'd been reluctantly roped into. Once she clicked on it, she was offered a list of other groups she'd been invited to. Every so often, someone would try and add her to a Facebook group of old girls – she hated that phrase – from St Catherine's. Up until now, she'd ignored them. But all the memories which had been stirred up in the last few days – reading her mother's letters, hearing Jill's side of the story – had made her curious. Would Jessica be on there?

The group had over three hundred members, so clearly there were plenty of women who looked back on their school days with much fonder memories than she did. She scrolled through the list of names. There were a few she recognised from her year group – most people had included their maiden name alongside their married one – and then she saw her. Her married name was Jessica Claremont-Stone.

Clicking through onto her name revealed very little except the posts she'd made in the group. Still, it felt like pushing a bruise to read her chirpy little messages about her precocious children and government-adviser husband. She'd shared photographs from their school days, too. Mostly of her and a friend or two at what must have been her parents' country pile. Gabbie remembered Jessica's parents from that day in the restaurant with her mother, and her father from the day of her thirteenth birthday party when he'd collected Jessica and then taken her and her mother to dinner to thank them.

It would be so easy to send her a private message. *How are you? Remember me?* If only she had the courage to ask Jessica why someone like her, who had so much, had been so utterly cruel to other people.

Right now, she'd much rather spend time with a friend who had been the exact opposite of that. She sent a text to Tricia.

> Have you got any plans tonight? Can I come over for a chat?

The reply came back almost immediately:

> Come over now. I'm at home on a study day.

Gabbie wasn't about to interrupt precious study time. She knew how annoying it could be when people assumed that 'working from home' meant 'available anytime'.

> It's not urgent. I don't want to interrupt your studying. I can come later.

The text has barely sent when Tricia called her. 'Come over now. Really, it's fine. I'm such a swot these days that I'm way ahead on this module. It's what happens when you have the social life of a carrot. A half-hour break and a coffee with you would be great. I've got the kettle on already.'

Gabbie was so impressed with the effortless way Tricia did that, set clear boundaries every time. Kind but clear. A half hour coffee would be perfect.

Once she got there, she told Tricia about her heated conversation with Jill and what it had revealed about her mother. Tricia didn't look as shocked as she'd expected her to have been. 'You knew already?'

Tricia shrugged. 'Not all the details. But it's a small village. People talk. A lot.'

That made Gabbie feel even worse. Had she been the only person who didn't know what had been going on? 'It brought up a lot of things for me. About school mainly. I had a pretty rough time there.'

Now Tricia did look surprised. 'Really? But you always made it sound as if it was the best place on Earth.'

Gabbie was embarrassed to remember the things she'd said to the local girls about her school. Every time she was home for the holidays, she'd felt as if she had to earn her way back into the group she'd left behind. Stories about school – most of them pure fiction – had been one of the few weapons in her arsenal. 'I suppose I wanted to forget about it all when I was at home. I hated it there. I missed my mum and I didn't fit in. There was a group of girls who made my life hell. One in particular was absolutely vile.'

Tricia shook her head in disbelief. 'Why didn't your dad take you out? Did you tell him?'

It was so complicated she didn't think she could even rationalise it to herself. 'I did in the beginning, but then my mum died and he was with Jill and I was just so angry. I just tried to keep my head down and push through it.'

It had got a little better as she'd progressed through the school. Most of the girls who had tormented her had bored of it as they got older. Only Jessica had kept an icy distance from her.

Tricia reached out and squeezed her arm. 'I'm so sorry, Gabbie, I wish you'd told me all of this years ago.'

Gabbie shrugged. 'Yes, well. I guess it's not just my mother who had a double life.'

Tricia's voice was gentle. 'All mothers make mistakes. Don't judge her, or yourself, too hard. She loved you, just like you love Olivia and Alice. It doesn't mean that everything goes smoothly.'

Though she could hear the truth in Tricia's words, she couldn't feel it. Because – with her own history – she should have done better with Olivia. 'The thing is, I do understand why Olivia wants to go to that party so much. Wanting to be part of the crowd is normal at that age. I should know that better than anyone.' She paused. 'I looked up one of those girls from school on Facebook earlier. The main one. The one who made my life hell.'

Tricia raised an eyebrow. 'The queen bully? Wow. I hope she's having a miserable life.'

Gabbie smiled. 'Looks pretty good actually. Although everyone's life looks perfect on Facebook, right? I was thinking of messaging her.'

Tricia's eyes widened, then a smile spread across her face and she clapped her hands. 'Good for you. What are you going to say?'

It was an irrational urge and not one Gabbie had ever had before. So many truths had been brought to the surface over the last few days that the desire to get to the bottom of this one was surprisingly strong. 'I just want to know why she was so awful to me. I mean, at the beginning it was just general unpleasantness. She was like it to lots of people. It was a power thing, I suppose. But after my mother died, she was so cruel. It was like I'd done something to her but I never knew what. Should I ask her?'

Tricia's obvious interest in this made it even more attractive. 'I don't know if you are going to get anything from it, but why not? Why shouldn't people like that be held to account? She could still be bullying someone now – a work junior or her kids' nanny. It might bring her up short. Do it now if you like and I can hold your hand.'

If she didn't do it now, she might not have the courage later. And Tricia was right, Jessica should be told how her behaviour had affected – still affected – her. 'Okay. Let's do it.'

Between them they composed a short message to Jessica. It was easier with Tricia beside her, making her laugh with her almost Shakespearean suggestions of curses to rain on Jessica's virtual countenance. Eventually they crafted something they were both happy with and – though it was only three sentences long – even typing it made Gabbie feel as vulnerable as she had at thirteen.

*Hi Jessica. I don't know if you remember me from school? You made my life hell and, as an adult, I find myself wondering why. Was it something in me, or something in you?*

Checking it for the third time, Gabbie's borrowed bravado wavered. 'Can I really send that?

Tricia shrugged again. 'It's up to you. But what have you got to lose?'

She did want to know. Her thumb hovered over the send button.

Tricia nudged her. 'Just do it.'

She pressed send and let out her breath. 'Done.'

Tricia patted her hand onto the side of her coffee mug in lieu of applause. 'Well done.'

Being with Tricia made her feel stronger. There was something about her that made Gabbie trust her. It also made her feel guilty for not being more honest. 'There's something else I haven't told you. The reason we're here. Why I wanted to speak a solicitor.'

Tricia must have been desperate to know, but she managed to keep that out of her face. 'Oh, yes?'

'We've lost our house. Well, Liam lost our house. He has huge gambling debts and it all caught up with him last week.'

'Wow.' Tricia looked far more shocked than Jill had been. 'I wasn't expecting that.'

'You and me both.' Gabbie tried and failed an ironic smile.

'I'm so sorry, Gabbie. Did you know? That he was gambling?'

'No. Not a clue. Unbelievable, right?'

Tricia held up her hands. 'The first time Craig cheated on me it was a bolt from the blue. And it had been going on for months. I know just how easy it is to not see something you don't want to.'

Gabbie's phone was still in her hand and it lit up with a message. 'Oh my goodness. Jessica has replied already.'

Tricia shifted forwards in her seat. 'What does she say? Read it out.'

Gabbie scrolled through the short message. '"Hi Gabbie. I have wanted to speak to you for a long time. There are things I need to say, but I didn't have the nerve to get in touch. Where are you living? Can we meet?"'

The mere thought of seeing her in the flesh sent a shiver through Gabbie. Yet she was intrigued to know what Jessica would want to say. 'Shall I meet her?'

Tricia was not so conflicted. 'Yes, of course. Aren't you curious?'

'I guess so.' She typed a response, telling Jessica that she was staying in Suffolk at the moment, but could meet her when the family returned to London.

The three dots came back immediately to show that Jessica was typing and Gabbie held up the screen to show Tricia, who mimed excitement with her hands up to her face.

'"I'm in Suffolk, too. I live near Beccles. I can come to wherever you are. Can I come in the morning?"'

'She really wants to speak to you.'

This felt very sudden. 'Shall I put her off?'

Tricia shrugged. 'Up to you. But I think it's best to do these things sooner rather than later. Before you get a chance to chicken out.'

She was right. Maybe that's why Jessica wanted to meet urgently, too. She sent a reply with Jill's address, suggesting that she come around midday.

The reply was brief.

*Thank you. I'll see you tomorrow.*


Gabbie flopped back on the sofa. 'I can't believe I'm going to see her tomorrow. An hour ago, I hadn't even spoken to her in decades. I don't know whether to laugh or cry.'

Tricia smiled. 'The power of the internet.' Then her face took a more serious expression. 'And, while we're on the subject of online communication, there's something I need to talk to you about. I don't know if now is the right time with everything you've got going on, but I know that I would want to know if it was me.'

Gabbie's heart sank to her toes; the expression 'need to talk' never ushered in good news. 'Of course. What was it?'

Tricia looked into her coffee mug, uncharacteristically reticent. 'I'm a little bit embarrassed to raise this with you, but your Olivia sent my Matt a photograph.'

From the expression on Tricia's face when she looked up again, she clearly wasn't talking about a holiday snap. Gabbie's heart thumped as she asked the next question. 'What kind of photograph?'

'I think the kids call it a nude.'

Tricia screwed up her face and gave a kind of half laugh as if to soften the blow, but Gabbie felt as if she'd been punched in the stomach. It couldn't be true. 'Are you sure it was Olivia?'

Tricia's embarrassment was palpable. Did that make it more or less bearable? 'To be honest, I haven't seen it. But he was sure. And it came from her number. I told him to delete it straight away and send her a message to tell her not to do it again, but the poor lad was mortified. He's nineteen; she's sixteen. He's worried he gave her the wrong signals when they were at the pub. He said he was just trying to make her feel welcome. They only swapped numbers because Elsa wanted to set up a WhatsApp group for the people at the pub the other night to share their photos. He has a girlfriend and you know how he feels about people cheating on their partners.'

This was getting worse by the second. Though she'd only seen Matt for a matter of seconds, she could understand how excruciating it must have been for him tell his mother what had happened. 'If it was Olivia, I'm so sorry. I'll obviously talk to her about it. To be honest, I don't know what to say.'

Now that Tricia had told her, she looked relieved and back to her normal, relaxed self. 'She's still a kid. Kids make mistakes, don't they? I thought you'd want to know, though.'

It felt like another branch on the bonfire being built around her. 'Of course. Yes. Thank you. I'll deal with it.'

Above them the heavy tread of teenage feet came thudding down the stairs. After pushing the door to the sitting room open, Elsa started when she saw Gabbie sitting there. 'Oh, hello.'

Gabbie was expecting Olivia to appear behind her. 'Are you girls having a nice time?'

Elsa wasn't meeting her eye; Tricia looked confused. 'Olivia isn't here.'

Had they crossed paths? 'Oh, what time did she go home? I thought you'd been together today?'

Tricia looked at her daughter, who was not about to win any awards for a poker face. 'Elsa? What's going on?' Have you seen Olivia today?'

Elsa flushed. 'I saw her this morning. But then I wanted to come home so…'

She left the sentence hanging in the air. This morning? So where was she now? 'Elsa, where has she gone?'

Elsa looked as if she wanted to run from the room. She looked at her mother for help. But her mother was stern. 'Elsa. What is going on?'

Elsa crumbled in front of them. 'I'm not supposed to tell you yet. She's fine. And I can tell you' – she glanced at the clock on the wall – 'in about an hour?'

Gabbie felt sick. What was going on? She opened her mouth to ask but Tricia got there first. 'You tell us now, Elsa. Where has Olivia gone?'

Elsa deflated like a balloon the day after a celebration and turned towards Gabbie with a plaintive expression. 'Please don't tell her that I told you. She's gone home. On the train. To go to the party.'

# TWENTY-THREE

*1st July 1993*

*Dear Dad,*

*I am sorry about getting into trouble. I won't do it again.*

*No, I don't want Jill to come and take me out for the day. I am fine. We only have a few weeks until the school holidays anyway.*

*I don't really have anything else to tell you right now.*

*Love Gabbie x*

Planning to run away and actually doing it were two different things.

The outside door to the changing rooms led out towards the playing fields. This was to her advantage. Alan the security guard and his huge white German Shepherd – Bruce – patrolled the buildings overnight, but the playing fields were left unguarded. If she could get out the door in the early hours of the morning and skirt the fields, she should be able to make it to the exit.

That would be the next problem. Getting out of the huge locked gates. She wasn't a natural athlete and, even if she'd been an able climber, the smooth wooden gates wouldn't have given her much purchase. In this, though, she found a surprising ally.

After lunch the girls were encouraged to take a walk around the grounds to 'aid digestion'. Standing alone as usual, Gabbie was staring at the gates when Jessica came up beside her.

'Thinking of running away, are you?'

She felt her face redden at being so easily discovered. Not wanting to see the nasty gleam that she knew would be in Jessica's eye, she kept her face forward and stayed silent.

This didn't deter her tormentor. 'You'll never make it over those gates with your fat legs.'

Still she stayed silent, despite the unshed hot tears the burned at the back of her eyes. Why wouldn't Jessica just leave her alone?

'It's a good idea, though. You should do it. There's a big hole in the fence down there; even you could fit through it.'

Jessica laughed and walked away. Gabbie hadn't seen where she was pointing, but even the idea of a hole in the fence gave her hope. Just as she was about to investigate, the whistle blew for afternoon lessons.

The last part of the plan was how she was going to get home. She had money hidden at the bottom of her sock drawer and she knew the route to the local station because it was on the outskirts of the nearest town. She would need to go into London and then out again, the fear of which was still not as strong as the desire to get out of this place. What could possibly happen?

She knew that she needed to do this soon, before she lost her nerve. So, the following night, she packed up some warm clothes, her money and some snacks for the journey and slipped out of the dorm just before midnight.

Though the hallways were lit at night by the weak light of table lamps, the changing rooms were in total darkness. It took her a few minutes to feel her way around the walls to the heavy outside door, which opened with a loud creak, sure to alert someone to her escape. She stood for a while, heart beating, straining to listen for footsteps in the corridor. When none came, she slipped outside.

By the light of the stars, the stretch of playing fields looked even bigger than they did by day, when they were covered by girls wielding hockey sticks. Gabbie made for the main gate, determined to find this hole in the fence.

How naive had she been for it not to have occurred to her that Jessica might've been lying? For at least half an hour she searched first one side of the gate and then the other, moving further around the perimeter each time, scratched by brambles, soaked by the dew on the leaves, the cold seeped through her school coat and made her shiver. She was deep inside the bushes, feeling the coarse fence panels with her hands when she heard Miss Foster's strident voice. 'Gabrielle. What are you doing out here?'

Shielding her eyes from the bright torchlight as she emerged from the sharp foliage, Gabbie swallowed before she spoke. 'I was... I was just...'

'We know what you were doing. Fortunately for you, your friend alerted me to your plans.'

It was then that she saw a smiling Jessica, standing behind Miss Foster, looking like the cat that got the cream.


She'd been allowed to go to bed, but spent the night tossing and turning, unable to sleep for fear of what would happen in the morning. Despite the worst-case scenario – getting expelled – being exactly what she wanted, it was still frightening to think of, yet again, being hauled in front of Mrs Spearman.

Immediately after breakfast, that was exactly where she was sent. As she tiptoed along the corridor towards Mrs Spearman's office, she heard whispers in voices she recognised. Her father was already there. Why had he brought Jill with him?

Pausing at the entrance to the room, she strained her ears to hear what they were saying. Clearly, they were trying not to be overheard.

Her father spoke first, his voice a strained hiss. 'I still can't believe she was trying to run away. Is she that unhappy here? I thought we'd sorted all that out. She said she wanted to come back.'

Jill's voice was a more reassuring murmur. 'She did say that. You can't blame yourself. We're here now and we can get this sorted out. She can come back with us if she wants to.'

There was a pause before her father spoke again. 'But then we would need to tell her. About us, I mean.'

Gabbie's stomach flipped over. What did that mean?

The click of the English mistress Miss Smallman's high heels at the other end of the corridor startled Gabbie into standing up straight and turning the corner to see her father and Jill waiting on chairs outside Mrs Spearman's office. He was dressed in a suit, she in a formal dress, as if she were going to a job interview. In one hand, her father held a saucer with a cup of tea which was balanced on his knee. His other hand was being held by Jill.

# TWENTY-FOUR

Olivia had had a pretty cosseted life. Liam was always telling Gabbie that she needed to let her be more independent, but Gabbie had been happy to run Olivia and her friends to places in the car rather than let them take public transport. She just worried about who else might be on the train or bus with them.

Walking back home, she tried Olivia's phone five times before she got through, leaving voicemails each time. Then she stopped dead in the street and punched out a text message.

> I know that you're on the train home. You have to call me. Or I'm calling the transport police to have you picked up.

She had absolutely no idea if they would even do this for a person of Olivia's age. Rationally, she knew that Olivia would be fine. She was sixteen years old and it was the middle of a summer afternoon. But the other part of her brain – the catastrophic, masochistic, anxious part – was imagining all kinds of terrible things. Strange men on the train, a wrong turn to the wrong platform, even falling onto the tracks. It took a while before her brain located the most likely problem: what if

Olivia turned up at the house and realised that it had been repossessed?

Just before she reached the front door, Olivia rang. 'You can't stop me. I'm already nearly there.'

Despite her daughter's caustic tone, Gabbie could have wept with relief. 'Olivia. I'm going to call your dad and ask him to pick you up. Where exactly are you? What was the last station you passed?'

She was answered with a kind of guttural growl. 'I don't need picking up. Don't pull Dad out of work. I'm fine. Stop treating me like a child.'

Gabbie took a deep breath. Arguing with her right now was not going to get them anywhere. 'Olivia. Tell me where you are.'

'No. I'll call you later, Mum.'

And she hung up.

Gabbie was at the house now, so she let herself in before trying Liam's number. No answer. She tried twice more, then left a voicemail asking him to call her urgently.

She found Jill in the kitchen, drying coffee mugs. 'Olivia has put herself on a train home. I need to go and get her.'

Jill paused with her hand and the tea towel on the inside of a bone china floral mug. 'Of course. But why has she gone and done that?'

Gabbie tried to keep her breathing even. 'This damn party that she wants to go to tonight. I told her she couldn't go and so she just did it anyway. I'm so upset with her. On top of everything else right now.'

She could hear the wobble in her voice. Since the shock of Jill's revelations about her mother and then Olivia's nude texts to Matt, today had just got progressively worse. How had she missed all of this happening?

Jill opened a cupboard to put the dry mugs away, then turned back with an expression that was surprisingly sympathetic. 'Try not to panic. She's just being a teenager. You remember what it's like to be that age and feel like everyone is against you. Why don't you call Liam and ask him to meet Olivia at the other end?'

If only it were that easy. 'Because I don't know where he is. I've tried calling but there's no answer. I've left a voicemail asking him to call me urgently.'

Jill's tone changed. 'Lost himself, too, now, has he? I could make a good guess where he could be.'

She wasn't about to get into this with Jill. 'All I want to do is find Olivia and bring her back here. I'll try and call Liam again from the car.' She had a sudden thought. What if the reason he wasn't answering the phone was because he was intending to turn up at the house and ask Jill for the money himself? She could just imagine what kind of reception he'd get. 'Look, if he turns up here, don't get into a conversation with him about any of it. Not until I'm back.'

'Here? Why would he come here?' Realisation dawned on Jill's face and there was a hard edge to her voice. 'If he turns up here expecting anything from me, he'll have another think coming. I really will tell him to get lost.'

The more she thought about it, the more Gabbie was convinced that this was exactly what Liam was likely to do. But she couldn't worry about that now. She needed to get to Olivia. 'Please, Jill. I'm just going to grab Alice and go. If Liam does appear, just keep him here.'

Jill's frown softened at the mention of Alice. 'Why don't you leave her here with me rather than dragging her down the motorway on a search party?'

It would be easier to go alone, but Gabbie knew Alice would want to come. 'It's okay. I'll take her with me. But thanks for the offer.'

Alice was in her bedroom with a huge doll's house in front of her. She seemed a little out of breath.

'Are you okay, sweetheart?'

'Yes. I've just been to the toilet.'

Gabbie resisted asking her how many times she'd been to the bathroom today. But she would definitely make another appointment with the GP. 'That's a fabulous doll's house. Where did it come from?'

'Auntie Jill's friend brought it round while you were out. She said I could have it. Where's Olivia?'

'Olivia is on the train. I'm going to get her. Do you want to come?'

Alice looked at her suspiciously. 'Will Daddy be there?'

That was trickier to answer. Until she'd spoken to Liam, Gabbie didn't want to make any promises that she couldn't keep. 'I'm not sure. Maybe. Why don't you come with me and we'll see if we can find him, too. You can come as you are; you just need some shoes.'

She was surprised when Alice shook her head. 'No. I'm going to stay here.'

Yesterday, she'd asked twice when they were going to see Daddy. Where had this change of heart come from? 'Are you sure? With Jill?'

Alice nodded and returned to the dolls she was positioning in the downstairs kitchen of the doll's house. 'Okay. See you later, Mummy.'

It would be easier to go on her own, and Jill had offered to look after Alice. She kissed Alice on the top of her head. 'Okay, baby. I'll see you later.'

She'd thrown her bag in the car and was just about to go back in to tell Jill that Alice wanted to stay with her after all, when Liam rang.

As soon as she picked up, he spoke. 'Hi, Gabbie. How's things? I got your message. What's urgent?'

She didn't have time to ask him why he was out of breath. 'Olivia has run away.'

'What?' For a moment, she enjoyed the panic in his voice

as she slipped behind the wheel of the car. Had she led with that to make him feel, just for a moment, how she did all the time? 'What happened? I'm getting my coat on now. I'm coming.'

She felt a trace of guilt for making him panic. 'It's okay. She's on a train back to London. I just need you to pick her up. I don't want her to try and go to the house. She has a key. A key that won't work, obviously.'

She heard a sigh of relief at the other end. 'Okay. Okay. I can do that. What time and where?'

That was trickier. 'I don't know for sure. She said she was nearly there.'

'Have you looked on her phone tracker?'

*Of course.* Why hadn't she thought of that? 'No. I'm an idiot. I just panicked.'

'You're not an idiot. I'll look now. Don't worry, I'll get her.'

The red-alert-level worry was subsiding as she spoke to him, but – initial shock over – she was still feeling terrible. 'I did the same thing when I was a child, Liam. I never thought this would happen. I never thought my daughter would ever want to run away from me.'

His voice was soothing. 'Hey. It's not about you. It's this party she wants to go to. You know what she's like. She just fixates on things and doesn't think of the consequences.'

It took every ounce of self-control not to ask him where Olivia got that trait from. 'I know. Just find her, please. I'm leaving now.'

'Okay. I'm getting my coat on as I speak. I love you.'

She let that hang in the air for a moment, not sure how to respond. 'I'll see you soon.'

At least being out of work meant that Liam could go immediately. She knew that he was staying with a friend of his from the gym – a single guy with a spare bedroom – but she wasn't sure what he was doing with his days. He had promised her that he would keep on top of things with the bank but, realistically, how long could a few phone calls take?

Still, it felt good to be able to share the anxiety – and the search party – with him.

Focused on the motorway as her car ate up the miles between her and home, Gabbie couldn't shake the idea that this was somehow her fault. She knew how upset Olivia was and she'd chosen to try and close it down rather than explain the situation to her properly. Not wanting to worry her, she'd probably made it worse. Alongside her worry about Olivia, she kept replaying Jill's words about her father. He'd thought he was doing the right thing, too.

This was the problem with being a parent: no one really knew what they were doing. It didn't matter if you were talking about potty training or pimple cream, weaning or curfews, sleep routines or sex education – there was no one way, no right way, no way to know for sure that you were doing it right. For a while, between the ages of eight and thirteen, she'd hit a sweet spot with Olivia. She was old enough to be independent, young enough not to be too far out of reach. By now, she'd hoped that they would be able to level with one another, that Olivia would be open and truthful.

Although, Gabbie hadn't been truthful with her, had she?

By the time she pulled off the motorway, she was even less sure where she should head for. Ten minutes from home, a call came in from Liam. 'I've got her. She's safe.'

## TWENTY-FIVE

Heat and the smell of coffee hit Gabbie as she opened the door. They'd been to this bistro many times over the years, from when Olivia was small and had to sit in one of the wooden high chairs folded near the door. There was a small crowd at the counter and Gabbie had to resist the urge to elbow her way through to find her daughter. Liam said she was safe, but she wouldn't be able to let her heart calm down until she'd seen her with her own eyes, held her in her own arms.

There they were, sitting in the corner. She could only see Olivia's back hunched over the table, then Liam caught sight of her and waved, which made Olivia turn.

'Excuse me.' Gabbie inched around a group of lads looking at the blackboard menu behind the counter, cracking jokes to the young girl taking their order. Beyond them, she was focused only on Olivia's tear-stained face. What had happened?

'Mum.' Olivia held out her hands and Gabbie almost tipped over a chair in her haste to take her in her arms. The chrome arm hit her sharply in the hip and the chair rocked dangerously before Liam reached out to steady it.

'Oh my darling, I was so worried.'

For a few moments, Olivia couldn't speak, she just cried into Gabbie's shoulder, clutching a damp paper napkin in her hand. Eventually, she sniffed and pulled herself back into her seat.

'I was so cross about the party, I thought I'd just go anyway. I figured it was worth whatever punishment you'd give me afterwards as long as I got to go.'

This was the problem with Olivia. She never thought about consequences. Everything was on impulse, letting someone else sort out the mess afterwards. This was not the time for a lecture though. 'So you took the train?'

She nodded. 'But I couldn't get hold of any of my friends so I went to the house. But my key wouldn't work. I got cross and I twisted it too hard and it got stuck. I tried to call Dad but then I realised that my phone was out of charge and I didn't know what to do. When Dad arrived I was so relieved that I just couldn't stop crying.'

She collapsed into tears again and fell back onto Gabbie's shoulder. Gabbie held her close, rocking her gently, matching her daughter's tears with her own. Slowly, slowly she felt the fear seep out of her. Her baby was safe.

Liam returned to the table with a coffee for each of them. She fought the urge to ask him where he'd got the money from. 'Feeling better now Mum's here to make it all right?'

He smiled at Gabbie, as if to ensure that she'd taken the compliment. This wasn't an opportunity for him to score points with her. Still, he must have been worried, too. 'Thanks for finding her. I've been worried sick.'

From her shoulder, Olivia's voice was still damp with emotion. 'I'm so sorry.'

Liam reached out and rubbed Olivia's arm. 'It's all right, sweetheart. We were sixteen once, too. And we all do stupid things sometimes, even as adults.'

Even if he hadn't been looking directly at Gabbie as he spoke, the subtext wasn't lost on her. How dare he use this situation to make a point about himself? 'I need to get back on the road really, otherwise I'll be falling asleep at the wheel. I know that you originally said that you could stay with one of your friends, Olivia, but I'm really not sure about you going to this party when neither your dad or I will be nearby to come and get you if anything happens.'

Olivia shook her head, her face white with fear and exhaustion. 'It's okay. I don't want to go now. I just want to go home. Why can't we go home? I want my own bedroom tonight. But I don't understand why our house is all locked up and my key didn't work?'

Gabbie looked up at Liam. Had he not told her anything? What had they been talking about before she got there?

Before she could confuse matters by asking, he jumped in. 'I explained that, Olivia, didn't I? There are some structural problems with the house and we can't stay there at the moment. Once it's all been repaired and checked, we'll be able to move back in.'

'But why have they changed the locks?'

You could say what you wanted about their daughter, but she wasn't stupid.

But Liam was ready with an answer. 'It's an insurance thing. I don't really understand it myself.'

Leaning away from her, Olivia frowned at Gabbie. 'Why didn't you tell me that, Mum? When I was asking why we had to stay at Jill's? Why didn't you just explain?'

Gabbie didn't have a choice of lies at her fingertips like Liam. And she was tired, too tired to lie. 'The thing is, love—'

'The thing is, it's going to cost quite a lot to sort it all out, so I've been really worried about money. I asked your mum not to tell you because I was embarrassed, but I've lost my job. Cutbacks at the bank. That's why I didn't come up to Jill's with you.

I've been going to interviews. I didn't want to worry you and Alice about it all, because it's going to be fine.'

Gabbie's mouth almost fell open like a character in a comic strip. How did these lies fall so easily from his lips? Had he already been planning this cover story, or was he able to make it all up on the fly? Clearly he'd had a lot of practice.

And his lies didn't only get him out of a hole, they won him the sympathy of his daughter. 'Oh Dad, I'm so sorry. That must've been horrible for you.' She stood and put her arms around him. Over her shoulder, Liam mouthed 'sorry' at Gabbie.

Is this how it had felt to be her dad all those years? Knowing that his wife had been spending nights on end with other people – other men – and yet having to take the flak from his teenage daughter as to why she'd missed out on another visit from her mother?

Olivia pulled away from her dad and looked at Gabbie. 'Is that why you've been in such a funny mood these last few days? Because you were worried about Dad?'

She wasn't aware that she'd been in a 'funny mood'. But right now it was easier just to go with the flow. 'I suppose so.'

Olivia sat down next to her and reached out for another hug. 'I'm sorry if I've made things more difficult for you, going on about that party. I just thought you didn't want me to go because you were worried about me. Dad said I should under-stand that it's difficult for you to see me as a grown up. He said you get anxious about me being out so late.'

How had he turned this onto her again? Liam at least had the grace to look embarrassed. 'Well, I said both of us really.'

Right then, she wanted to tell Olivia the whole truth. That Liam wasn't the saintly father he was trying to paint himself. But she looked so vulnerable and so young, that Gabbie didn't want to worry her any more than necessary. Maybe it was enough to tell her that the house needed work. At least Liam had admitted he'd lost his job; it was a start.

'I need to let everyone know that you're okay. I'll go outside and contact them.'

Firstly, she sent Jill a text to explain what had happened and reiterate that they'd be coming back tonight. She was planning to just text Tricia to let her and Elsa know that Olivia was safe, but Elsa had been so upset that she decided to call.

Tricia sounded almost as relieved as she might be for her own daughter. 'Oh, thank goodness. I'm really glad she's safe.'

Hearing Tricia's voice made Gabbie feel emotional all over again. 'Me too. We're just going to finish our drinks and then we'll be on our way back.'

'I don't know if you've mentioned the photo to her yet, but please tell her that Matt hasn't shown it to anyone. And he's deleted it from his phone. I can't help but think that that might have convinced her to leave.'

The nude picture. In the worry of the last couple of hours, Gabbie had forgotten about that. Tricia was right, the more people knew, the more mortifying it would be for Olivia. There was no need to tell Liam. She and Olivia would be in the car alone for the next two hours; it might be the perfect time to discuss it. 'Thanks. I'll tell her.'

The heat in the cafe hit her as she walked back in. In the corner, Liam and Olivia were laughing about something together. A week ago, this sight would have warmed her heart so much that she might have slipped her phone from her pocket to take a candid photograph of the two of them. Olivia was always complaining about her doing that, moaning that it didn't give her a chance to pose for the camera. But that was exactly why Gabbie did it. Not wanting a posed picture, she wanted to just catch the moment, with them looking as they really did. She'd often wished she had more photographs of her mother – videos, even. This generation would never know how lucky they were to be able to capture so many moments to treasure forever.

Now, though, she didn't take the snap. This was not a moment she wanted to remember. This whole period of her life was something she wanted to bury and never recall. Would that ever be possible?

She joined them at the table and picked up her jacket. 'Come on, then, love. We need to get back. Alice will want to give you a hug and check that you're okay.'

Olivia looked at her dad. 'Are you coming, too?'

Liam looked at Gabbie and she ignored him, shaking her head at Olivia. 'Your dad has things to sort out here. But he'll come and see you and Alice soon.'

He reached out and squeezed Olivia's arm. 'Really soon. I promise.'

His promises didn't mean very much, but this wasn't the time for getting into that. 'I'll call you.'

He leaned forward to kiss her and she turned slightly so that his lips met the side of her cheek rather than her mouth; even that was a concession because Olivia was watching.

Once it was just the two of them in the car, she wanted to talk to Olivia about the message she'd sent to Matt. Gabbie still couldn't get her head around why. Hadn't she been desperate to get to the party to see her boyfriend? Sending provocative photographs to another boy – man – that she'd only just met didn't make much sense.

She'd wanted so much for her daughter to be confident about who she was and what her place was in the world. But sending nude photographs of herself to boys she'd just met? That was not what she'd meant.

# TWENTY-SIX

Gabbie waited until they were on the motorway before speaking to Olivia about the photo she'd sent Matt.

Part of that was cowardice. She'd enjoyed their closeness in the cafe; it had been a while since her daughter had hugged her that hard. Even now, sitting on the passenger seat, scrolling through some nonsense on her phone, there was less animosity emanating from her than there'd been for a while.

But she needed to do it and it would be best to get it out of the way before they got home and Olivia saw Elsa again. How to start?

'I'm glad you got to see your dad. I know you've missed him.' Gabbie glanced across and was rewarded with a smile.

'I have missed him. I wish you'd told me that he lost his job. I feel bad that he's been going through that on his own. You can tell me stuff like that. I can handle it.'

If only she knew. 'Well, actually, there is something else that I need to talk to you about – something serious.'

Olivia's head snapped to look at her. 'Is it to do with Dad? The reason that he lost his job? He's not ill, is he?'

Why was her first thought for her father? It was strange to

think that Olivia was three years older than Gabbie had been when her mother died. Seeing it from that perspective made her realise how young she'd been when it happened. How naive.

'Your dad is fine. This is to do with you. I've had a conversation with Tricia.'

Another side glance saw Olivia's face whiten. Clearly, she knew what was coming.

'She said that Matt got a text from you? With a photograph?'

Olivia covered her face with her hands, her voice muffled by her fingers. 'I'm so embarrassed. It was a mistake. It wasn't meant for him.'

Gabbie didn't know if this was better or worse. 'Who was it meant for?'

A groan escaped from the fingers before Olivia pulled her head out of her hands and let it bang back onto the headrest. 'Please don't make a big deal out of this, Mum. We really don't need to talk about it. Everyone does it now.'

Though she'd planned to take this slowly and gently, the 'everyone' out of Olivia's mouth made that very difficult. 'Not a big deal? To send naked photographs of yourself to someone you barely know? Think about what you're saying, Olivia.'

'But I do know him. Not Matt – that was a mistake and, yes, I am mortified. But I meant to send it to my boyfriend.'

Gabbie couldn't make sense of the fact that her sixteen-year-old daughter was trying to normalise sexting her boyfriend. This was a scene from a nightmare. 'Why did you do that? How could you possibly think that was a good idea?'

If she'd expected her daughter to crumble into regret, she was sorely disappointed. If anything, Olivia was getting cross with her. 'It's your fault. I had to send it. You wouldn't let me go to the party and there's going to be a ton of other girls there. I had to keep him interested. And everyone's doing it.'

She had to keep him interested by sending him sexual

images of herself? Why did they all do this? Pleasing their partners, putting their needs before their own. Her and Liam. Jill and her father. And now her precious girl. And they couldn't just blame it on their partners. Because they did it to each other, too. Meeting others' expectations. Fear of upsetting. Putting themselves last.

But it stopped here.

'Did he ask for this? Did he pressure you? Because that's not okay, Olivia.'

'No. He didn't. I chose to do it. I'm not some idiot, Mum.'

Gabbie really hadn't wanted to get angry with her, but Olivia's reaction was throwing her off completely. 'I just can't believe you've done this. It's illegal.' She'd been to the scary talk about the dangers of social media at Olivia's school last year. A police officer had pulled no punches as she'd explained the distinct possibility of being put on a sex offenders register for doing exactly this: her stern tone meant for the students but terrifying the parents, who had shifted a little closer to their sons and daughters and collectively believed that it would never happen to them.

Still, Olivia didn't seem remotely contrite. 'It's not illegal. I'm sixteen. I'm not a child.'

Physically, she was right. Her body was that of a woman; centuries ago, she would most likely have become a mother herself by now. But emotionally? 'I know you're not a child, but you haven't experienced the world yet. There is so much you haven't seen. So much you don't know. About the world. About people.'

Was this her fault for being a – what had Liam called it? – helicopter parent? For being cautious and overprotective? What was the right level of protective?

Olivia let her head fall back again as she groaned. 'You always think you know better than me about everything. But it's my body, isn't it? I can do what I want with it.'

Of course Olivia's body was her own, but she was still making herself, still working out who she was in the world. 'But this is something that will stay there forever. Once these images are out there, you can never take them back. They could be all over the internet. Your future friends, boyfriends, employers, will all be able to see them.'

'He wouldn't share them with anyone else. It's just for us.'

Gabbie wanted to cry for her naivety. The trust. Believing that this boy would never be tempted to show a friend what his girlfriend had sent him. And what about when they broke up? 'You can't possibly know that, Olivia. You have no control over what he does with them.'

That was how Gabbie felt, too. She had no control here. When Olivia was younger, she could have grounded her, taken her phone away, banned her from seeing him. But the time for that kind of power was slipping from her hands like sand through her fingers.

A change in Olivia's expression suggested that something had occurred to her. 'Are you going to tell Dad? Please don't. I'll be so embarrassed.'

For the first time, Olivia looked worried about what she'd done. Why was she so much more bothered about what Liam thought than what Gabbie thought? 'I can't keep something as big as this from your dad, Olivia.'

And that was the truth of the matter. She wouldn't keep big secrets from her husband, even though he had kept something huge from her.

'Dad's got enough to worry about. He's got to get our house back. I don't want to stay here anymore. I want to go home. I want to be with my friends. This was supposed to be the start of the best summer ever and you're keeping me away from everything. You're being so out of order. Don't you want me to keep all my friends?'

If only Olivia knew how painful her words were as they hit

Gabbie. The last thing she ever wanted was for her children to feel like this: lonely, isolated, longing to return home.

It was impossible having this conversation in the car. What had she been thinking, not waiting until they got home? They travelled the rest of the way in silence until they pulled up the drive of Jill's house.

Gabbie shut off the ignition, but Olivia didn't move. 'I mean it, Mum. I don't want to be here. I have one friend and now I'm embarrassed to speak to her because of the text I sent her brother. Why can't I just stay with Dad? Why are you making me come back here?'

The emotion overtook her words and she started to cry. Gabbie reached for her and tried to pull her into an embrace. Initially, she resisted, but as the sobs took over her body, she released her anger and let herself fall into Gabbie's arms.

Gabbie rocked her gently as she'd done when she was small, pressing her lips to the top of her head. 'It's going to be okay, sweetheart. I'm going to make it all okay.'

Olivia's words were mumbled into the top of Gabbie's chest. 'I want everything to be like it was.'

Like it was? How far would they have to go back? Olivia probably meant a week, but this had been going on for longer than that. What part of their past was far enough back to not be tainted with Liam's gambling, his lies? 'I know. Me too, me too.'

Olivia raised her head and looked at Gabbie through red-rimmed eyes. 'So when can we go home?'

She couldn't put off speaking to Jill again. She would have to make her see how important it was for the girls to get back home. 'Just give me a few days. I'm trying my best, Olivia, I really am.'

Jill must have heard them pull up, because she had the front door open. 'Welcome home. I've made some hot chocolate for you all.'

That actually sounded like heaven, right now. 'Thank you.'

Jill glanced behind them. 'Did you not bring Alice home, too?'

What was she talking about? 'What do you mean? I left Alice here with you. She said she wanted to stay here and wait.'

Jill stared at her. 'No. You told me she was going with you.'

She *had* said that, but that was before she'd spoken to Alice in her bedroom. 'But then she didn't want to come. I told you...'

Ice shot through her as she remembered. She hadn't told Jill anything. She'd been outside when Liam had called and she'd jumped straight into her car. *Oh no, oh no, oh no.*

She ran into the house, screaming at the top of her lungs. 'Alice? Alice, baby, where are you?'

Jill followed behind, twisting her hands, her face as pale as death. 'She's not here. I've been into all the rooms with fresh laundry this afternoon. I didn't know she was here.'

Gabbie was already at the top of the stairs. 'Alice! Alice!'

But she was met with silence.

Pushing the door to Alice's room, all she could see was the doll's house, its front wide open and the dolls lying on the floor. Then she tried her own room. Again, nothing. But a page that looked to be torn from a sketchpad was lying on top of her laptop, covered in a shaky rounded script that she knew as well as her own. She lunged forwards and snatched it up.

*Dear Mummy*

*I am looking for Daddy because he doesn't know where the house is.*

*I don't want him to get lost.*

*Lots of love Alice xxx*

# TWENTY-SEVEN

*10th July 1993*

*Dear Mr Cooper,*

*Further to our recent meeting, I wanted to send my sincere hopes that time at home will enable Gabrielle to reflect on her recent behaviour.*

*I hope that she will decide to return to school in September. However, I also wanted to take the opportunity to remind you that fees are paid termly in advance. Therefore, should she decide not to return, fees would still need to be paid up to and including the end of next term.*

*Yours sincerely,*

*Mrs E Spearman*

*Headteacher*

There was no way she wanted to go home with them now.

How long had it been going on? Had they been having an affair all this time? Before her mother had even died?

She could barely look at either her father or Jill as they sat in Mrs Spearman's office.

'Taking into consideration everything that has happened to Gabrielle in the last few months, I think it would be best if she came home with you and saw out the rest of the term at home. We would be happy to have her back in September if you think that she's ready.'

They hadn't had long to speak together before being called into the office, so her father looked relieved at this decision. 'Thank you. Yes. We can go home and speak about this. Thank you for your understanding.'

Jill offered to come with her to pack up her things, but Gabbie refused. The bedroom was empty as she threw everything she had into a suitcase. Again. When she opened the drawer in her bedside cupboard there was a hastily scribbled note in Jessica's handwriting. *Good riddance to you and your disgusting family.* Her tears blurred the writing. What had she done to deserve such hate?

She'd tried so hard to make friends. To be brave. Not to upset her mother. Not to disappoint her father. And this was where she'd ended up. She didn't want to be here and, if her father and Jill were together, she didn't want to be at home either.

The journey home was conducted in silence. When she got home she was in for another surprise. In her absence, the house had been decorated. Gone were her mother's vibrant wallpapers and modern paintings. Instead, every wall, every surface was bare and beige. It was as if they'd removed every memory of her from the house. Gabbie ran to her room, ignoring her father's call, and threw herself on the bed.

When hunger sent her downstairs two hours later, her father was sitting alone.

'Has Jill gone?'

'Yes. She thought it was best.'

And what Jill wants, she gets.

Lying on her bed earlier, Gabbie had turned it over and over in her mind. How long had it been going on between them? Had they been having an affair before her mother's accident? Had her mother known? She'd even tortured herself with visions of her mother fleeing the house in a state of hysteria, escaping from the sight of Jill and her father wrapped around one another.

From whatever angle she looked at it, her father – and Jill – had betrayed her mother and she would never forgive either of them. In her head, she'd composed a vicious speech, only undecided on whether to unleash it on her father tonight or wait until, inevitably, Jill returned tomorrow.

But then another idea had occurred to her. What if she didn't reveal what she'd overheard? Would they continue to pretend that their 'friendship' was purely platonic? Could she keep them apart by feigning ignorance?

She took a seat beside her father and he turned towards her, his arm resting on the back of the sofa. 'Why did you try and run away, Gabbie? Is someone being horrible to you again?'

He looked genuinely concerned. It would have been the easiest thing in the world to fall into him and tell him everything. But she needed to stick to her plan. 'I just wanted to see you. I want it to be just you and me, Dad. I don't need anyone else. Just you and me.'

He brought his arm down across her shoulders. 'So you do want to leave the school, now? That's fine, sweetheart. We can do this somehow. You know that it's tricky with me working away so much, but Jill has kindly offered—'

'No.' She cut him off before he could even say it. 'I don't want Jill to look after me. I don't want her here. I just want you and me. If I can't have that, I'll just go back to school.'

He started to rub at his temples. 'You've got to help me out here, Gabbie. You try to run away from school. You know that I can't be here to look after you all the time. I don't know what you want.'

*I want my mother*, was all she could think. *I want my mum.*

# TWENTY-EIGHT

Terror tore through Gabbie faster than she tore out of her bedroom. Downstairs, she could hear Olivia throwing open doors and cupboards. 'Alice, where are you?'

How had she been so stupid? What had possessed her to get in that car without telling Jill that Alice had decided to stay home? Why had she had that stupid conversation with Jill about Liam? And why, oh why, had she not been honest with the girls from the start? She took the stairs so fast that she almost slipped and had to grab the banister. Jill reached out her hands. 'Slow down. Slow down.'

Gabbie thrust the paper at Jill; her voice came out as a roar. 'I can't slow down; my baby is missing. I've lost my child.'

As Jill scanned the letter, Olivia ran towards them from the other end of the hallway. 'She's not down here. I've run around the garden but I can't see her anywhere. Oh, Mum. Where is she?'

There was a sharp intake of breath behind her. Jill looked up from the trembling letter. 'Oh no. Gabbie. She must have heard us talking. You said that Liam might be coming here, and then I said... Oh, Gabbie, she must think Liam is lost.'

Gabbie grabbed at her own hair and pulled it, trying to make her brain work. 'We need to start looking in the village. I'll start at the shops. Jill, you stay here in case she comes back. Olivia, call the police.'

Olivia's voice was small and scared. 'Shall I call Dad?'

*Liam.* She hadn't even thought about him. 'Yes. Call your dad and tell him to come.'

Jill already had her phone in her hand. 'I'll call the police. You go.'

Where had she put her keys? They weren't in her bag. Or her coat. She wanted to scream. 'Where are my keys?'

Jill was holding them out to her. 'They were in the sitting room. Just breathe. We'll find her.'

Breathe? She felt as if her heart was being ripped from her body. 'Just call the police. Tell them to find her.'

'I will. Are you okay to drive? Do you want me to...?'

'Just call them.'

She was out the front door and into her car in seconds, gulping back sobs that she didn't have time for. Because of her trembling hands, it took three attempts to get the car key in the ignition. Jill was right, she needed to calm herself enough to drive; she'd be no use to Alice if she wrapped herself around a lamp post. She forced herself to pause and take three deep breaths. *Please let her be safe. Please let her be safe.*

Ten seconds was long enough to wait. Clutching the steering wheel, the gravel crunching beneath the wheels of the car, she pulled slowly out of the drive, looking all around her. It was impossible to look and drive at the same time. She slammed on the brakes and ran back towards the front door, leaving the engine running. She raised her fist to bang on the door but it opened so quickly that she nearly punched Olivia.

'Mum, I can't get hold of Dad on the phone. It just keeps going to voicemail.'

Gabbie clutched at her daughter's arm. 'Don't worry about

that now. You need to come with me. You can look while I drive.'

Jill appeared behind Olivia. 'Do you want me to—'

Gabbie was already running back to the car, so she shouted back over her shoulder. 'No. You stay here.'

Olivia was crying hard as she buckled herself into the passenger seat. Like Gabbie with the keys, it took her more than one attempt. 'It's all my fault. If I hadn't left, you would've been here. She wouldn't have run away.'

Much as she wanted to console her, Gabbie didn't have the capacity right now. The lanes towards the village were narrow with thick foliage either side. In places, the trees reached towards one another and formed an archway which, right now, made them look like an ominous passageway. 'Keep looking for your sister.'

Gabbie couldn't bear the thought of Alice walking down here alone. Had she put on her coat? Taken one of her dolls for company? There wasn't much traffic down here, but sometimes a car – a tourist, or a delivery van or a young, reckless driver – would take the corners too fast and crunch into the trunk of one of these ancient trees.

Olivia was turning her head from the windscreen to the passenger window; her voice sounded strangled. 'I'll never forgive myself if something has happened to her.'

Gabbie couldn't bear to let her mind go there. She reached out her hand and felt for Olivia's, which she squeezed. 'We're going to find her. She's going to be okay.'

'I'll do anything. I'll be so good from now on. As long as she's safe.'

It broke her heart to hear her daughter bargaining for her sister's life. 'This is not your fault, Olivia. It's my fault. I should have told Jill that Alice was in the house and I didn't.'

She still couldn't believe her stupidity. What kind of a mother did that?

'But you were coming to find me. So it *is* my fault.'

Olivia was the only one of them *not* to blame. Gabbie should have told Jill that she was leaving Alice, and Liam... well, none of this would have happened if he hadn't betrayed them all. 'She's looking for Dad.'

Olivia was too scared to pick up on the anger in Gabbie's voice. 'But where would she look for him?'

'I don't know.' Her brain flicked through the places in the village like files in a cabinet. Where would she have looked for Liam if she was Alice?

Chewing on her nails as she scanned the trees and bushes, Olivia was clearly doing the same thing. 'What about the pub? She'd have passed that when she was out with Jill early this morning. Would she remember how to get there?'

This was ridiculous. Of course Alice wouldn't know how to get there. She was eight years old. A tiny little girl, who could be behind any of these trees and bushes. Fear gripped Gabbie like a vice. They needed more people.

Olivia's phone rang in her hand. 'It's Jill. I'll put her on speaker.'

Gabbie shouted from her side of the car. 'Jill? It's Gabbie. Have you called the police?'

'Yes. They're sending someone over right now. They need a picture of her to send out to any other local officers.'

Images of lost children on posters and news reports flashed into Gabbie's brain and she pushed them down again. 'I have photos on my phone. I'll get Olivia to send one to you.'

'It's fine. I have one on my phone from yesterday. When she was holding up her painting.'

Jill's voice cracked at the other end. It almost started Gabbie off – she'd never heard her stepmother cry. Even at her father's funeral, Jill had kept herself composed and dignified.

'Tell the police that I'm looking down the lanes but we can't see anything.'

A horn blasted behind her; an impatient man waved his arm at her in anger. She knew she was driving too slowly – but how else would they have a chance of catching sight of Alice? A moment later, the driver had clearly had enough of waiting; as soon as they turned the next corner, he pulled into the opposite lane and accelerated past, shouting as he did so. All she could make out was, 'You stupid woman.'

Yes, she wanted to say, I am a stupid woman. Much more stupid than you realise.

Olivia's voice trembled. 'Why is he driving so fast? He needs to slow down.'

Gabbie knew what she was thinking and it make her feel even more sick. 'Try your dad again, sweetheart. Tell him we need him to come.'

For the second time today, Liam wasn't answering his phone. Why, when it was usually in his hand constantly? Where the hell was he?

'Shall I send him a text message?'

'Yes. Good idea. But don't say Alice is missing, just tell him that it's urgent that he calls you.'

Even saying those three words aloud – *Alice is missing* – was surreal. Alice was her good girl. She was never naughty, never rude, never demanding. From a tiny baby, she'd been the easiest child in the world. And the sweetest, kindest girl you could know. A wave of grief threatened to pull Gabbie downwards, but she pushed it down. *Not now.*

They reached the end of the lane at a T-junction. The high street was right and the pub was left. For a small village, there were so many places Alice could be. 'Call Tricia on my phone and put it on speaker. We need some help before it starts getting dark.'

Tricia answered in two rings. 'Hi, Gabbie. Are you home yet? Elsa was wondering if Olivia wanted to come over and I thought we could go and get a drink at the pub?'

Her last conversation with Tricia felt like a year ago. 'Alice is missing.'

Those three words again, so simple yet so deadly.

'What? Missing where?'

'I don't know. We got back from London and she'd gone. We think she's looking for her dad.'

'Why the hell would... Okay, that doesn't matter right now. I'm grabbing my keys and getting in the car. Where have you looked already? Have you been to the playground?'

*The playground.* Of course, why hadn't they thought of that? 'I'm going there now. Can you check the pub or the high street? Jill has called the police so I hope they'll be there soon.'

'I'll go to the pub. We'll find her, Gabbie. This is a nice village. Someone will see her.'

Gabbie squashed down another sob and smiled at Olivia's hopeful eyes. It might be a nice village, but there were still fast cars and a deep river and strangers. And it was getting dark. They had to find her soon. 'Thank you. I'm hoping you're right about the playground.'

# TWENTY-NINE

During the day, playgrounds are full of the cries of chubby toddlers and their harassed mothers; in the evenings, the occasional shout or laugh of teenagers lounging around the swings and benches. During lockdown, one of the saddest sights had been Gabbie's local park, cordoned off with red and white tape, children banished. The melancholy emptiness a reminder of all they'd lost.

The park in the village amounted to two swings and a slide attached to a climbing frame. When she'd brought Alice here two days ago, they'd been the only people there. Now, it was just her and Olivia. Though they could see from a distance that Alice was nowhere to be seen, they jogged towards the red, blue and yellow equipment to make sure.

Olivia recovered her voice first. 'She's not here.'

Heart thumping as she regained her breath, Gabbie held onto the chain of the swing that Alice had chosen two days ago, alternating between begging to go higher and screaming to slow down. Maybe it was Jill's revelations about her father, but memories of her own childhood were coming to the fore. *Push me, Daddy. Higher! Higher!*

Like Alice, she'd wanted the rush of speed, yet been frightened by it. Her young daughter was so much like her. It was no
surprise that she would put herself at risk to look for her dad,
that she would want for everyone to be safe and together.

'Where shall we look now?'

Olivia's face was expectant, trusting that Gabbie would
know what to do. If only she did. Where was there? Where
would Alice have gone? *Think. Think.* 'Let's get back in the car
and drive to the high street. You can try your dad again.'

She should have called Liam herself, but she didn't know if
she could. Hearing his voice might make her unravel altogether.
Where were the police? Jill had said that they were on their way
– shouldn't they be there by now? Where was she?

Gabbie already had her phone to her ear, but she shook her
head. 'Voicemail again.'

Where was he?

Her own phone rang in her pocket and she fished it out.
Tricia. 'Hello? Have you seen her?'

Tricia also sounded out of breath. 'No. I'm sorry. She's
nowhere near the pub. Not at the park either?'

'No. We're going to drive to the high street. Maybe she's
found her way there?'

She didn't really believe that. How would Alice – who
complained if she had to walk home from school – have walked
as far as the small collection of shops? But she had to be
somewhere.

'Okay. That's a good idea. I'll drive down the lanes to Jill's.
If I park in the layby, Elsa and I can take a look around in case
she's wandered off for a rest.'

*Or if she's been knocked clean off her feet by a reckless
driver. Or if she's dropped her doll as someone pulled her into
their car. Or if she's fallen into the river and drowned.* Was there
any scenario in which this didn't end badly? Gabbie wanted to

double over and give in to the fear, but there wasn't time. 'Okay. Thank you. The police should be there soon.'

She was clinging onto their arrival with the same trust that Olivia had in her. She only hoped that her beliefs were more well-founded.

'We'll find her, Gabbie. It's going to be okay.'

While she appreciated the sentiment, they both knew that there was no way that Tricia could know that for sure.

As they walked towards the car, Gabbie called Jill. There was no answer. She tried again. Maybe she was with the police, but surely she'd know that Gabbie would want to be kept informed? Her irritation gave way to new fears. *They've found her. Jill needed to identify her because...* She shook her head. No. Alice was fine. She had to be.

She was in the car and pulling her seatbelt across when she realised that Olivia hadn't got in; she was still looking around as if she was waiting for Alice to catch them up, tripping along behind them complaining that her legs weren't as long as theirs. Gabbie wound down the window and leaned across the passenger seat to call to Olivia. 'Get in, love. We need to keep looking.'

Olivia leaned in the window. 'You drive to the high street, Mum. I'm going to walk around. We might miss her from the road.'

Gabbie didn't want to hang around; she needed to be looking, looking, looking. 'Are you sure? Will you be okay on your own?'

This time, there was no roll of the eye, no groan about not being a child. 'I'll be fine, Mum. I promise I'll be careful.'

Gabbie pressed her hand to her chest at her daughter's obvious understanding that she needed to know that she was safe. Maybe she was old enough to trust her to do more. And there were still a couple of hours before it got dark. 'Why don't you call Elsa and ask if her mum can drop her here to look with you?'

Olivia blushed and shook her head, twisting her hair with her fingers, her tell from childhood that she was embarrassed or unsure. 'No. It's fine. I'll do it on my own. I don't really want to see her, yet.'

Gabbie started the car; she really needed to get going. 'I don't even know if she's aware of the photo. Tricia said Matt hasn't told anyone. And we all make mistakes, love.'

What had seemed huge a few hours ago, now seemed as inconsequential as a smudge of ink on a page. Everything was fixable. Everything was surmountable. *Except losing a child. Except losing Alice.*

Olivia stood back from the window and gave her a little wave, something about it making her look like a little girl again. Gabbie pressed her fingers to her lips to send a kiss with her wave goodbye.

She drove as slowly as she could towards the high street, moving her head back and forth as she scanned the pavement either side of the lane. When she passed a young woman in a loose sundress, pushing an empty pushchair and holding the hand of a toddler – him planting each foot with a determined thump like a tiny drunk – she pulled over and called out through the passenger window. 'Excuse me. Have you seen a little girl along here? She's eight and has long brown hair.' *And she's beautiful and clever and kind.*

The woman shook her head, clutched the hand of the toddler even tighter. Was she looking at Gabbie with horror that she could be so terrible as to lose her own child? 'I'm sorry. No. Have you tried the playground?'

She was right to look at her like that. Gabbie *was* a terrible mother. So wrapped up in her problems with Liam that she hadn't paid attention to the one person who really needed looking after. How had she been so stupid? Why, oh why, had she not gone back into the house and told Jill that Alice would be staying home with her?

It was more than that. If she hadn't dragged the girls here to stay with Jill rather than ask a friend to take them in. If she'd let Liam come with them. If she'd found a way to let Olivia go to that damn party. If she'd asked Liam to look for Olivia rather than go rushing off to London herself. If she'd taken Alice with her as planned. *If. If. If.*

She'd played this 'game' before. When her mother died. Thinking of all the things she could have said or done that might've saved her. If she hadn't asked her to visit that weekend. If she hadn't made such a fuss about the school that her mother was worried. But – like she'd said to Olivia about Alice going missing – it hadn't been her fault.

There was a small free car park behind the church that everyone used and it was half-empty when Gabbie pulled in. There was only a sprinkling of shops along this side of the road: a hairdresser, the small supermarket, a greengrocer, a cafe and a shop selling cards and small gifts. She was ready to ask every shopkeeper, shopper or dog walker if they'd seen Alice.

As she walked out of the car park, she called Jill again. Still no answer. Before she could talk herself out of it, she tried Liam again. This time he picked up. 'Gabbie? Hi.'

Anxiety made her angry and she needed to direct it somewhere. 'Why haven't you been picking up your calls? Olivia has been trying to get hold of you.'

He sounded out of breath himself. 'Has she? Sorry, my phone coverage is bad here. What does she need? How are you feeling after the scare she gave us today?'

Gabbie didn't even care where 'here' was. The familiarity of his voice washed over her, more soothing than she'd expected. 'It's Alice. We can't find her. We think she left to look for you and we don't know where she's gone.'

A man who had just passed her glanced back in her direction; she must be talking loudly, but she didn't care. At the other end of the phone, there was a moment's silence, as if Liam was absorbing what she'd said. 'For me? Are you sure? I mean, she's not just hiding, is she? You know how great she is at that.'

Alice loved a game of hide-and-seek. Liam would play it with her for hours, curling himself into the tiniest and most imaginative of places, having to call her name out loud when she impatiently called out, 'Give me a clue, Daddy!' She'd learned from his ingenuity and, on the rare occasions that Gabbie would be pressed into playing, it was genuinely difficult to find her.

'No. She's not hiding. We've searched the house and the garden. I've driven around the lanes and to the park. Jill has called the police.'

'Where are you now?'

'I'm just about to go into the local shops and ask if anyone has seen her. I don't know what else to do.' The fear she'd been pushing down was threatening to strangle her.

Liam sounded as if he'd started running, his voice coming in steady, rhythmic bursts. 'I'm on my way. I'll be with you as soon as I can.'

Relief flooded through her. He was coming. All the tears she'd kept under control threatened to spill from her. 'Get here as fast as you can. We need you.' A sob escaped, which made the man look at her again. 'I need you.'

Knowing that Liam was coming spurred her on. She took a moment to blow her nose and catch her breath and was about to start in the supermarket when her phone rang in her hand. Jill. Finally. 'Hello? What's going on? Are the police there?'

Jill's breath was loud and erratic, her mouth so close to the phone that her voice crackled sharply in Gabbie's ear. 'I've found her. I'm holding Alice right now. But she's unconscious. There's an ambulance on its way. You need to come right now. Hurry, please. I can't wake her up.'

# THIRTY

The heat of the day had left behind a damp closeness which made it hard to hurry. Even worse, the ground beneath Gabbie's feet was so uneven that her ankles twisted and wobbled as she tried to get to Alice as fast as she could. 'Jill? Are you here? Where are you?'

It made her sick to think she'd driven past her on her way to the park. While they'd been crawling down the lanes, fruitlessly looking for signs of Alice, she'd been lying out here all alone. Olivia had been right; they should've been searching on foot.

'Jill? Can you hear me? Am I getting closer to you?'

This time there was a response. 'We're over here.'

She pushed on closer towards the voice, brambles catching on her arms and face. How had Alice come this deep into the wood? How frightened must she have been once she realised that she was lost?

Pushing back a curtain of low hanging branches, Gabbie saw a low concrete wall which was attached to some kind of structure with a window which looked familiar. On the other side were the bright yellow jackets and green uniforms of two paramedics. To the left, Jill with her hand in front of her mouth, staring down at where they were both knelt on the parched ground. Between them, a small pair of legs wearing the red patent shoes Alice had begged for at their last trip to the shopping centre near home. Oh, how Gabbie wished they were back there, before any of this had happened.

'Alice.'

The word came out strangled and weak, but it was enough for Jill to turn towards her, relief flashing across her face before it returned to worry. 'You're here. Thank God.'

A stocky male paramedic had his back to her; the other was leaning over Alice. Now she was closer, Gabbie could see that Alice was on a stretcher and they were about to lift her up. The second paramedic was a dark-haired woman who didn't look much older than Olivia. She looked up at Gabbie. 'Are you her mum? Are you coming with us? We're going now.'

Gabbie couldn't take her eyes from those tiny red shoes. 'Yes. Yes. I'm coming. Is she okay?'

'She's breathing and there's no blood or anything broken. Let's get her into the hospital as quickly as we can.'

They lifted the stretcher and now she could see Alice's face for the first time, the emotion that came out of Gabbie sounded like that of a wounded animal. 'Oh, Alice, baby.'

She passed her keys to Jill, asked her to find Olivia and take her home, and stumbled after the paramedics in the direction of the ambulance, which was on a track off the main road. As soon as Alice was safely on board, the male paramedic – he told her his name was Leigh – helped Gabbie up so that she could sit next to Alice and talk to her while his colleague – Sue – drove them to the hospital on a blue light.

Leigh looked tough, but his manner was gentle. 'Alice's grandmother said that she isn't receiving any treatment or medication at the moment. Is that correct?'

For most of her life, Alice had been fit and healthy, able to shake off any colds or bugs that did the rounds at school. 'That's correct. But I was supposed to take her to the doctor yesterday. She's been drinking a lot and going to the toilet more often than usual.'

She half expected him to wave that away, but he wrote everything down. 'Anything else? Headaches? Tummy aches? Sickness? Tiredness?'

Alice had been tired, even offering to go to bed. 'Yes, she has been tired.' She should have kept that appointment yesterday. Should have pushed for a doctor to see Alice sooner than that. She'd known that something wasn't right.

Laid out in the ambulance, Alice looked as if she was asleep, but she was as pale as the sheet beneath her, her breath soft and rasping. Gabbie held her clammy hand and leaned in close. 'Hey, baby girl. Mummy is here. I'm right next to you. You're going to be okay. Everything is going to be okay.'

Was she saying it to persuade Alice or herself?

The journey to the hospital was no more than ten minutes, but it seemed to last a lifetime. At the other end, Alice was rushed inside and Gabbie followed as fast as she could; she never wanted Alice out of her sight again.

In the examination room, everything happened so fast. It was hard to take in everything that was happening; just a blur of syringes, tubes and wires. A woman wearing a pale blue uniform and a kind smile stood by her. 'Hello, I'm Dawn. I just need to ask you a few questions. I'm picking up on some symptoms you told our paramedics. You said that Alice has been very thirsty lately? And going to the toilet more than usual?'

'Yes. To both of those. I was supposed to take her to the doctor yesterday, but we had to come here and—'

Dawn was kind. 'That's okay. Has she been overly tired at all?'

'Yes. But there has been a lot going on the last few days. We had a long car journey and she's been unsettled because...'

Gabbie stopped babbling. As if the nurse needed to know all of that. 'Do you know what's wrong? Why is she unconscious?'

The doctor who had been examining Alice stood back from the bed and spoke to the nurse beside him. 'She needs insulin and IV fluids immediately.'

He joined Dawn and matched her kind smile. 'Hi. I'm Dr Russell. I'll be treating Alice. Would you like to talk here or shall we go into another room?'

There was no way she was leaving Alice. 'Here is fine.'

'Okay, so Alice is in diabetic ketoacidosis, which means that she has too much acid in her blood. It's caused by her blood sugar levels being too high for too long.'

It was as if he was speaking from a distance; her legs felt as if they might not keep her upright. 'Is it serious?'

'It can be. Usually, there are symptoms before the stage that Alice is now in. Lack of energy, being very thirsty, going to the toilet more than usual, blurred vision. Have you noticed anything like that today?'

That explained the questions from the nurse. 'I haven't been with her today. I had to take my other daughter... I mean collect my other daughter... She was missing. We've been looking for her for the last hour but she could have been gone longer than that. There was a big confusion and—'

'It's okay. We can talk about this later. I am assuming there's been no diagnosis of diabetes before this?'

'No. Nothing like that. I'm sorry, I had no idea she was...' Gabbie didn't know how to even finish the sentence. She'd had no idea. That said it all.

The doctor nodded. 'There's no need to apologise. It can develop quickly in a child Alice's age, and sometimes symptoms are missed for a while. Let's get the insulin into her and we can see where we are after that.'

He wasn't making sense. 'What do you mean, where we are?'

Dr Russell coughed into his fist. 'Apologies for not being clear. Because we don't know how long Alice has been unconscious, we don't yet know how serious the situation is.'

There was a buzzing in Gabbie's ears. 'Serious?'

His voice was calm but his words were grenades. 'A diabetic coma can be life-threatening. But let's not get ahead of ourselves. She's here now and the nurses are setting up the insulin IV as we speak.'

Gabbie swayed as she looked from him to Alice. Dawn, the nurse with the clipboard, put a hand on her arm. 'I think you'd better sit down.'

Not since the day she'd found out her mother had died, had Gabbie felt so utterly alone. She'd called Liam to let him know that Alice was in the hospital, but he was still an hour away. He'd said all the right things – *she'll be okay, she's in the right place* – but the platitudes didn't touch her; he wasn't looking at their daughter, laid out on a hospital bed, hooked up to an intravenous drip. She needed him here. Now. She sipped at the water Dawn had insisted she drink and watched Alice's face for signs of recovery. Over and over, she heard the doctor's words like the rhythm of a drum. *Life-threatening.*

Forced church services and choir practice at school had made her less than keen on organised religion, but now Gabbie begged God to save her child. *I will do anything. I will be good. I will watch over her forever. Please, please don't let her die.*

How had their lives imploded so quickly? A week ago, the worst thing that she'd had to deal with was Olivia's moods or Alice's friend being mean. A tight deadline for a translation job. That annoying tutoring request from Mia's mother. And now? No money, no home, no idea of what to do next. And even those things were like nothing compared to this. Her beautiful baby girl lying here so still. *Please, please don't let her die.*

When Alice's lips first began to twitch, she'd willed it so hard that she thought she was imagining it, but the nurse who had just arrived to check her over confirmed it. 'Hi, Alice. How are you feeling? Your mum is here. Can you open your eyes for me?'

It was as if her eyelids were too heavy, but slowly, slowly, she opened them to reveal her beautiful blue eyes. 'Mummy?'

'I'm here, baby. I'm right here.' A river of relief coursed through Gabbie as she leaned forwards to show Alice her face, trying to pour her love and support out through her eyes. 'You're in the hospital but Mummy is here and I'm holding your hand. You're safe, sweetheart, you're safe and I'm here.'

The nurse squeezed a peg open and closed in front of Alice. 'I'm just popping this onto the end of your finger to take your readings, Alice.'

Gabbie watched her. 'If she's awake, does this mean she's okay?'

The nurse watched the screen to take the necessary readings, but she glanced at Gabbie and smiled encouragement. 'It means that the insulin is doing its job. I'm going to ask Dr Russell to come and check her over.'


Gabbie didn't leave Alice's side while the doctor checked her over and spoke to her, asking how she was feeling. While she wanted to stare at Alice, drinking in her polite responses and smiles, she also watched the doctor's face for any signs of pleasure or concern. When he smiled, she could have kissed him.

'Well, I think you're a very lucky little girl. My guess is that you hadn't been unconscious very long when your grandmother found you.'

Alice frowned and looked at Gabbie. To her, 'grandmother' meant Liam's mother, who they saw once a year at best.

'Auntie Jill. Auntie Jill found you.' And Gabbie would never be able to repay her.

The doctor explained that Alice would need to stay in overnight for observation and that they would be getting a visit from the diabetic nurse shortly to talk about type 1 diabetes, medication and treatment. All of that would be a lot for Alice to deal with, but, right now, all Gabbie could feel was overwhelming gratitude that they hadn't lost her. She sent up a silent prayer of thanks.

As soon as the doctor had gone, she called Olivia and let her speak to her sister. Then Jill came on the line and tears ran down Gabbie's face at Alice's, 'Thank you for finding me, Auntie Jill.'

A nurse had to interrupt for another round of observations on Alice, so Gabbie took her mobile into the corner of the room and lowered her voice. 'Jill. The doctor said you saved her life. If you hadn't found her when you did...'

'Don't think about that. She's back with us. That's all that matters.'

Gabbie couldn't think about anything else. 'How did you even know that she was there?'

'I didn't know for sure, but I'd been trying to think of a place she might have found. You used to love it there when you were a child. Do you remember? You called it the little house?'

She'd thought it looked familiar. How had she forgotten that that place had even existed? She knew now that it was a gun emplacement from World War Two. A concrete installation which would have housed a huge gun at some point in its past. But to a young Gabbie, it had been the perfect place to lay out a picnic for her dolls while her father indulged her by sitting cross-legged at the edge of a tablecloth and waited his turn for tea. Where had that memory been hiding?

'That feels so long ago.'

'That's because it was. I've known you a long time, remember.'

There was something in her tone that Gabbie couldn't quite read. 'Well, I don't know how I'm ever going to thank you.'

'You don't need to. Just give that little girl a big squeeze from me. Hang on, Olivia wants you back.'

There was some rustling as the phone was handed over to Olivia. 'Can I come to the hospital? I really want to see her.'

'Yes. Ask Jill to bring you. I'm just going to call your dad and let him know she's awake.'

Alice caught the last of the conversation. 'Can I talk to Daddy when you call him?'

'Of course. But he'll be here soon and you can talk to him in person. He's going to give you one of his biggest cuddles ever.'

Gabbie felt as if she could do with one of those, too.

# THIRTY-ONE

**Date: 13th January 2006**

**From: Gabrielle@WaymentTranslations.Fr**

**To: C.Cooper@JBRlegal.co.uk**

*Hi Dad,*

*Nice to hear from you. I hope that you and Jill are well. Sorry that I didn't make it home for Christmas but there was so much to do here. The translation agency has just taken over another company based in Paris, so I might be flying back and forth a couple of times in the next few weeks. A chip off the old block, eh?*

*I'm loving living in London. Thanks for the offer of a deposit on a flat, but I'm happy renting at the moment. I should also let you know that I've started seeing someone. His name is Liam and it's pretty serious. Next time I come home, I'll bring him to meet you.*

*Love Gabbie x*

Gabbie was so used to her father's house that it almost surprised her to see Liam's reaction.

'Wow. This place is huge.'

She shrugged. 'Don't forget what I said about my dad. It's easier just to go with what he says. Otherwise you end up in a huge discussion of him telling you why he's right.'

She was overdoing this, but she knew how Liam could be and how her father might react. It surprised her how much she wanted the two of them to get along.

The last six months with Liam had been a whirlwind. Although she'd had a couple of relationships at university, this felt completely different. He was a grown-up. He knew the good restaurants to take her to, the plays that everyone was talking about, the bars and clubs where they'd be most likely to spot a celebrity or two. He'd brought fun to her life like she hadn't experienced since her mum.

Her father met them at the door and pulled her into a hug. Ironically, they'd been closer since she'd left home; wrangles about him wanting to give her money aside. Then he held out his hand to shake Liam's. 'Welcome, young man.'

Liam flashed the smile that won over everyone from waitresses to traffic wardens. 'Pleased to meet you. You have a lovely home.'

That was a good start. Her father was proud of this place. She squeezed the hand that Liam placed in hers as they followed her father inside.

Jill was waiting for them in the front sitting room, cakes and sandwiches laid out on china that Gabbie hadn't seen before. She stood up stiffly to greet them. 'Hello, Gabbie. And you must be Liam?'

'Guilty as charged.' Liam bobbed forwards and kissed her on the cheek.

Jill blushed before holding out her hand. 'Please, sit. I've made some lunch, but if there's anything else you'd like, let me know.'

The last was directed more at Gabbie, who felt a familiar irritation. 'This looks fine, thanks.'

'How was your journey?'

Liam took a plate from Jill. 'Fine. I just got a new car, so it was nice to give it a run. I don't get out into the country very often.'

Cars was another favourite topic of her father's; Liam was keeping to the script very well. 'I noticed that. Very nice. Business must be good. What do you do?'

'I'm in finance. Working for a bank.'

Gabbie needed to steer the conversation so it didn't become a grilling for Liam. 'I noticed the new rose bushes outside, Dad. They look good.'

Her father took the plate of sandwiches that Jill had selected for him. 'Thanks. We've just had the back garden landscaped. Well, I say "we". Jill did all the planning really.' He smiled at his wife. The two of them were still clearly in love.

Gabbie coughed. 'That sounds nice.'

Her dad turned his smile on her. 'I'll take the two of you for a tour when we've finished lunch. Jill insisted on a row of sunflowers because they were your favourite when you were little, Gabbie. Do you remember?'

'All children like sunflowers, don't they?' As soon as she said it, Gabbie felt guilty for the look of hurt in Jill's eyes. Something about being here made her act like a teenager again.

Liam came to her rescue. 'I know nothing about flowers at all, Jill, so you'll have to explain everything to me like you would to a child.' Thank goodness for his charm, pasting over the cracks of her awkwardness.

Jill smiled at him. 'It would be my pleasure. We're planning on doing some work inside the house, too. It's been a while since the upstairs bedrooms have been done. Maybe you could help me with some ideas, Gabbie?'

Why did Jill do this? Constantly trying to reach out to her? It would be so much easier if she just accepted their relationship for what it was. Cordial and polite. 'I'm no good at interior design, I'm afraid.'

Her father laughed. 'I guessed that from the awful little flat you're living in. Maybe you can persuade my daughter to let me help her out, Liam.'

This was one of the things they were here to tell them, but she wasn't ready for that yet. She wanted her dad to get to know Liam a little first. 'We've just booked a holiday, actually. We're going to Cape Verde.'

Jill picked up the teapot to refresh everyone's cups. 'How lovely. We went there a few years ago. The beaches are beautiful.'

Liam grinned. 'That's what I've heard. I love to travel, see different places.'

'You should speak to Clive' – Jill nodded towards Gabbie's father – 'he's been all over the place with his job.'

Her father reached for a cream slice. 'Not quite the same as a holiday, though. All I ever got to see was the airport and the inside of a boardroom.'

'Gabbie has told me a lot about your travels. You must have had a very interesting career.'

Her father shrugged. 'It was. But it took me away from home an awful lot and time is something you can never get back.'

He looked at Gabbie, but it was too uncomfortable to meet his eyes. Things were better between them, but she could never forgive him for sending her away.

Again, Liam picked up the conversation. 'Maybe you could give me some advice about business, sometime. I'm trying to get a portfolio of stocks together at the moment. I'd like to play the markets. Get some capital together.'

Her father frowned and Gabbie knew what was coming. 'That sounds risky. Aren't you better off staying where you are in the bank? Working your way up?'

Now Jill was pressing Liam to take another sandwich, so it took him a moment to respond. 'The bigger the risk, the bigger the pay off. I'd like to own a house like this one day. Preferably before I'm thirty.'

Gabbie knew that Liam was trying to pay her father a compliment, but this wasn't the way to go about it. Still, she didn't like the glance that had passed between her father and Jill. 'Liam is very clever, Dad. I'm sure he'll be able to make it work.'

'I have been doing my research, learning everything I need to know. Once I've got an initial investment, I'll be away.'

She really wished he hadn't said that. It was obvious from her father's darkened expression what he was thinking. 'I see.'

It was time to change the subject. 'That's enough about work. Why don't you show us the garden before we start on the cake?'

The change of scene helped. As they walked the new pathways and flower beds, Jill explained to Liam about the plants they could see and those that would come up later in the year. Gabbie and her father walked a few paces behind, just out of earshot.

Her father reached for her hand like he had when she was small. 'It's lovely to see you, Gabrielle. It's been a long time since you were last here.'

It'd been less than a year, but Gabbie wasn't going to argue. 'I've been busy, Dad. I've been to Paris and back a few times with work and then I've been with Liam.'

She looked ahead to where Liam was pretending to be

immensely interested in some kind of small tree that Jill was telling him about.

'How long have you been seeing him now?'

'Eight months. It feels like forever, though. He's really great, Dad. He spoils me and takes me places all the time.'

Her father's voice was gruff. 'Do you love him?'

They'd never had a conversation like this before and Gabbie's face warmed in a blush. 'I do.'

'And will he look after you? Is he dependable?'

'Oh, dad. It's not the 1950s. I can look after myself.'

'It's important, Gabbie. I know you think he's fun, but you need a lot more than that in a relationship.'

She could see him looking at Jill now and it was irritating. 'Once you get to know him, you'll love him as much as I do.'

He nodded and was quiet for a moment. 'Jill was looking forward to seeing you today, too. You could make a little more effort with her.'

They'd had this conversation before. But today Gabbie was willing to be a little more accommodating. 'Okay. I'll talk bedroom design with her later if you like.'

He squeezed her hand. 'I would like. And so would she. Also' – he paused again, scratched at his beard with his free hand – 'you might want to sort out anything of your mother's from up there that you want kept.'

She was surprised at that. 'I thought it had all been thrown away when Jill moved in,'

Her father frowned and clearly chose not to rise to her tone of voice. 'There are still a couple of things. Although I'm sure there's another box somewhere that I can't find.'

After the walk, the mood in the sitting room was a little lighter as Jill cut the cakes she'd made and passed everyone a slice. Now seemed as good a time as ever. Gabbie reached across the sofa and put her hand onto Liam's knee. 'Well, then.

What we really wanted to tell you today was that we're planning to move in together.'

Her father choked on the carrot cake he'd just bitten into. 'You're only twenty-six, Gabrielle. There's plenty of time for all that. I thought that you didn't want to put down roots yet. Isn't that what you said to me?'

She *had* said that to him, but that was when he'd wanted to pay the deposit on a flat for her to buy rather than rent. It was easier than telling him the truth; that she didn't want his money.

Liam shifted forwards in his seat. 'It's okay. We're only renting. And it makes financial sense. If we share somewhere we can pool our resources and we'll have more spare money to make the most of living in the city.'

She could practically feel her father twitching. 'It's dead money, though, isn't it? Renting? You're just lining someone else's pockets.'

This was one of her father's favourite hobby horses, but Liam didn't take the hint of her squeezing his hand and he continued outlining his plans. 'Like you said, we're young. We don't want to tie ourselves down to a mortgage yet.'

'Anyone for another slice, yet?' Jill's interruption was hardly subtle, and neither was the warning look she gave Gabbie's father. Although it was saving her, Gabbie still felt irritated at Jill's involvement.

The rest of the afternoon was civil but awkward. Jill and her father had to be the only people on the planet who didn't warm to Liam as soon as they met him. Why couldn't they see how much life he had in him, how he adored her, how much fun they had together? That was probably what it was; they were so boring they wouldn't understand him. Of course they wouldn't like him. Because he was exactly like her mother.

## THIRTY-TWO

When Liam strode towards Gabbie – where she was standing in the corridor to show him where they were – there was a part of her that wanted to run towards him with open arms. Liam had always made everything better, easier. But times had changed. None of them would be here if it wasn't for him and she wasn't about to let him forget it.

He seemed uncertain how to act, too. 'How is she?'

'Come and see for yourself.'

As soon as they entered the room, their daughter's eyes lit up at the sight of him. 'Daddy! You're here!'

Gabbie's traitorous heart contracted at the sight of Alice's pleasure. To be fair, Liam had always been a wonderful dad. Everything was fun with him: the way he would make pictures with the girls' food if he was in charge of lunch, the stories he would tell them at bedtime about them and their friends having outlandish adventures. Every time she watched him with them, her heart would fill with love for him.

'What were you doing running away and scaring Mummy like that, sweetheart?'

Alice folded her arms. 'I wasn't running away. I was looking for you, Daddy. I thought you'd got lost.'

Liam looked up at Gabbie with a frown and she waved away the question in his face. 'A miscommunication. Alice heard me say that I couldn't get you on the telephone. She thought you were on your way to the house.'

He still didn't look as if he understood, but he turned back to Alice. 'Mummy should have told you that daddies don't get lost. Silly Mummy.'

Gabbie had to bite down on her lip not to reply. Of course it was her fault and not his.

Olivia came back from the canteen with two takeaway lattes and, when she saw Liam, her shoulders dropped in relief. 'Oh, thank goodness Dad is here.'

Gabbie wasn't surprised Liam was such a big presence in a room; his absence had been felt by all of them. He reached out for Olivia while still holding Alice's hand. 'All my girls together, at last.'

He used to say this all the time. One of their friends had made a joke once about his lack of sons, but Liam had always been adamant that he was happy to have 'three gorgeous girls' in his life.

Alice closed her eyes. The doctors had warned them that she might be really tired until her blood sugar levels were where they should be. Liam swept the hair from her eyes and stroked her forehead with his thumb; the tenderness brought tears to Gabbie's eyes. How could she be so angry with him and yet love him at the same time?

Sitting watching Alice on that bed had been so terrifying, and it had been awful to be alone and helpless. Having Liam here was like a warm blanket being wrapped around them all. She'd been so angry with him since they came here that it'd been impossible to think about how they were going to get through this. Like the picnics at the gun emplacement with her father, she'd resisted the good memories with him and thought only of mess he'd got them into. But now, watching him with the girls, she could only see the man she'd married. The thoughtful husband. The fun dad. The caring family man. Had she been too harsh, leaving him to deal with all the house stuff on his own? He'd done a terrible thing, that couldn't be denied. But was it bad enough to end their marriage? In sickness and in health – wasn't his gambling a form of sickness? He'd promised that he would get help so that he would never do it again. Should she stay and help him get better?

Olivia leaned in and rested her head on Gabbie's shoulder. 'I'm exhausted.'

Gabbie put an arm around her, feeling again the pang at how tall she was now. How much longer did they have together as a family of four? Olivia had two years at college before she would leave for university. Though the circumstances were different, Gabbie hadn't lived with her father and Jill since she'd graduated. If Olivia did the same, that would give them two more years like this. It wasn't enough. It would never be enough. She kissed the top of her head. 'I'm tired too, love. I'm going to stay here with Alice tonight, but I can ask Jill to come and get you if you want? You can go home and get some sleep.'

She felt Olivia's head nod against her shoulder. 'Is Dad going to come back to the house too?'

They looked over to where Liam was whispering, or singing, to Alice, who was either asleep or nearly there. 'I don't know, but I expect so. I don't think he'll want to be far from Alice tonight, either.'

'I don't think I ever want to have children.'

'Really? Why's that?'

'It's too scary, isn't it? Worrying about them all the time.'

She wasn't wrong. 'It is. But it's wonderful, too. Trust me.'

Olivia lifted her heard and looked at her, her eyes bright with the potential for more tears. 'I'm sorry that I've been so awful, Mum. I've been so horrible to you and you don't deserve it. You're a really good mum. The best.'

It was all Gabbie could do not to cry herself. 'Thank you, sweetheart. And you haven't been horrible. Well, not all the time.'

She was rewarded with a small laugh as Liam stood and joined them. 'I think she's asleep. Shall we go and get a sandwich from the canteen or a friendly vending machine?'

Even stepping out into the corridor to find Liam had made Gabbie nervous. 'I don't want to leave her.'

'I'll stay with her, Mum. I like her more when she's asleep.' Olivia smiled again. Gabbie liked this new easiness between them. If only it hadn't taken such a terrifying event to bring it about.

The corridor was empty and this time she let Liam take her in his arms and hold her close. His familiar smell and the feel of his outstretched hand on her back was all she needed to start crying again, relief leaking from her like water from a pressure valve.

When she was herself again, she pulled away and found a balled-up tissue in her bag, wiped her eyes and blew her nose. 'The diabetes nurse is going to come and talk to us in the morning. About her treatment.'

Liam nodded. 'Okay.'

He always took bad news like this, as if he needed time to absorb it before he'd tell her what he really thought. Her reactions had always been more immediate. 'This is going to be a huge thing for her to deal with. Diabetes. I was looking on my phone earlier. We will have to check her blood sugar every day, pay close attention to everything she eats. She might need to inject herself. She's going to have to live with this forever.'

Initial relief over, the enormity of the diabetes diagnosis was beginning to take root in her brain. This was life changing. How could he look so calm?

'We'll get her through it, Gabbie. She's got us.'

That wasn't hugely comforting. How much use had she been so far? 'I feel terrible, Liam. The paramedic, the doctor, the nurse all asked me what symptoms she'd been having. This must have been coming for weeks or even months and I haven't noticed. I mean, I did notice something was wrong and I made an appointment, but then we came here and I didn't keep it. And then I forgot to tell Jill she was in the house and she went looking for you and I didn't even know where she was. All of this, it's too much for her to have to deal with. She's still so little. I can't help but think it's our fault.'

Liam hadn't seen her lying there on that stretcher, her face so pale. Hadn't felt the terror of getting her to the hospital before it was too late. Perhaps that was why he could be so calm about it all. 'We haven't done this to her. It's just circumstances. We're doing the best we can, love.'

And there it was again. It wasn't just circumstances. If he hadn't lost their house, they wouldn't be here. And that hadn't just 'happened'. But she didn't want to start arguing now, with Alice and Olivia on the other side of the door. And it did feel so nice to have him here. To feel as if she wasn't dealing with this alone. She just needed a little longer to rest before getting back into the chaos. She reached out and squeezed his arm. 'I'm so glad that you're here with us. It was only when I was sitting with Alice earlier that I remembered that your car was repossessed by the lease company. How did you manage to get here so soon?'

He put his hand over hers and returned the squeeze. 'I got a taxi. I just wanted to get to you as soon as possible. I couldn't bear the wait for a train.'

She understood – she would have felt exactly the same. But there was something not right here. She tried to keep her tone level. 'I thought you said your bank account was empty? Where did you get the cash for a taxi?'

He stiffened, but his expression didn't change. 'That's the last thing you need to worry about. Come on, let's get going and find something to eat.'

She didn't move. Here they went again. 'But I do need to worry about that, Liam. I didn't think you had any money?'

When she'd first asked the question, it had been genuine. But now she was suspicious. A last-minute taxi ride from London to here must be at least £200. As far as she knew, their joint bank accounts were empty. She'd been eking out the little money she had in her personal account since they'd left home. Where would he get that kind of cash in a hurry?

He reached out and put an arm around her. The arms that had felt so reassuring now felt manipulative. 'All we need to worry about is getting Alice better. Everything else can wait.'

Now she was the one who felt she couldn't breathe; this smoke and mirrors was suffocating. 'Of course Alice is our priority, but everything else can't wait, can it? We need to speak to the bank and you need to give me the paperwork for the house. I've spoken to a solicitor and she says that we—'

He held up a hand to stop her. 'You don't need a solicitor. I'll get a solicitor if we need one. All we need is the inheritance money you are owed from Jill. A fresh start. Then everything will be fine.'

How had he reframed this so quickly into money she was 'owed'? He was wrong. Everything wasn't fine and she wasn't going to let him misdirect her this time. 'Where did you get the money for the taxi, Liam?'

The rattle of a hospital trolley forced them to stand apart as a young boy attached to a drip was wheeled down the ward, followed by a relieved-looking woman clutching a bag in front of her who must be his mother. Life was so fragile, so quick to change. She sent another silent prayer of thanks that Alice was okay. They could be standing here right now having a very different conversation.

Once the mother and son had gone, Liam reached for her hand. 'I need to get something to eat. Why don't you head back to Alice and Olivia? We can talk about this later. I'll explain everything later. I promise.'

The door to Alice's room opened and Olivia stuck her head out. 'Can you get me a sandwich, too, please?'

'Of course. I'm on my way. Ham and cheese, right?' Liam put his hand into the small of Gabbie's back and pushed her back towards Alice's room. It was where she wanted to be, anyway. But that didn't mean that she didn't want to talk about everything else. She turned to say as much, but Liam must have read her mind. 'We'll talk later. I promise.'

# THIRTY-THREE

But there was no later. By the time Liam came back with plastic sandwiches from the only working vending machine he'd found, a porter had arrived to set up a camp bed so that Gabbie could sleep beside Alice. Olivia was yawning; the emotion of the day had taken it out of her.

Gabbie took the sandwich from Liam – wondering where he'd got the money for that, too – even though she still wasn't hungry. 'You can stay at Jill's with Olivia tonight. I've sent her a text. She said she'll come and pick you both up from here.'

She'd also read a lovely text from Tricia. Jill had been keeping her informed and had let her know that Alice was awake.

> What a relief. Please let me know if there's anything you need. Any time of day. Sending you love x

She'd smiled at the kiss at the end. Olivia always mocked her for doing that and she wondered if Elsa was the same.

She wasn't so keen on Liam's reaction to the offer of a night at Jill's. 'Thanks. It'll be nice to catch up with her.'

The expression on his face gave him away. 'Don't speak to her about money, Liam. I mean it. Now is definitely not the time.'

'Of course not.' He looked offended, but she didn't trust him. Would she ever really trust him again?

When Jill arrived at the hospital, she sent Gabbie a message.

> I'm here. Would it be all right to see Alice before I leave?

Gabbie felt bad that she hadn't suggested that. Hadn't included Jill in the family group standing guard over Alice. Had even asked her to drop Olivia off earlier without inviting her in. 'Of course.'

Even though they were in a side room, ward rules dictated a maximum of three visitors to a bed, so Olivia volunteered to wait outside. As Jill opened the door to Alice's room, she looked unsure of herself until Alice smiled at her. 'Auntie Jill. I'm here.'

In a few steps, Jill was beside the bed and hugging Alice close. It brought tears to Gabbie's eyes. All this time that she'd been sad that her children wouldn't have her mother as a grand-mother, and here was someone who had been waiting to do the job. She wanted to thank Jill again for saving Alice, but every time she started to speak to her, something – or someone – got in the way.

'Jill, nice to see you.' Liam's voice was so warm that it was obviously fake. Maybe that was why Jill's reaction was less than cordial.

She merely nodded at him. 'Liam. Glad to see Alice is okay.'

'Yes, a big relief. It sounds like we owe you a big thank you for your quick thinking.'

Jill waved it away. 'It was nothing.'

They were interrupted by the bell for the end of visiting

hours.

Alice was exhausted and quickly fell asleep after the nurse had done the final observations of the evening. She'd made Gabbie smile with her hundred questions for the patient nurse, asking him what all the numbers meant on the blood pressure reader and how he could know all that from the peg on her finger. She was definitely back to normal.

Lying beside her on the camp bed, Gabbie was frightened to close her eyes, wanting instead to keep watching her little chest rise and fall. The doctor's questions about Alice's health had cast a chill of guilt over her. Alice falling asleep in the car on the way to Jill's, her need for the toilet as soon as she'd got to the park – how long had this been coming? And how had she allowed herself to become so wrapped up in all the house issues to miss the GP appointment?

Beside her, her phone dinged with a message. It was Olivia.

> I really am sorry Mum. Please give Alice a goodnight kiss from me. I love you.

The last thing she wanted was Olivia lying awake wracked with guilt. She'd been foolish to take a train home without telling them, but this wasn't her fault. Gabbie switched her phone to silent so that her keys didn't make a noise when she typed her reply.

> Alice is fine and this isn't your fault. We'll be home tomorrow and you can help me to spoil her rotten.

She wanted to ask about Liam and how he and Jill had been around each other, but that wasn't fair to Olivia either. She knew how that felt, to be in the middle of adults. Was Jill right? Had her mother misled her to make her father the bad guy?

Another message popped up on her phone. This time from Jill.

> Are you awake? I'm outside the door to the ward.

The lights were down low on the ward, so Gabbie tried to pad as silently as she could past the nurse's station. The nurse on duty smiled and nodded as she passed. In contrast, the lights in the corridor were bright when she pressed the security switch and let herself outside.

Jill was in her coat, spattered with rain, the warmth of the hospital steaming up her glasses. For the first time ever, she looked older to Gabbie. Vulnerable, even. 'What are you doing back here? Is everything okay at home?'

Jill took off her glasses and rubbed at them with the finger and thumb of her leather driving gloves. 'I know what hospitals are like late at night; there's nothing to eat apart from vending machine snacks. I thought you might want something decent.'

She held out a square mint green lunch bag. Gabbie had barely thought about food in the last few hours, but she was suddenly ravenous. Unzipped, the bag revealed itself to be full of food in various sized plastic boxes. She could see olives, pitta bread, houmous: all her favourite things. 'This is so kind of you, thank you.'

Jill smiled. 'I made a banana loaf, too. I remember how much you like it.'

Gabbie blushed with guilt. Jill used to do this when she was younger. Make her lunches from her favourite things. Gabbie had rarely been as grateful as she should. Now that she was a mother herself, she knew how onerous it was to prepare meals night after night and the frustration of having an ungrateful child turn up their nose. And Jill hadn't even been her mother.

'Jill, I don't know how I will ever thank you for today. For saving Alice. If you hadn't been there...'

She couldn't finish that sentence, couldn't think of the consequences if Jill hadn't had an idea of where to look.

'You don't need to thank me, Gabbie. I love her and Olivia.' She paused, as if unsure whether to continue. 'I love all of you.'

Gabbie's awkwardness was physical. If this had been one of her friends, she would have hugged them for saying that. But her body was stiff with years of reluctance where Jill was concerned. 'I'm sorry that we haven't visited more. Since Dad died. I know the girls would've liked to see more of you.'

Jill's face wasn't giving anything away. 'I know how busy you must be. But you are welcome at the house anytime. It's your home. Your dad was always insistent about that.'

'Why did he send me away, then? I know you said he didn't trust my mum, but I don't understand why. And why he waited until I was twelve?' She hadn't planned to ask this now. But she was too tired to be reticent.

'Because he thought he was doing the right thing.' Jill motioned to the row of seats flipped up against the wall of the corridor. 'Do you want to sit for a while?'

Gabbie was torn. Even though Alice was sound asleep, she didn't like to leave her. But this conversation had been a long time coming. 'I can only be ten minutes.'

'That's fine. Come on, let's sit.'

The hinges that attached the chair seats to the wall squeaked as they pulled them down and sat beside each other. Gabbie waited for Jill to speak which, after a sigh, she did.

'Your father loved you very much, Gabbie. When you were tiny, he and your mother existed in a bubble of infatuation. She would dress you in the most beautiful clothes and parade you around the village. Everyone remarked on what a perfect little family you were.'

Gabbie tried to discern whether there was an air of jealousy in Jill's tone, but there didn't seem to be. 'So they *were* happy together?'

'They were. Very happy. But as you got older, your mother seemed to get... restless. Their life in London had been much more exciting than the village. I think she just got bored.'

That was hurtful. 'Of being a mother?'

'No. Not that. But I think she just wanted more from life. Variety. That was the thing. She needed things to be new and different all the time.'

Unbidden, Liam came to Gabbie's mind. Always busy, always looking for excitement, always wanting to surprise and entertain and amaze them all.

'But that doesn't explain why my father sent me away to school. My mother didn't want me to go. She told me so.'

'You're right. She didn't. But she didn't want to be at home looking after you all the time, either. When your father was away, she would take herself off to visit friends in London or other parts of the country. Sometimes back to Paris. When you were a baby, she would often take you with her or, sometimes, she would leave you with someone she knew.'

Gabbie had no memory of this. 'Who?'

Jill shrugged. 'I don't know. It wasn't the same person every time. And she and your dad would argue about it. Her reasoning was that it was always someone with a family. That it was good for you to socialise with other children. Especially as she'd told your dad she didn't want any more children of her own.'

So that was why she was an only child? Gabbie remembered asking her mother that question and only ever getting dramatic answers about how her mother couldn't possibly share the love she had for Gabbie with anyone else before she covered her in kisses and changed the subject. 'Why wouldn't I remember this? Being left with other families?'

'It was only when you were very little. As you got older, it was more difficult. That's when she started inviting people to the house.'

*That* she did remember. Her mother would have small parties of six or eight people. Gabbie would lay at the top of the stairs, peering down at their glamourous outfits and listen to the tinkling laughter. Her mother would prepare her a tray of treats – crisps and sweets and tiny cubes of cheese and pineapple – and make her promise to stay in her bedroom. 'Surely that wasn't terrible?'

Jill sighed. 'In theory, no. But your dad had no idea who these people were and there was a lot of alcohol. Maybe other things.'

Gabbie swallowed. 'I see.'

'It wasn't just the parties. She would invite these people – people your father had never met – to stay over in the house. While you were there.'

Gabbie hadn't thought about this in years, but she did remember occasions of sitting with her mother's friends at the breakfast table. As a child, she hadn't seen anything unusual about it. But now, with a mother's perspective, she saw it through a different lens.

Now Jill was staring at her hands. 'And then there was an occasion. She... Margot... your mother... she invited one of her friends – a man – to stay in her bedroom. And your father found some of his clothing. That's when it all came out. About the parties, the overnight guests. He was furious.'

Of course, he would be. Aside from her mother's unfaithfulness, a strange man staying overnight in the same house as his young daughter? 'What did he do?'

'I don't think he knew what to do. They argued for days. Eventually she won him around, promised that she would never do it again. Like I say, he was infatuated with her. But he no longer trusted her. He was so terrified that something would happen to you that he would beg me to watch out for you every time he had to go away. He even offered to pay me, but of course I refused money.'

Gabbie knew that her father and Jill had grown up together, but that she and her mother had become friends when he'd moved her back to the village that he'd grown up in. 'Is that why you spent so much time at our house? Because he'd asked you to?'

'Initially. But your mother was wonderful company. Funny and clever and always ready to try new things. I could see why he was besotted with her. And then there was you.'

Gabbie frowned. 'Me?'

Jill's eyes softened to a glassy sheen. 'You were such a beautiful child, Gabbie. So easy to please, so quick to laugh. When your mother was tired or if she had to be somewhere, I would play with you for hours.'

Gabbie remembered Jill at the house, of course she did. But in her distorted memory, she'd assumed her mother was the one who'd set up the imaginative play. That Jill had just been on the fringes. Jill had been so natural with Alice; painting and crafting with her, but it hadn't occurred to Gabbie that this wasn't the first time she'd had to find ways to entertain a little girl.

There was one more beat to the story, one more connection to get to the final outcome. 'I'm assuming she didn't keep her promise? About inviting strangers to the house? Other men?'

Gently, Jill shook her head. 'That's when he made the decision about sending you to school.'

When Jill had explained all of this that morning, Gabbie had struggled to accept it. For years, she – and her mother before her – had painted her father the villain. But now? Was it true that he had only been trying to keep her safe?

Jill was watching her for a while before she spoke again. 'Are you and Liam back together?'

The phrasing of the question – and abrupt change of subject – put Gabbie off balance. 'I'm not sure we were ever really apart.'

Jill raised an eyebrow. 'Oh, I see. Sorry, I must have misunderstood.'

For a reason that she couldn't explain, Gabbie didn't want Jill thinking badly of Liam. 'The thing is, he made a mistake. A pretty big mistake, but none of us are perfect, right?'

She wasn't expecting Jill to laugh. 'Sorry, ignore me. It's just that you sounded exactly like your dad.'

'What do you mean?'

'It doesn't matter.'

Suddenly it mattered more than it should. 'In what way like my dad?'

'That's how he referred to it every time your mother would disappear for a night or a weekend or even a week. "She made a mistake, Jill. And I love her."'

The corridor was unnaturally warm, so it wasn't the air temperature that made Gabbie shiver. 'What can I do, though? I love him and I love the children. I have to give him another chance.'

'But what about you? Do you love yourself, Gabbie?'

That was an odd question. 'What do you mean?'

'All I've heard you talk about since you arrived is how you need to be doing this or that for other people. The work that you've been sent with silly deadlines, that woman at the school expecting you to give up your time at the drop of a hat, bending over backwards to try and please Olivia when – to be honest – she was being rather spoiled and demanding. But what about you? Who is looking after you?'

Tears scratched at the back of Gabbie's eyes and her throat tightened. 'It's just being a mum, isn't it? You have to do these things. You have to put your children first.'

Jill was looking into her eyes as if she was looking for permission to speak, gauging how much she could say. 'But you don't have to put yourself last.'

Gabbie was too raw for this conversation, her fear for Alice's life too recent. 'I think I need Liam. Whatever he's done, I can't imagine doing this on my own. Raising the girls, making decisions, keeping them safe.'

It wasn't only Alice. The nude photograph Olivia had sent had shaken Gabbie to her core. This was a whole new stage of parenting that she wasn't equipped for. How was she going to do that on her own?

'Well, it's not for me to tell you whether to give him another chance. I learned that from your father, too.'

While they were speaking so openly about her mother and father's relationship, Gabbie had had a burning question she'd wanted answered for years. Maybe now she could ask it. 'Did you always love him, even when he was married to my mother?'

Jill took a deep breath. 'I always cared about him and then, when your mother treated him so badly, I think my feelings grew because I could see how unfair it all was. Then, when she died, he was so broken, that I just wanted to look after him. I wanted to look after you both.'

The air was thick with so many different emotions that Gabbie could barely breathe. 'I have to get back to Alice. In case she wakes up.'

'Of course.' Jill stood. 'When you're ready tomorrow, I can come and collect you both. Then I can watch the girls if you like? Give you and Liam a chance to talk?'

'Thank you.' As they stood in front of each other, this would have been the perfect time for her to reach out to Jill and hug her. Instead, she patted the lunch bag that she held in front of her. 'Thanks for this, too.'

'My pleasure.'

As she watched Jill walk away, she considered how much Jill had done for her over the years that she hadn't thanked her for.

But Jill wasn't the right person to talk to about Liam. She hadn't liked him from the start.

## THIRTY-FOUR

Alice spent an uneventful night in hospital, but Gabbie had barely more than two hours' sleep together. Between the footsteps of the nurse checking in on patients, her obsession with listening to Alice's breathing and her thoughts about Liam and the house buzzing through her mind, she was never still enough to stay asleep. When Liam came to collect them in her car, she almost wept in relief at the solid sight of him.

'Let's get you two home.'

She let him take her hand, his other arm around Alice, but the mention of home reminded her that she had to take the pin out of thinking about their next steps. Something had to be decided and it needed to be soon.

Jill had the front door open as soon as they pulled up the drive. How had it been only four days since they'd arrived here? This was a very different homecoming and Gabbie was surprised how pleased she was to see her. Handing over the lunch bag, she smiled. 'That was delicious, thank you.'

Looking embarrassed at the praise, Jill stood back to let them in. Alice wrapped her arms around her waist and squeezed. 'Is there any cake, Auntie Jill?'

Jill kissed the top of Alice's head. 'I think I can find some. Come and sit down.'

Gabbie was grateful that her daughter could show the love that she was struggling to. But she panicked at the thought of cake; even though the diabetic nurse had been really helpful – and have given her lots of information to bring home – she didn't have her head around what Alice could and couldn't have.

But, as soon as she was out of earshot, Jill winked at Gabbie. 'I've been researching diabetic cake recipes all morning. I've found one I think she'll like.'

Gabbie wished she could kiss Jill as easily and naturally as Alice had done.

In the middle of the sitting room, Olivia held a 'WEL-COME HOME ALICE' banner. All around the mirror above the mantelpiece were streamers and pictures that Olivia and Jill had created. Alice gasped when she saw them and Olivia held out her arms for her little sister to run into. Seeing the two of them wrapped up in each other, Gabbie had to look away and swallow the lump in her throat. Liam pressed his hand into the small of her back. 'We did well when we made those two.'

This should have been a moment for relief and love, to lick their wounds and talk about how lucky they'd been. Both girls were here, safe. Their family of four reunited. But there at the edges, real life was waiting to come back in the room. It was okay for her to pretend a little longer though, wasn't it? To enjoy this moment for now.

Tactfully, Jill had slipped out into the kitchen to give them some time alone. While Olivia was showing Alice all the pictures she'd printed of her favourite cartoon characters, Gabbie went to find her, following the scent of freshly baked banana bread warm in the air. On the kitchen table there was a pile of delicate bone china plates with gilt edging, onto which she was carefully placing slices of cake.

'Thank you so much for this Jill. The cake, the banners' – she swept her hand behind her back towards the laughter of her daughters – 'for everything.'

Had Jill changed in these last few days, or had she? Either way, Gabbie enjoyed the softer way they spoke to one another. 'Please stop thanking me, Gabbie. It's a pleasure to have someone to look after. This time with you all, it's been a gift to me.'

That lump in her throat was there again. There was still a lot to get through – with Liam, the house, their finances – but maybe, once she'd spoken to Liam, she'd ask Jill if they could stay for a while longer. There was more to be said between the two of them, too. 'The girls seem happy together in the lounge. I was thinking that I'd take you up on the offer to watch them while Liam and I go for a walk and have a talk.'

Olivia was old enough to look after both herself and Alice, but there was no way Gabbie would leave either of them unsupervised for a while.

Jill looks surprised. 'Of course, if you're ready for that. Don't you want to rest first? You've been through a lot in the last twenty-four hours. Liam can wait a little longer.'

Gabbie was exhausted, but she also couldn't rest properly until they'd sorted everything out between them. Pretending to be a happy family could only last so long. If she tried to rest now, she'd only be plagued by thoughts of where they were going to live, what they were going to do and, most importantly, whether she could trust Liam to keep his word and never put their whole lives at risk like this again. 'I just want to get everything sorted. Then I can rest.'

Jill picked up two of the plates to take through to the sitting room. 'I understand. And of course I'll stay with the girls. Why don't you and Liam go to the pub for some lunch? Susie and Paul have a new menu these days. Then you can take your time.'

Lunch was a good idea. It was a nice day and they'd be able to sit in the pub garden, out of earshot of anyone else. 'Thanks. I will. But first I'm going to try my first ever slice of diabetic banana loaf.'

Jill waved the plates she was holding. 'We'll get the girls to try it first and if it passes the Alice-test, I'll cut you the biggest slice you can eat.'

In the quiet of the kitchen, Gabbie took a minute to sit in silence, to let all the things on her mind settle around her into some kind of list. According to the large kitchen wall clock, it wasn't quite twelve yet; she could give it an hour before going out to lunch with Liam. As she looked at the clock, though, she had a creeping feeling that she'd forgotten something. She'd planned to order something for Tricia when she got home, a gift to thank her for being such a great friend in the last few days. Was it that? Or was it just the misfirings of a tired brain, a by-product of the guilt she still felt over missing Alice's symptoms?

Her train of thought was derailed by Liam pushing open the kitchen door. 'There you are. Don't you want to come and sit with us? It's so great to be with you all again. I've missed you all so much these last few days.'

'I just wanted a few minutes. It's been a lot.'

In two steps he was beside her and reaching out for her hand. 'I know. But she's safe now. She's home. You don't need to keep beating yourself up about it.'

Again, no remorse. Both Olivia and Jill – and Gabbie – had berated themselves for their part in Alice's disappearance. Though Liam could argue that he was not directly responsible, surely he could see that none of this would have happened if they'd been at home? 'We missed the doctor's appointment. Alice was supposed to see a doctor on Monday but we couldn't go because we were here.'

She tried to pull her hand away from him, but he held it tight. 'All the more reason to let me speak to Jill about the money. Then we can get home and make sure that Alice has the care she needs.'

This time she did manage to pull her hand away. 'We need to talk about that, Liam. Jill has offered to look after the girls so that we can have some space to talk. We could go and get lunch at the pub in an hour?' With the extra work she was taking on from the translation agency, she could just about justify a pub lunch.

'Good idea. I'm going to get back into the sitting room.' He held out his hand. 'Are you coming?'

'I'll follow you in a minute.'

As he closed the door, she closed her eyes. She just needed some space to think, to breathe. But again, she was interrupted, this time by the doorbell.

At the other end of the hallway, she heard the door open and Jill's voice. Moments later, she stuck her head around the kitchen door. 'There's someone at the door for you, Gabbie. She said you're expecting her.'

The mists in Gabbie's brain started to clear as she walked towards the woman on the doorstep. How had she forgotten their arrangement, made only yesterday? Her face was older and softer around the edges, but her thick blonde hair was unmistakable. Jessica.

# THIRTY-FIVE

Although she was a world away from the eighteen-year-old girl that Gabbie had last seen, grown-up Jessica looked exactly as she might have predicted. Flawless make-up, expensive jewellery and a simple yet stylish – and probably insanely expensive – linen suit. What she wouldn't have predicted was how nervous she seemed, twisting a large emerald ring on her right hand and blinking more than was required by the late morning sunshine. 'You look surprised to see me.'

*This* was the arrangement that had been nagging at her. How had it slipped her mind? 'I'm so sorry. My daughter was taken into hospital last night. I completely forgot that you were coming.'

Jessica's face fell. 'Oh no. How frightening. Is she okay?'

This was surreal. 'She's going to be fine. She's home now, but, well, it's been a stressful night.'

'I can imagine. Do you want me to go? Come another time?'

How could she send her away when she'd made the journey here? 'No, it's okay, come in. We can sit in the garden and talk. I won't have that long, though. Come in.'

'Only if you're sure.'

Jessica followed her down the hall and out to the back garden. Through the morning room, there was a door to the patio with a wooden table and six chairs. 'What a lovely house and garden.'

'Not mine, unfortunately. This was my parents' house. My stepmother lives here now.'

Jessica tilted her head to one side and frowned. 'So you've lost your father? I'm sorry. Me, too.'

'I'm sorry, too. I'm just going to tell my family what's going on. Can I get you a drink?'

Though she smiled, Jessica was still twisting the ring on her finger. 'I feel like I need a large gin, but I'd better stick to water.'

Jill was in the kitchen and her eyes widened when Gabbie told her who it had been at the door. 'The girl from your school? The one you had problems with? What's she doing here? How did she know where to find you?'

'Problems' was an understatement. Jessica had made Gabbie's life an absolute misery for at least two years. After that, she'd taken her attention elsewhere, but she'd never missed the opportunity for a putdown or a nasty comment. 'I sent her a message on Facebook yesterday. I don't know why, really. But she's here now.'

Jill looked concerned. 'Do you think this is a good idea? Especially today.'

What would have irked Gabbie as judgement yesterday, felt like care and concern today. 'I'm a big girl now; I don't think she's going to try and bully me.'

She'd meant it as a joke, but Jill wasn't laughing. 'I'm here if you need me.'

Back outside, Jessica was walking up and down the nearest flower bed, inspecting the flowering plants. 'These are beautiful. I'm a keen gardener these days; that's how boring I've become.'

Her self-effacing tone made Gabbie more nervous than the

confident arrogance she'd anticipated. She passed a glass of water to Jessica and motioned towards the table and chairs with her head. 'Shall we?'

The wooden chairs scraped on the patio as they pulled them out to sit down. Jessica sipped at her water, then stared down into her glass as she spoke.

'When I got your message yesterday, I was really shocked. I wasn't sure how to reply. I'm a mother now and I know how I'd feel if someone did that to one of my children.' She paused and it seemed to take a real physical effort to lift her head and look at Gabbie. 'I know it doesn't help, but I want you to know how sorry I am. It doesn't excuse it, but I was angry at you. Really angry.'

This wasn't making any sense. 'Angry at me? What did I do to make you angry at me? I was as quiet as a mouse when I started at that school. And you were this confident, popular girl who had a gang hanging on your every word.'

Jessica winced. 'I don't mean at the beginning. Yes, I'm not proud of the way I behaved then, either. But I mean the part where I was really horrible. After it happened. After the accident.'

This still didn't add up. 'But why were you worse after my mother's accident? What did that have to do with anything? How did that affect *you*?'

Jessica frowned and turned her head to the side as if she was trying to read Gabbie's face. 'You know that that it was my father driving the car the night she died?'

She couldn't have shocked Gabbie more if she'd thrown the glass of iced water over her. Gabbie hadn't even realised that someone else was driving the car when her mother died. Though she trawled her brain, she couldn't remember what her father had said at the time. Whatever it was, she'd had no concept that there had been anyone else in the car at all.

Jessica had her hand to her mouth. 'You didn't know? I'm so sorry. I just assumed... I thought you would know.'

This was so outlandish that Gabbie didn't even know if it was true. 'Are you sure? I mean, why did you not tell me that at the time? You never mentioned it once.'

Jessica lowered her gaze, then forced herself to look at Gabbie again. 'Because I was ashamed. Looking back, I think that's why I needed to make you frightened of me. So that you wouldn't tell anyone. When I found out that your mother was having an affair with my father, I hated her. I'm guessing you already know I hated him, too, for what he'd done to my mother. Looking back, I took all that hurt and anger out on you. Again, all I can do is apologise and promise you that I feel terrible for the way I behaved.'

She spoke so carefully and precisely that Gabbie knew she must have practised this speech several times before she came. Still, it wouldn't sink in. Her mother had been having an affair with Jessica's father? That friendly man who had taken her and her mother to dinner after her birthday party? Had it started before or after that day?

She shook her head. 'I didn't know about my mother's affair with your father. And I didn't know that she was in the car with him when she died.'

So much made sense now. The change in Jessica after her mother's death. Jill's campaign to remove all trace of her mother from the house. Until this moment, she hadn't fully believed the version of her mother that Jill had presented to her. But here was cold hard evidence. Her father had kept all of this from Gabbie to protect her. But all it had done was drive a wedge between them.

Jessica looked mortified. 'I'm so sorry. I just assumed...'

She didn't need to finish her sentence. How had it felt for thirteen-year-old Jessica? She'd been one of the girls at the birthday party, awestruck by the glamour of Gabbie's mother.

And then to find out that she'd slept with her father? *I hated her.* She hadn't lost her father but she'd lost her faith in him. *I hated him, too.*

As a teenager, Gabbie had seen Jessica as a nasty spiteful monster. As an adult, she could peel back the hard shell and see the broken, disillusioned child beneath. Of course she'd hated Gabbie; she was a constant reminder of the woman who'd wrecked her family. It must have taken a lot for Jessica to come here – she could've just ignored Gabbie's message or sent a brief reply. Still, thirteen-year-old Gabbie didn't deserve to have her let Jessica completely off the hook.

'You did make my life at school hard, especially after my mother died. I can see now why you were so angry, but I too hope that neither your daughters or mine are ever as unhappy as I was in those years at St Catherine's.'

She'd never allowed herself to imagine Alice or Olivia in the same position she'd been in. It was too painful. Thinking of herself back then, she wanted to reach down the years and put her arms around that little girl. Tell her younger self that she would survive, that she would be okay.

Hand trembling in front of her mouth, eyes filling with tears, Jessica's voice wasn't much more than a whisper. 'I am so, so sorry, Gabbie. Truly, I am.'

Was it fair to torture adult Jessica for the past? 'Thank you for your apology and for explaining what happened. It does help me to know that it was nothing in me that made that happen. It wasn't my fault that you didn't like me.'

As she said those words, Gabbie realised the truth of them. It hadn't been her fault. There'd been nothing wrong with her. Tears dripped from the end of her nose and she wiped them away with the back of her hand.

She closed her eyes and let the grief pass over her like a shadow. Let go of those feelings of self-doubt and self-criticism. She remembered the picture from the box that she'd looked at with Olivia and Alice three days ago. A skinny, self-conscious Gabbie in a school blazer, standing in misery at the school gate on her first day. *It wasn't your fault, little Gabbie. It wasn't your fault.*

When she opened her eyes again, she saw that Jessica had her face in her hands, her shoulders jolting with every sob. 'It was nothing to do with you. It was all my fault.'

How could Gabbie not feel sorry for her? 'It wasn't all your fault. Our parents... they made decisions – sometimes very selfish decisions – and we were too young to deal with them.'

Even the decisions that weren't selfish, like her father keeping the truth about her mother from her, had had consequences that had rippled throughout her life. She could see that now.

Jessica fumbled for a tissue in her bag and blew her nose. 'I've felt guilty for a long time about this. I don't know how to make it right.'

What could she do? It was a lifetime ago. 'You don't need to do anything. Now I know the truth, I can understand a little more.'

Jessica's face crumpled into further tears, but she fought to keep her voice steady. 'Even before your mother, my father had other affairs. The way I picked on other girls... I was just so angry with the world. But I'm raising my girls to be kind. To challenge bullies. I'm doing the best I can to be a good parent.'

Wasn't that all they could do? But Gabbie hadn't learned from the mistakes of her parents, had she? She hadn't told her girls the truth.

Jessica picked up her bag and stood up. 'I won't keep you from your daughter any longer. Thank you for seeing me today. I can't tell you how much it means to me to have seen you and apologised. I know it doesn't take away what I did, but I'm grateful all the same.'

There was something so vulnerable about her that Gabbie

could do nothing other than put her arms around her. They stood there for a few moments, bully and victim, both damaged by the choices other people had made. Maybe one day, she'd be able to fully forgive her.

After waving Jessica goodbye, promising that she would at least think about meeting up again in the future, Gabbie washed her face in the bathroom and reapplied her make-up, not wanting the girls to see that she'd been upset.

At the bottom of the stairs, Liam was waiting for her. 'Is everything okay? With your friend? Jill said she was from your school.'

Liam would know the implications of her having to face Jessica. 'Yes. She came to apologise to me. She was the bully. She wanted to say sorry.'

'Wow. That nasty girl you had to share a room with? That's huge. How do you feel?'

She wasn't sure. Numb? Relieved? Upset? Confused? All of the above. 'Like I want to hug our girls close and never let go. Let's give it an hour or so before we go to lunch. I just want to sit with Alice and Olivia for a while.'

Liam looked as if she'd just given him a stay of execution. 'Good idea.'

He held the door to the sitting room open, where she could see Jill and Alice drawing pictures of Olivia, who kept pulling funny faces – much to Alice's delight – to make it difficult for them. She'd been halfway between the two of them in age when her mother had died. If she'd been in her father's position, would she have told them the truth?

# THIRTY-SIX

The village pub was unchanged from Gabbie's childhood memories. Though her father had spent his business hours dining in five-star restaurants with wealthy clients, he'd liked nothing more than a pint of ale in his local. There had been rare occasions when it'd been just the two of them, sitting in this same garden, possibly – by the rotten state of them – on these very same benches. Her dad would buy her a lemonade and a packet of ready salted crisps; he'd have a pint of ale and a packet of pork scratchings, laughing at her disgust for the smell and the ear-splitting crunch. How had she only just remembered this?

'Is it still warm enough to be outside?' Liam was smiling as if this was a regular jaunt to the pub, instead of a summit meeting on their future.

The air had cooled despite the efforts of the weak sun above them. Still, she would rather sit out here, in the far corner, away from anyone's ears. 'I'm fine. I have my coat.'

'Great. I'll go in for some menus. Dry white wine and soda?'

It'd been her drink for the whole time he'd known her. Usually there was a comfort in their knowing each other so well. But her world had shifted on its axis: nothing was the same any longer. 'Actually, I'll have a beer. A bottle of Beck's.'

He raised an eyebrow. 'Beck's it is.'

While he was inside, she chose the furthest table from the pub with a stripe of sunshine across it. The bench was still damp from overnight rain and it seeped through her jeans to the backs of her thighs. Before Liam came back, she needed to work out what she actually wanted. It had been good to have him here and the girls had been delighted to have him back. It would be the easiest thing in the world to just slip into their old routines, fight to keep their home together, but how could she do that without a cast-iron guarantee that he would never do this again?

Her phone buzzed in her pocket. A picture of Alice and Olivia making more paper families and giving her the thumbs up with a text from Jill.

All's fine here. Take as long as you need.

How eagerly Jill had taken to the role of grandmother, as if she'd only been waiting for the green light from Gabbie. By keeping her at arm's length, Gabbie had denied all three of them this relationship. When they moved back home, she'd make sure that they saw more of each other. *If* they moved back home.

'There you go. I got them to put a straw in it for you.' Liam grinned as he handed over a bottle of beer with a paper straw poking out the top like a bottle of pop.

The smile slid from his face when she didn't return it. He produced a glass from the pocket of his jacket, before swinging his long legs over the attached bench and pulling a menu from under his arm. 'We have to order food at the bar.'

Her eyes skimmed the list of meals – lasagne, burgers, usual pub fare – without really reading them. Letting it drop, she took a deep breath and caught his eye. 'We need to talk, Liam. Properly.'

His face was so sad that she almost felt sorry for him. 'I know.'

'I've spent the last few days so angry with you for what you've done. Not just the gambling, but the lying. I can't get my head around how deceitful you've been.'

He had the decency to hang his head. 'I know. I deserve that.'

'Were you ever going to tell me about the money my father gave you for the deposit on our house?'

His eyes widened. 'Jill told you?'

She nodded, but waited for him to say more.

He shuffled backwards on the bench and scratched the back of his head, letting out a long breath. 'That was so long ago.'

She'd had the same thought. So long ago that he'd first lied to her. 'Why did you accept it, Liam? You knew how I felt about accepting money from my father. And to take the money and not tell me?'

It had been a day and an eternity since Jill had dropped that bombshell; she was still taking it in. What possible excuse could he have for that?

'You know what your father was like, Gabbie. How persuasive he was. He made me feel... well, he made me feel as if I'd be letting you down if I didn't take the opportunity to buy the kind of house you deserved. And we had Olivia by then. He kept saying we couldn't have a baby in that flat we were in.'

She did know what her father had been like, but that still didn't excuse what he'd done. 'You lied to me. You said you'd got a great mortgage deal and a bonus at work.'

He held up his hands. 'Both of those things were true. I didn't lie.'

'But you didn't tell me the truth. Omissions are lies, too.'

He looked up at her, those dark brown eyes that she'd

thought she knew so well. 'I know I've made mistakes, Gabbie. Huge mistakes. But they're all in the past. I can't lose you. I'll do anything you want to keep us together.'

She didn't doubt his desire. What worried her was whether he would keep to his word. 'I need to know – really know – that you are never going to gamble or do anything like this again.'

He leaned across the table, reaching for her. 'I promise you.'

She wasn't about to take his hand. He had to know she meant business. Another couple took the table a few feet away but they sat on the same side of the bench, so that they could sit close together. Hopefully they were far enough away not to hear their conversation, but Gabbie lowered her voice just in case.

'How was the Gamblers Anonymous meeting?'

He shrugged. 'Okay, I suppose.'

That didn't tell her anything. 'How often are they?'

He took back the hand he'd reached out towards her and pulled at his earlobe. 'Not often. Weekly, I think.'

She knew the answer before she asked the question. 'You are planning on going?'

'The thing is' – he paused as if searching for the right words – 'it's not really for people like me. GA is for real addicts. Those people, the ones at the meeting, were at rock bottom, Gabbie. It was horrible.'

She almost laughed. Was there anything more rock bottom than losing your house? 'Liam, you have a gambling problem. You've lost our home.'

'I know, Gabbie. But that's over. I won't do it again. You'll see.'

Again, Liam tried to reach for her, but she pulled her hands out of reach. 'You're an addict. You need help. You have to go to that group. Or another group. You need to get treatment.'

The irritation in his sigh surprised her. 'It's not an addiction. But, yes, okay. Whatever you want. I'll go to the group with the man who lives on his mother's sofa and the woman whose kids are in care. If that's what you want me to do, Gabbie, I'll do anything you want. I just need us to be okay?'

His impatience prickled her. The bottom line was that she still didn't know that she was doing the right thing. But, for the sake of the girls, she knew that she had to try. 'If you prove to me that you've really changed, I'm willing to give you a chance. But I want full control of our money, Liam. I want access to all our accounts from today and I need to know about every single transaction. Because this will be the *only* chance, Liam. You *cannot* screw this up.'

She pushed away the voice of Tricia in her head. *Fool me twice.*

Liam's eyes filled with tears. 'I love you so much. You won't regret this.'

This time when he reached for her across the table, she let him take her hand. But she wasn't ready for a big show of reconciliation. She wanted to take this slowly, carefully. 'I need to eat something. I just want a cheese sandwich. What do you want? I'll go and order.'

But he was already on his feet. 'No, no. I'll go. I'll decide what I want on the way.' He took the menu from her and almost tripped over the bench in his eagerness to take her order.

Once he'd gone, Gabbie sipped at her beer and looked around the garden. She clearly hadn't needed to worry about being overheard by the couple on the next table: they only had eyes for one another and she watched as the woman held up her face to be kissed. Maybe they were at the beginning of a relationship. How beautiful those early days were. How fragile.

Liam was taking a while ordering the food. She should probably feel relieved now that she'd made the decision to give him another chance, but it would be some time before she knew for sure that she'd done the right thing. Awful though the last few days had been, she believed that Liam meant to try and she owed it to the girls to give him a chance. She slipped out her phone to look again at the picture Jill had sent, then scrolled through the other photographs on her phone. Family snaps from their holidays and days out, full of their joy in being together. A breeze blew across the back of the pub garden and she pulled her coat closer around her, peered closer at a picture of Liam on the last-minute trip they'd taken to Whitstable last summer. It was a shot on the beach, with Olivia and Alice either side of him, an ice cream in each of their hands. It was difficult not to wonder how deeply in debt he'd been at that point. How many secrets were behind those eyes?

'Food all ordered.'

Gabbie hadn't even noticed his return and she jumped at the sound of his voice.

'Thanks.' Looking at photos had actually made her feel more uncertain than she was before. 'Actually, I need a quick trip to the ladies'. Won't be a moment.'

The inside of the pub had had a refit from the last time she'd been in here and, for some reason, the ladies' toilet was now the gents'. In her confused state, Gabbie looked around without success before catching the eye of the young guy behind the bar to ask him where the ladies' toilet was now.

She always felt as if she needed to explain that she wasn't just passing by and availing herself of the facilities. 'Hi. I'm sitting outside. My husband just came in and ordered some food. Can I use the toilet?'

He pointed to the other side of the bar. 'Through the door, up the stairs, on the right.'

'Thank you.'

The face reflected back at her from the cracked mirror on the bathroom wall looked older than the one in the photos on her phone from only a few months ago. Hopefully it was the harsh lighting making the lines at the corners of her eyes so deep, her skin so pale. She pulled a length of toilet tissue and blew her nose. A tube of foundation from her bag managed to smooth out her face, but her eyes still betrayed the emotional exhaustion of the last few days. Maybe she should leave the rest of that beer and get herself a glass of water instead.

Back in the bar, the young barman was wiping the counter and whistling to himself. He smiled as she made her way towards him. 'I've just found your husband's wallet.'

She recognised the Tom Ford wallet she'd splashed out on for him for Christmas two years ago. It was unlike him to be so forgetful. The barman held it out towards her with a grin. 'Is it your turn for the twenty-pound pint, now?'

Maybe it was the tiredness that made Gabbie confused about his joke. 'Sorry?'

He looked barely old enough to drink in the pub, let alone be working there. 'Just joking. That's what my dad calls it when someone pays for their drink with a twenty-pound note and asks for their change in pound coins.'

She still didn't understand. 'Sorry, I still don't get it.'

He looked as if he wished he hadn't started the conversation. He nodded to the beeping fruit machines in the corner. 'For the slots. People want the pound coins to put in the machine. Like your husband. That's where the wallet was.'

Gabbie froze. Pound coins for the slot machines? That was why he had taken so long to order food in an almost empty bar? Needing to be sure, she tried to keep her face passive. 'Oh yes, I see what you mean. Did he win, then? Am I going to get a nice dinner out tonight?'

He laughed, clearly thinking this was just a bit of fun. Because it was for most people, wasn't it? A slot machine, a bet on the Grand National, a friendly game of cards. 'Not tonight, sorry. I think he put it all back in. Might be fish and chips again.'

The laugh she forced tasted bitter in her mouth. 'Oh, well. I'll make the most of my sandwich then.'

She turned before he could see the tears that she was doing

her utmost to swallow down. Liam had just sat in front of her and promised – promised! – that he would never gamble again. That he wouldn't let her down. Then he had come straight in here and poured pound coins into those machines like water. Why had she believed him? What an absolute fool.

# THIRTY-SEVEN

As Gabbie left the pub and walked towards Liam, the anger in her belly increased with every step. By the time she drew level, she was a volcano ready to erupt. Liam turned towards her and the smile froze on his face. 'What's the matter? Is it Alice?'

The laughter of the couple on the other table now felt like mockery and she no longer cared about lowering her voice. 'Slot machines? You sit there and tell me you will never gamble again and you've been in there on those damn slot machines?'

His faced paled, but his expression didn't change. 'No. What makes you think—'

'A twenty-pound pint, is it called? All that change and I'm guessing it's not in your pocket? Or in here?'

She waved the wallet in the air, knew that she was getting louder because the couple were looking in their direction. Liam was shaking his head. 'No. There's some mistake. What do you mean? Who said…?'

*Still* he was lying to her. 'Why did I not think to ask where you got the money from for this lunch? Win on the horses, was it?'

Liam changed tack, his voice a masterclass in calculated

calm. 'No, listen. It's not that. I just' – he rubbed at his face as if he was cleaning it – 'it was just a couple of quid in a machine. Everyone puts their change in a slot machine when they're in a pub. It's just a bit of fun. It's not gambling. It's not a problem.'

She wanted to throw herself on the floor and howl. 'Of course it is! That's exactly what it is. A gambling problem. Which you told me you were getting help with. Which you promised you wouldn't do again. I can't believe you lied to me. Again.'

Liam glanced in the direction of the couple, who were doing their best to pretend that they weren't enjoying the show. 'Gabbie. Sit down. People are looking. Let me explain.'

He still hadn't answered her question. 'So, come on then, Liam. Where are you getting the cash from for this lunch? And your taxi? How did you have a twenty-pound note for your drink and gamble?

Liam was running his hands through his hair, trying to look as if he had no idea where this outburst had come from. 'Gabbie. Sit down. You're acting crazy. This is delayed shock from yesterday. From Alice. Sit down.'

How dare he use Alice to shift her focus away from the questions she wanted answering? Where had the money come from? The cogs in her brain were moving slowly, but at least they were moving now.

She waved the wallet again. 'And what am I going to find in here? Your winnings?'

As she thrust the wallet towards him for emphasis, it flipped open and two squares of paper fluttered out like tiny white birds. Liam made a lunge towards them, but was too slow to get more than one; Gabbie snatched the other from the air.

The square of white paper had a blue printed heading. She'd never actually been in a betting shop before; wouldn't know how to even place a bet on a horse race or sports game. But she'd seen the name 'William Hill' on the sign of a bookmaker's. Knew how betting odds were written like improper fractions. Recognised Liam's scribbled handwriting at the bottom of the slip. *Win.*

Liam's face reddened under the weight of her stare. 'They're old ones. I don't know why they're still in there. Just throw it away.'

She held the slip out of his reach. She could read the date too. And this one was yesterday's. 'You're lying. Every word from your mouth is a complete and utter lie.'

Liam held his hands out towards her. 'Please, Gabbie. Listen, just listen. Sit down.'

But she shook her head. More thoughts were assailing her. The earring that she hadn't been able to find in her jewellery box. Her mother's emerald earring. Surely he hadn't... 'Did you sell any of my mother's jewellery?'

'No.' His voice was loud and he glanced at the other table, where the couple were finally leaving. He was softer the second time. 'No. But I had to do something. I needed money to live. You just disappeared back here and left. It was okay for you, you had a comfortable bed to sleep in, but I was sleeping on a lumpy sofa at Tim's with no idea how I was going to get off it. You left me on my own and then you said you wouldn't ask Jill for any money. I had to do something to get us back on track. So I tried to win some money so that I could... What else could I do, Gabbie? I was desperate.'

Was he really expecting her sympathy? 'And what about today? In the pub. Telling me that everything was going to be different and then walking straight in there and putting money into a slot machine. I could have walked in at any moment, Liam. Or is that part of the thrill?'

The breeze was picking up and Gabbie's hair whipped around her face. Now the romantic couple had left, there was no one left in the garden to hear them scream at one another. Liam's face was white; he'd never heard her speak like this before. Had she ever spoken to anyone like this before? She thought of Jessica this morning, the years she'd put up with her bullying and never once stood up for herself.

Liam opened his mouth to speak, then stopped and really looked at her. Seemed to make a decision. 'Look, you're right. I've really, really screwed up. I just couldn't see another way to get out from under it all and I made another bad decision. But that's it. I mean it. Let's draw a line and go from today. Everything will be different from today. No more gambling. I'll go to GA. You can have all the accounts. You can control all our money. I'll have nothing.'

He was like a man in a sinking ship, scooping water and throwing it over the side. But the holes were too big. How could she believe a word he said? 'I can't trust a thing you say to me.'

His voice came in bursts of breath, like a drowning man. 'But you can. You can. I will be honest about everything. Please, Gabbie. Look, this is how honest I am. I asked Jill for money. I know I said I wouldn't, but I did. This afternoon. When you were with your friend in the garden. I don't need to tell you that, but I'm telling you because I want you to know that I am being completely honest now.'

Did he think this was helping? Heaping more betrayals onto those she already knew about. Like wave after wave, they kept coming. 'I told you not to ask her. I told you not to ask Jill for anything, Liam.'

'I know. But I am desperate, Gabbie. I'm trying to save my family, here. What else would you have me do?'

Did she really need to spell it out to him? 'Tell me the truth. Be honest with me. Don't keep secrets. Don't take every penny we have and throw it away on a stupid bet. Don't lose our home. It's not difficult, Liam.' She screwed her eyes shut, not able to bear looking at him. 'I can't believe that I was going to give you another chance. I was going to forgive you for the girls' sake. What a stupid, stupid fool.'

'You're not stupid. I know that you love me and you can still forgive me. We can still fix this. All of this. Jill said no to me but I've seen the way she is with Alice. With Olivia. If we get them to ask her—'

'No!' Gabbie no longer cared who could hear her roar. 'You will not get the girls involved in this. You will not have them cleaning up after you. This is your fault and you will fix it.'

He actually had his hands together as if in prayer, beseeching her for forgiveness. 'I will. But I need money to do that. And Jill's money is your father's money. It's our money. Money he would have left to us. You said he didn't care about you, sent you away to school. Don't you think he owes you? Jill owes you?'

She couldn't believe her ears. He was using things she'd told him in the dead of night a few months after they'd got together. About her mother, her father, her experience at school. And now he was using this to leverage her support in asking Jill for money. 'Us? Money he would have left to us? There is no "us", Liam. And how dare you talk like that about my father? About Jill?'

He clearly realised that he'd gone too far. Now he was pulling at his hair and pacing in front of her. 'I'm sorry. I'm sorry. I didn't mean that the way that it sounded. Please, Gabbie, don't back away from me. Just give me a chance to explain.'

Until he said it, she hadn't realised that she'd been stepping away. When he stood up and reached for her, she shook her head. 'Leave me alone.'

She was hot. Suffocated. Couldn't breathe. She needed to get far from here, from him. Turning away, she stumbled in the direction of the car park, her feet slipping on the wet grass. Liam called her name; she needed to get far enough away that she couldn't hear him any longer. When she got to the car park, she realised that he had the car keys. So she kept going, crossed the road, walking, walking, walking. She was so agitated, so upset, so angry that she didn't know what to do with herself. She didn't want to go home to the girls in such a state and she definitely didn't want to stay here with Liam.

Her breath came in short angry bursts and she wiped at her blurred eyes with the back of her hand. She'd believed him. Trusted him. And he had let her down. Was this how her father had felt? Had her mother begged forgiveness time and time again, only to betray him with someone else? How had he felt the day of her mother's accident? Knowing that her last act on this earth had been to betray him one last time?

She couldn't keep walking nowhere like this. She needed to sit, to rest, to think. There was only one place she could think of to go.

# THIRTY-EIGHT

The graveyard at St Matthew's was small and most of the graves dated back hundreds of years. In the far corner, there was a gate which led to a larger, modern cemetery and this was where Gabbie's father was buried. She'd been surprised to find in her father's will that he'd already purchased this burial plot, wanting to stay close to the village he'd loved even in death. It was all the more surprising because her mother had been cremated and her ashes scattered in France. This, too, had been in her will.

The flowers in front of the headstone were fresh. Jill came here regularly to keep it neat, but this was only the second time Gabbie had been here. The first being the day they'd laid him to rest; the second, several months later with the girls so that they could lay flowers on his birthday. Beside the grave was a wooden bench and she sat there and waited for her heartbeat to settle to a regular rhythm. There was no one nearby to hear her speak aloud. 'Why didn't you tell me, Dad?'

Even on the heels of Jill's truths about her parents' marriage, Jessica's revelation about her own father's affair with Gabbie's mother had knocked her sideways. It had been hurtful enough when her mother had cancelled visits to the school which Gabbie had looked forward to, but now even those visits that she'd made were coloured with questions about whether they'd been an excuse to see Jessica's father afterwards.

Jessica. She'd never thought she would feel sorry for her, but yesterday she had. What was worse? To know from a young age that a parent was deeply flawed and live with that, or to idolise – as she had done with her mother – and to have that statue of memory toppled when they were no longer here to answer for it?

So many people had been hurt by the actions of her mother. Even now, she struggled to take it in that her mother had been so different to the woman she'd thought she was. Well, not different in every way. Jill had been generous in her description of how much fun she'd been to be around. That part was true. Could Gabbie hold onto this? Keep her precious memories of her mother unsullied by this other side that no one had ever shown her? 'You should have told me the truth, Dad.'

What was the truth? That her mother had put him through hell? That she couldn't be trusted to look after her only daughter? That he'd sacrificed his own happiness to ensure that everyone else was okay? But she *hadn't* been okay.

'I'm so angry with you. I've been so angry with you for so long and you never gave me a chance to talk to you about it. Why didn't you trust me? Why didn't you tell me the truth?'

This was pointless, but somehow it cleared her mind. Getting these questions out of her head and into the cold sharp air. The last time she'd stared at this gravestone, three years ago, she'd seen her father through completely different eyes. The blame for her boarding school days, his obvious disapproval of her choice of husband, his annoyance with her for her treatment of Jill: all these things had driven a wedge between the two of them that had widened with each passing year.

The births of the girls had brought them a little closer. She hadn't been about to deny him the chance to be a grandfather. And he'd been a good one: jokes and gifts and cuddles. Yet this had made her even more angry about the past, when he had worked all the time and she'd been sent away to school.

And now? Now she didn't know what to think. What to feel. How much of her anger at her father had been because of her adoration of her mother? An adoration that, it seemed, had not been justified.

'I'm sorry. I know that doesn't help now, but I am. I didn't see it. I didn't understand.'

What would their life together have been like if Gabbie had known the truth? If her father had explained the true circumstances of her mother's death, and of their marriage. Would she – could she – have understood at thirteen? Would she have shown her love for him more? Forgiven him for sending her away? Understood his marriage to Jill?

She closed her eyes again as she remembered how awful she'd been to both of them over the years. All the time she'd known they were together, but ensured that Jill was kept at arm's length whenever she was home from school. How she'd made it clear to her father that she wasn't ready for another woman to take her mother's place. All those years he'd put her happiness before his own.

And then, when he and Jill had married, she'd left home, putting physical distance between her and them both. How must that have been for him? She couldn't imagine how terrible it would feel for her to lose Olivia, or Alice, and see them only once or twice a year. She'd – knowingly or not – been punishing him for a crime that he hadn't committed.

'I am sorry, Dad. I wish we'd had more time. I wish I'd made more effort to make it right.'

What had Jill said to her when she'd told her about her mother? *I'm telling you while you still have a chance to do the right thing.* Gabbie had thought that was what she was doing.

Protecting the girls, keeping the family together. But it wasn't the right thing, was it? Not for her. And not for them.

She leaned forwards and hugged her knees. 'I don't know what to do, Dad. But I know I don't want to make the same mistake as you. I don't want to sacrifice myself to make it okay for everyone else.'

She hadn't realised the truth of this until it was out there, hanging in the air like the smoke from her father's cigars. She didn't want to carry everyone any longer. Didn't want to be the sensible, straight foil to Liam's circus act. But how was she going to make that happen without hurting everyone else?

Footsteps behind her made Gabbie sit up and wipe at her face. Talking aloud when you were on your own was one thing, but she didn't want a stranger listening to her. She sat up straight and waited for them to pass.

But the footsteps kept coming in her direction, until she heard a voice that she recognised. 'It's okay. It's only me.'

# THIRTY-NINE

Gabbie turned in relief at the sound of Tricia's voice and watched her pick her way through the patches of mud to join her beside the grave. 'What are you doing here?'

'I've been sent on a special mission. Jill was worried about you. Olivia can track you on her phone. She could see you were here.'

Of course. 'Is Liam back at the house?'

'Yep. Jill said he was in a bit of a state. He was going to come after you, but she suggested that you might prefer to see me right now.'

Her emphasis on 'suggested' made Gabbie smile. As did the thoughtfulness behind Jill having called Tricia. 'Sorry to drag you away from whatever you were doing.'

'It's no bother. Although you might have picked a more salubrious setting.' She nodded at the grave. 'Have you been having a bit of a chat?'

Gabbie looked back at the gravestone. 'Yes. I just don't understand why people keep such big secrets. I feel like my whole childhood was a lie. I know that sounds like a complete cliché but that's how I feel. My parents weren't the people I thought they were. How am I supposed to feel now?'

Tricia grimaced as she sat down on the wet bench. 'People get things wrong, I suppose. They think they're doing the right thing. Especially parents. The odds are so high for getting it wrong that it's probably a foregone conclusion that we will. What's that Philip Larkin poem?'

It was true. How often had she got it wrong with her two? Especially in the last week. 'Liam has been gambling again. He promised me that he wouldn't, but he has.'

Tricia raised an eyebrow. 'Ah. I see.'

It was so difficult to explain how she was feeling right now; there were so many conflicting emotions vying for control. 'I was so angry with him when I came to stay here with Jill. It was such a shock. Not only the gambling, but the fact he'd lied. I still don't really know how long it's been going on. I mean, if we hadn't lost the house, I might still be in the dark about it all. I can't believe I didn't notice.'

In the last couple of nights, she'd been trying to work out whether there'd been signs that she'd missed. But, just like poor Alice's symptoms, she'd been blithely unaware. How could that be?

'Don't be hard on yourself. Life is so busy, we're all focusing on the next thing on our list. If you're not looking for something, you're unlikely to find it.'

Was that true, or was Tricia just being kind? 'But the thing is, I thought... I guess I just expected that we would work it out somehow. When we got married, I was pregnant with Olivia.' It hadn't been that long after she and Liam had moved into their first flat together. She could still picture the look of horror on her father's face. What she'd taken for judgement and disapproval had now refocused as fear and concern. 'I know that my dad and Jill didn't think it would last, but I really believed it would. I loved him. I still love him.'

She gasped at the last words. She did still love him, but that love was giving her more pain than joy.

Tricia reached out an arm across the bench and rubbed at Gabbie's back as if she was a baby who needed soothing. 'I know, sweetheart. It's so hard.'

She searched Tricia's face as if for an answer. 'I'm not sure that I can stay with him if I can't trust him, Tricia. I can't live like that.'

Tricia's face stayed kind and supportive; there was no judgement there. 'Of course you can't. And you shouldn't have to. No one should.'

She would say the same if a friend asked her advice, but it wasn't just about her, was it? She couldn't make this decision based on her feelings alone. 'I'm worried about the children, though. They absolutely adore Liam.'

She thought again of her mother. The joy she'd had in her company, the fun she'd brought to everything. When she'd died, it was as if a bulb had blown in Gabbie's life.

'And the girls love you, too. You're their mother. You've been there for them at every point in their life. Do you think they'd want you to be unhappy?'

Gabbie felt a twinge of guilt. That was exactly how she'd wanted her father to feel, wasn't it? Making his life difficult by making him choose between her and Jill. How much time had she wasted, holding him responsible for her loss? By keeping her distance from him, physically and emotionally?

Tricia was right that her girls would not want her to be sad. But neither would they want to live in a separate house from their dad. She remembered Olivia's words when they'd first arrived. *If you leave Dad, I'm staying with him.* Nothing was worth losing her children. Nothing. 'I can't do it, Tricia. I'm not strong enough to pull our family apart. The girls will blame me, I know they will. Especially Olivia.'

Tricia nodded. 'So, what are you suggesting? That you stay

together and you just silently ride the wave of his wins and losses? Never quite sure if your car will still be on the drive or whether a man dressed in black is going to come knocking on your door?'

She'd never told Tricia about the car. Was her life such a stereotype now? She couldn't live like that, either. She couldn't. But still, her girls' trusting vulnerable faces kept appearing in her mind. 'I just don't want to put them through the pain of a separation.' She couldn't even think about the word 'divorce' yet. 'Especially right now. Olivia is starting A levels and Alice is so young.'

Plus there was the whole issue of Alice's diabetes diagnosis. Gabbie didn't want to give her any more stress.

Tricia was nodding. 'I understand that. We're mums: our first instinct is to protect our young. But we need to look after ourselves too. When someone betrays you, you can't just soldier on as if nothing has happened.'

Gabbie knew where Tricia was coming from. But her situation was different. 'Liam hasn't cheated on me though. It's different. He has a problem.'

She was worried that Tricia would be offended by her obvious reference to her own husband's infidelity. Yet she merely smiled. 'It's not different, Gabbie. For my ex-husband it was women. For yours, it's gambling. Either way, they put their mistress before us.'

The truth of this went through Gabbie like a bolt. Liam had put his gambling before her, before all three of them. And this hadn't happened once. It had happened for years. And it was happening now. *Fool me twice.* 'Oh, Tricia. I don't know what to do.'

Tricia still had a supportive hand on Gabbie's back. 'It took me months of therapy to really grasp this, but you don't need to keep setting yourself on fire to keep others warm, Gabbie. Children are far more resilient that we give them credit for. And they won't be losing their dad. They will still have both of you. You deserve to be happy, too, Gabbie.'

It was easier for Tricia to say this. She didn't know Liam. She hadn't seen him spend hours creating a Father Christmas escape scene for Olivia by poking torn red fabric into the door hinges and making flour footprints on the floor. Hadn't witnessed his excitement when he'd proposed by wrapping her engagement ring like a Russian doll into ever decreasing boxes. Hadn't listened to him create the most incredible bedtime stories for Alice with voices and hand puppets and lots and lots of laughter.

Even as she remembered these precious moments, though, they brought in their wake a realisation. Liam was good at these things. The grand gestures. The spotlight moments. Meanwhile, Gabbie had been the one to run the children to playdates, make sure that uniform was ordered, school dinner money paid. Was it any wonder that Olivia would rather stay with the parent who delivered excitement and fun?

Hadn't *she*?

Leaving Liam would be the hardest thing she ever did. But staying would be even harder. The girls deserved a life of certainty and safety. And they deserved the truth.

# FORTY

When she got back to the house, the first thing she did was check on Alice.

'How are you feeling, sweetheart?'

Alice, her hands covered in more yellow paint than the smudged sunflower on the paper in front of her, looked surprised at the question. 'I'm fine, Mummy. Do you like my picture?'

She picked up the page to show it off, paint dripping onto the newspaper below, her smile as bright as the colours she'd chosen. Both Gabbie's children were so resilient; they amazed her every day. Another thing they got from Liam. Would he bounce back this time, too? 'That's beautiful. You're so clever.'

Alice accepted the compliment effortlessly, then nodded at her sister. 'Olivia's drawing me.'

Although Olivia was only drawing to stay close to her sister, Gabbie was surprised by how good the sketch was when Alice forced her to turn it around. She frowned, 'I know it's rubbish.'

Her self-criticism hurt Gabbie's heart. What happened to children between Alice's age and Olivia's? Why couldn't they keep that self-belief? 'Well, I think it's wonderful. You've really captured her. In fact, I'd love to put it into a frame.'

Olivia blushed and shrugged. In that moment, she looked like a little girl again. Sixteen was still so young. Gabbie knew they had some difficult conversations ahead, but she needed to cherish moments like these, however fleeting.

She'd snuck in the back door when she returned so, when Liam pushed open the door to the morning room and saw her standing there, he looked surprised, then hurt. 'You're back.'

She nodded. 'Yes. Can we go and sit in the other room and talk?'

On the way home from the graveyard, she'd rehearsed her words as she'd walked, refusing Tricia's offer of a lift home for that very reason. Even so, it wasn't easy to say them to Liam's face.

'I know that we still need to sort out the financial situation and the repossession of the house, but it's over between you and me, Liam. I can't live like this. I can't be with someone that I can't trust.'

He looked as if she'd slapped him. 'What do you mean?'

'I want a separation. I want a divorce.'

He paled before her eyes. 'You can't be serious. You can't leave me.'

She was ready for this reaction, had played it over in her mind as she'd skirted the river on her way back here. '*You* left *me*, Liam. When you went back to gambling.'

Tricia was right; there was no difference between her husband's affairs and Liam's addiction: they were just different mistresses. She could tell by him shaking his head in disbelief that he didn't quite see it that way. 'But I did that for us. I told you. I wanted to get the house back for you and for the girls.'

How was he still trying to justify this? 'By putting whatever money you had into the hands of a bookmaker? By stealing my mother's emerald earring? Is that how you were doing it for the girls?'

He flinched. 'That was an impulse. And it's only pawned. I'll get it back.'

This was the first time he'd admitted to it. 'So you did take it? What else is there, Liam? Will I discover that my ring from our holiday in Rhodes is missing? The bracelet you surprised me with in the Lake District?'

The look on his face told her everything she wanted to know and it made her feel even more sick. It wasn't the items themselves – though she'd loved to wear them – it was the memories wrapped around them. Family holidays, romantic breaks; Liam had insisted she have a new piece of jewellery every time they went away. When they'd first been together, it had been costume jewellery. Later, it had been the real deal. Now it was gone.

'I'll get it all back.'

'I don't want it back. How could I wear any of it now, knowing what you'd used it for?'

'I used it for us. Don't you understand? I don't enjoy this. It's not fun for me. It's agony, but it's the only option I had. When you said you weren't asking Jill for the money, you backed me into a corner. What did you expect me to do?'

So it was her fault again? It was like talking to Olivia about that damn party. Just round and round the Ferris wheel until she was so confused that she gave in. But not this time. 'I expected the truth.'

'I know I've screwed up. But, please, Gabbie. You have to forgive me. You have to give me a second chance.'

This was tough, but she *had* to stand firm. 'I did give you a second chance; I was trying to forgive you. But then I find out that you're still lying to me. The betting slips in your wallet. The money in the pub slot machine. What else don't I know?'

He moved towards her on the sofa, as if he'd seen a chink in her defences and was eager to exploit it. 'But this is the same thing. The same problem. It's all mixed up together. I was just trying to get it all sorted out. Get us back to where we were. Once the house was safe, I swore I would never do it again.'

His voice was bordering on mania. Desperation dripped from every vowel. He believed every word he said. To him, it made perfect sense. And that was why she couldn't have him in her life. 'It's over, Liam. I can't ever trust you again.'

'No.' It was a virtual howl. 'You can't leave me. I can't live without you and the girls. You are my whole world.'

These were empty words. If they'd been his whole world then why had he needed to risk everything for more? 'You won't ever have to live without the girls. They're your daughters. I'd never keep them from you.'

'But I need you, too. Gabbie, I love you so much. And I need you. If you leave, I don't know what I'm going to do, what will happen to me.'

He grabbed her hand and she let it rest in his, limp and unresponsive. Still, he seemed to take it as a sign of hope. 'Please, Gabbie. I love you so much. This is us. This is me. You know how much I love you. You know that I would never want to hurt you.'

'And yet, you did.'

'And I will spend my whole life making it up to you. I will never put a foot wrong. I will tell you where I am at all times. I will never ever lie to you again.'

Empty promises. Did he know it as well as she did? She pulled her hand from his grasp. 'It's over, Liam. I can't live like that, in fear of where you are and who might be knocking on our door. The girls can't live like that, I won't have that for them. They need a home that is safe, inviolable, that no one can take from us. And all the time you are there, we won't be safe.'

The sound that came from Liam was like a wounded animal. She hated hurting him like this. She still loved him. But she wouldn't ever be able to trust him again and, without trust, a relationship was nothing. And that was the next step.

'We also have to tell the girls the truth.'

He had curled in on himself, but his head snapped upwards at this. 'No. They don't need to know. It would just hurt them more and what's the point of that?'

She still loved him enough to hope that at least part of his reason for wanting to keep it from them was his desire not to cause them pain. But they both knew it was also about protecting himself. 'The point is that I'm not going to lie to them. We can do it together or I can do it on my own. But they need to know the truth.'

'They're going to hate me. I hate me. I hate what I've done to us.'

'You can still be a good father. They adore you, both of them. If you are honest with them, they will still love you.'

Her voice caught as she spoke. How different might her childhood have been if someone had just told her the truth? She'd been sent away to hide it from her; a misguided attempt at protection. Shielding someone from the truth wasn't protection. Only honesty could keep them safe now.

She could tell by the look on Liam's face that he was finally getting it, finally understanding that she meant what she said. When he'd stepped up to the slot machine in the pub, he had taken an even bigger gamble that she would never find out. And he'd lost.

It wasn't easy. He'd been her solid foundation, her safe place, her *home* for so long. But focusing on him meant taking her eye off the ball with the girls. She'd almost lost both of them in the last forty-eight hours. She'd have to work hard to get enough money for them to live and she needed to focus on the girls. She couldn't babysit Liam, too. Jill's words came back to her. *And who is looking after you?*

. . .

When Liam decided that he didn't want to be there when Gabbie told the girls the truth, he merely affirmed that she was doing the right thing. Leaving it to her, as always, to do the difficult part of parenting. The hard conversations. The strong boundaries. She thought again of her dad. What she'd seen as unrelenting rules had actually been the firm arms of love.

Still, she didn't know how she was going to approach it with them. Should she tell them about the gambling or was that too much for them to understand? But was any less than that a contradiction of her determination to only tell them the truth?

She had to look away when Liam said his goodbyes to them, promising that he would see them soon. She couldn't bear his face over their shoulders as he hugged them to him. Whether or not he was trying to manipulate her, it still hurt the same. It doesn't matter how dysfunctional a relationship is, it can still break you when it ends.

Slipping away to the kitchen, she heard him telling the girls how much he loved them, followed by Alice's lisp, 'And Mummy, too.'

Was she imagining the break in his voice? 'And Mummy, too.'

Once he'd gone, she found Jill keeping a low profile in the kitchen, nursing a mug of tea. 'How are you doing?'

Gabbie slipped into the seat opposite. 'Like I'm about to break into a million pieces.'

Jill nodded. 'It's not easy being the one who holds it all together.'

She knew, to her shame, that Jill was speaking from experience. 'I'm leaving Liam. I told him earlier. It's over between us.'

Saying it aloud was an out-of-body experience. Like this was all happening to someone else. If Jill was surprised, she didn't show it. 'I see.'

Like a boat without an anchor, a balloon without a weight, she was both free and lost at the same time. 'So who knows what happens now? I have no house, no husband. I'm on my own again with nowhere to call home.'

Jill reached out and took hold of Gabbie's hand. 'No, you're not. You've never been on your own. And this will always be your home.'

Gabbie brought her other hand around Jill's and held onto it tightly, as if it were a safety rope dangling from the edge of a cliff. It took a few moments before she could speak. 'I'm so sorry for the way I've treated you. Not just recently. The whole time.'

Jill's eyes were full, too. 'Don't worry about that now. You've got yourself and the girls to think about.'

The girls. How was she going to do this? 'I don't know how to tell them. How much do I say?'

Jill squeezed her hand. 'Why don't you start with Olivia? She sees more than you know. Take your lead from her.'

# FORTY-ONE

To give Gabbie some time alone with Olivia, Jill offered to bake fairy cakes with Alice, who didn't need asking twice.

'We need to make my special dye-betic ones, Auntie Jill.'

'Of course. We'll find a recipe on my iPad.' Jill nodded at Gabbie before following Alice to the kitchen and mouthed encouragement. 'You can do this.'

Olivia was sitting on the sofa in the front room, thumbing through her phone. Gabbie pressed the door shut and sat beside her. 'Can we have a chat?'

Olivia's eyes were fearful when she looked up. 'Is it about you and Dad?'

Jill was right, Olivia did see more than she was letting on. 'Yes. It's about me and Dad. And about what's been going on.'

If Olivia looked scared before, she looked terrified now. 'I knew there was something. You said it was going to be okay.'

'I know I did. It was wrong of me. I was trying to protect you, but I've realised now that it's more important that I tell you the truth. It's a lot, though, Olivia. So I need to take it slowly and you can ask me any questions that you want to.'

Olivia nodded. 'Okay.'

Where to start? 'The thing is, we've got some big money problems which are difficult to solve.'

'You've told me that already. That there's problems with the house that need to be fixed and that Dad's lost his job.'

Gabbie took a deep breath. 'Well, there's more to it than that. It was gambling. Your dad gambled our money and he lost. He lost a lot of money.'

Olivia's eyes widened. 'Like horse racing? At a betting shop?'

'Sometimes. And sometimes on his phone or on slot machines.'

She paused and waited for Olivia to take this in. She was shaking her head. 'I don't understand.'

Neither did Gabbie, so how could she explain it to her sixteen-year-old daughter? Liam was such a coward, leaving this to her. 'It's an addiction. An illness. You know like some people are alcoholics? Well, your dad is like that with gambling.'

Olivia's bottom lip began to wobble. 'Is this why we're here? Have you left him?'

This was the biggie. 'Well, the thing is. We've... your dad lost so much money that the bank has taken our house.'

The whimper that came from Olivia was like that of a lost child. It was horrible having to do this to her. She was sixteen. She shouldn't have to know that her father was so selfish that he'd lost everything they'd ever owned. No, not lost. Lost she might have forgiven. He had spent it.

'I'm so sorry, sweetheart. I know that this is a lot for you to take in. But I think that you deserve the truth.'

Olivia nodded. 'Is that why you didn't want me to go home? For the party?'

'Yes. I couldn't run the risk of you going to our house, or hearing about any of this from someone else.'

Olivia pulled at her bottom lip, a sign that had precipitated tears since she was very small. 'Can we never go home? Where are we going to live?'

'At the moment, I don't have the answer to that question. Once we've sold the house, I'll know how much we have for a deposit and how much I can afford to get a mortgage for and then we can choose somewhere together. It'll be small, but we'll make it nice.'

As Gabbie spoke, she realised that there was a part of her looking forward to choosing something small, something manageable, something that could never be taken away.

'I'm scared.'

'It's okay to feel scared, because this is different, it's a change and that can be scary. But I am here. I'm not going anywhere. Whenever you need me, I'm here.'

Olivia was still pulling at her lip. 'But what about you, Mum? Won't you be lonely?'

He heart squeezed at her eldest daughter's care for her. 'How can I be lonely when I have two beautiful girls in my life?'

How flippant did that sound? Not only that, Olivia would be leaving to go to university in less than two years. Gabbie didn't want her to feel that she needed her to stay. She reached out and took Olivia's hand. 'I'm going to be okay. I have friends and I have Jill and, you know what, I have myself. I'm stronger than I look.' She smiled and Olivia returned her smile.

The door pushed open and a flour-covered Alice appeared. 'What are you doing in here? Do you want to make cakes with us?'

Jill, wiping her hands on a pristine tea towel, followed. 'Shall we get back to it, Alice? Let Mummy and Olivia finish their chat?'

Gabbie reached out for Alice. 'It's okay. You can be part of our chat. Don't go.' The last was to Jill, who had started to back out of the room. 'Stay with us.'

Jill perched on a chair and Gabbie pulled Alice onto her

lap. 'I've just been telling Olivia that we are going to move to a new house.'

'Why? I like our house.'

Gabbie loved it too. There were so many memories there. 'Because we need to save some money, so we need to get a smaller one.'

Alice tilted her head to the side as she considered this. 'You can have the money in my china pig. It's really heavy now.'

'That's so kind, sweetheart, but we will have enough to get somewhere.' She hoped that was the case. There wasn't enough equity in the house to remortgage, but there should be enough for rental deposits at least. Which brought her onto the next part. 'Daddy is going to live in another house.'

Alice frowned. 'Why?'

Gabbie had rehearsed this in her mind, but it was easier to say the words when she wasn't looking at her daughter's vulnerable face. For the second time, Olivia was the one who came to the rescue. 'Do you remember when you and Gracie had an argument and you didn't want to play together?'

'Yes. She took my bracelet and said it was hers. And she wouldn't give it back until her mummy made her. But now we're friends again.'

If only relationships were as easy as they were at eight years old. Olivia continued with her analogy. 'Yes, but you needed to be apart for a while first because you were really cross. Well, our mummy and daddy need some time apart, too. And then maybe they can be friends again.'

She looked at Gabbie with such hope in her eyes, that it almost hurt. Gabbie wasn't sure if this was the right thing to say, but then she didn't know what would happen to her and Liam in the future. Maybe this was okay. 'The most important thing is that Mummy and Daddy both love you very much. And that will never change.'

It was a lot for Alice to take in. 'Will we live here with Auntie Jill?'

Gabbie glanced at Jill. She clearly hadn't been expecting that, either. 'No. We need to find somewhere close to our old house. Otherwise, how would you get to your school and see your friends?'

'I could go to school here.' Alice's tone was so matter-of-fact it almost made Gabbie laugh.

'Well, Olivia needs to be able to get to college.'

Olivia shrugged. 'I could go to college here, too. Elsa said that the college she's going to has a really great common room. And a huge media suite for people doing subjects like mine.'

How had she raised such resilient children? 'Let's talk about this later. I just wanted to make sure that you both know what's happening. You'll be living with me, but Daddy will always be there whenever you need him. Is that okay, Alice?'

The head tilt was back, then Alice nodded slowly. 'Okay, I'll try it.'

That made all four of them laugh. Olivia held out her hand to her sister. 'Come on, then. Show me where this cooking is happening.'

As they left the room, she heard Alice giggle. 'In the kitchen, silly.'

Gabbie flopped backwards on the sofa and sighed. 'That wasn't easy.'

Jill's smile was warm. 'You've made the first step, though. Well done.'

'I'm not sure it's completely sunk in for them yet, but the girls were amazing. You were right, they're stronger than I realised.'

'That's because of you. You've given them a firm foundation.'

It would have been so easy for Olivia to have struck out again, been upset with her. Instead, she'd handled the information like a grown up. Was that all it had needed? For Gabbie to trust her with the truth? Would she have acted differently herself, thirty years ago, if she'd known everything? 'Thank you for being here like this. I meant what I said earlier. I am really sorry for the way I've treated you.'

Jill waved away her apology. 'You were a child. And you'd lost your mother. It's in the past.'

A simple apology wasn't enough, but she would find the words to tell Jill everything she felt sometime soon. 'Liam told me that he asked you for money this morning.'

Jill wrinkled her nose. 'Ah. I did wonder whether or not to say anything to you, but you looked as if you had things under control.'

She *was* beginning to feel more in control. 'I've been such a fool. Leaving all the money management to him. You must think I'm so weak.'

Jill shook her head. 'It's not weak to trust someone. And you're loyal, like your dad. But there comes a point when you have to decide whether that person deserves your loyalty.'

She was right. 'I'm going to get onto the bank straight away and then call the solicitor to make an appointment. I want to make sure that I really understand it all. I might even see if I can do a course or something.'

Jill laughed. 'That sounds good. But maybe you can let yourself rest for today?'

Gabbie stretched herself backwards onto the sofa and closed her eyes. 'A rest sounds good. I'll start tomorrow. Have a look at some houses online, too.'

Jill smoothed the bottom of her apron. 'What do you think about Alice's idea? About living here, with me?'

Gabbie opened her eyes. 'You don't need to do that. The bank will sell our house. There will be money there for me to get a deposit on a small rental for me and the girls.'

'I know. And I understand if it's not what you want. But

maybe you could stay for the summer. See how it feels. And then, if you all like it here, you can stay for good. I've really enjoyed having you all here. Getting to know the girls.' She hesitated. 'Getting to spend time with you.'

Was it such a crazy idea? There would be so much to sort out in the coming weeks that the thought of having somewhere to stay was very attractive. 'But I'd have to sort out school for Alice and see if they have space for Olivia at Elsa's college.'

A hopeful smile played at the edges of Jill's mouth. 'I could help you look into that. Just so that you know what your options are.'

Could they do this? 'Are you sure you want the three of us invading your home?'

Jill held out her hands. 'It's your home, Gabbie. It always has been.'

It hadn't felt like home in a long time, but right now it felt like the safest place on Earth. Why not stay? See if it works. 'Thank you. Maybe we could stay a while and see how it goes. For all of us.'

Jill's hand went to her throat, her eyes filled. 'I would like that. Very much.'

One of them had to make the first move and Gabbie knew that it had to be her. She was the one who'd pushed Jill away, resented her, blamed her. All this time she'd grieved for a mother that she'd only half known, when she could have had a mother who'd waited on the sidelines for decades.

As she stood, Jill got to her feet too and opened her arms. Gabbie stepped into them.

She was home.

# EPILOGUE

## TWO YEARS LATER

*Dear Mum,*

*Letter as promised! All my new friends think it's totally weird that we are writing to each other like this instead of emails. I tried to explain that letters are important to you, but they still think we're nuts.*

*When you and Dad left, it was really strange. I went back to my bedroom to unpack (thanks for the secret sweets by the way!) but I felt really alone for the first time ever. I never thought I'd say this, but I wanted Alice to come and bug me about something! After about ten minutes, there was a knock on the door and one of my housemates introduced herself and said that a couple of them were going into the quad to the coffee shop and did I want to come? They were so nice and friendly. It was such a relief!*

*So, basically, I'm writing to tell you that you were right. Now that I've met some people and been to my first lectures, I'm really enjoying it here. There are so many different clubs and societies to join that my only problem will be fitting every-thing in. I could tell that you were worried when you left me here. And I know that you didn't have a good time when you left for boarding school, but this is so different.*

*Did you know that Auntie Jill sent me a package already? Banana bread and her homemade pasta sauce. She said that she might visit with you when you come up next? She also said that you've been decorating your and Alice's bedrooms. Are you going to do mine too?*

*Dad has been sending me text messages and memes. He seems happy in his new job, so you were right there, too. He will be okay. He sent me the medal he got for two years' attendance at GA, too.*

*So, the only person I need to worry about is you. Mainly because – how are you going to survive without me? Ha ha. As you were right about me and Dad both being okay, I'm going to believe you that you are fine, too. I've only been away a week and I've already realised how many things you do that I haven't even noticed. In case I forget to say it when you come and visit, thank you. You're the best mum I could ever have.*

*Lots of love,*

*Olivia xxx*

# A LETTER FROM EMMA

I want to say a huge thank you for choosing to read *My Stepmother's Secret*. If you did enjoy it and want to keep up to date with all my latest releases, just sign up at the following link. Your email address will never be shared and you can unsubscribe at any time.

*www.bookouture.com/emma-robinson*

Thank you for reading Gabbie's story. Gabbie is a people-pleaser who puts herself last on her to-do list and tries to keep everyone happy. Speaking to friends and looking at my own life, I think it's really common for many of us to feel anxious about saying no and setting boundaries and, sometimes, this can be to our serious personal detriment. If you recognise elements of yourself in this, too, I would wholeheartedly recommend the people-pleaser episode of the *Best Friend Therapy* podcast beloved of Tricia in this book, and also the book *Please Yourself* by Emma Reed Turrell.

When I was planning the plot for *My Stepmother's Secret*, I needed a backstory for Gabbie which explained why she was unaware of her mother's affairs. Inspiration came in the form of reading research on Boarding School Syndrome which was sent to me by my very clever friend Alison Lutz. While there must be many people who had a positive experience at boarding school, it was a fascinating – and disturbing – read to learn about the effects of this type of school in a child's formative years. It has certainly made me look at some of the people in power in our country with fresh eyes.

My last key research was in the area of gambling addiction. I don't think I knew as much about this as I did about alcohol and drug addiction, yet it is something which ruins thousands of lives. After speaking to former addicts, I became so much more aware of how hard it is to avoid seeing advertisements pushing gambling on the high street and on TV. It prompted me to speak to my children about the dangers of gambling and how you can never beat the dealer.

Thank you again for reading *My Stepmother's Secret*. I hope you enjoyed Gabbie's journey home and, if you did, I would be very grateful if you could write a review. I'd love to hear what you think, and it makes such a difference helping new readers to discover one of my books for the first time.

I love hearing from my readers – you can get in touch on my Facebook page, through Twitter, Goodreads or my website.

Emma

www.emmarobinsonwrites.com

 facebook.com/motherhoodforslackers
twitter.com/emmarobinsonuk

# ACKNOWLEDGEMENTS

I was lucky enough to have TWO talented editors to work on this book. Isobel Akenhead, thank you for all your invaluable help with the early stages of this and all of my other books. Susannah Hamilton, thank you for taking up the baton and for your insightful plot ideas – I already know that we are going to write some great books together!

Thank you Kim Nash and the PR team for all your support. Alice Moore, I LOVE this cover, thank you so much. Also, a huge thank you to Gabrielle Chant for the copy edit and Laura Gerrard for proofreading – your eagle eyes are much appreciated!

The research for this book covered topics as diverse as gambling, house repossessions, translation, bailiffs and boarding school. For all of your help, and willingness to answer my questions, thank you Theresa Allen, Lee Coughtrey, Carrie Harvey, Alison Lutz, Sophie Watling and Chris Wayment. Any mistakes are mine.

And lastly, as always, my family: for not looking for a new wife/daughter/mother when I abandon you to hang out with the people who live in my head.